Best wishes
Sarah

Chailey's Daze

by
Sarah Burtenshaw

Bloomington, IN   authorHOUSE™   Milton Keynes, UK

AuthorHouse™
1663 Liberty Drive, Suite 200
Bloomington, IN 47403
www.authorhouse.com
Phone: 1-800-839-8640

AuthorHouse™ UK Ltd.
500 Avebury Boulevard
Central Milton Keynes, MK9 2BE
www.authorhouse.co.uk
Phone: 08001974150

First published by AuthorHouse 5/1/2006

ISBN: 1-4259-1992-8 (sc)

Printed in the United States of America
Bloomington, Indiana

This book is printed on acid-free paper.

For my two beautiful daughters, Allison and Natasha
who are the centre of my life and my reason for being.
I will love you forever.

Chapter 1

"You want me to what?" I yelled into the phone.

8:02 a.m. and I hadn't even touched my coffee or chocolate chip muffin and Sandy, the police dispatcher, was already pushing my buttons!

"I need you to attend 157 London Street to see why an eighty-year old lady is lying naked outside on her front lawn. She told the neighbours that she was sunbathing. Officer Spencer will meet you there."

I could tell that Sandy was trying her hardest not to laugh, however, I could also hear the other dispatcher's lack of restraint. To be precise, someone was giggling hysterically in the background.

"Fine!" I slammed down the phone.

My name is Chailey Smith and I work for the Cookfield Police Department as a Mental Health Nurse, which means that any police calls involving mental health issues are responded to by myself or the other part-timer, Jody Brooks, a.k.a. bitch supreme. Our job is to help the police meet the needs of the mentally ill. We alternate shifts, share the same office and fight for the affection and favour of our part-time cranky secretary, Flo. Jody and I despise one another and I try to minimize our contact as much as possible so it helps that she works only eighteen hours a week. Jody is everything I'm not – she's tall, blond, slim, and beautiful, drives this year's model car and is sought after by every healthy male who happens to walk within her shadow. She's like a modern-day version of Medusa, the Greek mythical goddess who turned people to stone when she looked at them. Okay, so the men don't turn to stone but something turns as hard as a rock when she lays eyes on them. She isn't married currently, having left two heart-broken husbands in her wake while she pursues her quest for the ultimate relationship. Princess Jody has enough money that she really doesn't have to work so we all know why she is employed at the biggest meat market in town.

As for me, I'm a mere five-foot, two-inch thirty-five year old who my grandmother described as "pleasantly plump," hardly a flattering description for an Internet dating advertisement. My hair is brown with blonde streaks; at least it is this week and I've been told that I have great eyes. Most importantly I am younger than Jody however, I don't have oodles of money like her and have to drive a 1994 beige Toyota Corolla, a car that I adore. To make ends meet, I also work part-time for a security company. Like Jody, I was also married. Unlike her, I continue to duke out my divorce in the courts. My divorce lawyer is number two on my speed dial.

The Mental Health Nurses are expected to go on all police calls that have even a smidgen of mental health concerns therefore the dispatchers think that all the police calls with naked men and women should be sent our way. And they are never *good* naked calls. A naked octogenarian was not my idea of the way to start a day. Perhaps a naked man half that age waking me up would be okay. I seemed to have as much chance of that happening as this woman would in getting a sun tan since it was pouring down with rain. Typical May weather for our city making it feel bleak and dreary, somewhat like my love life.

I got back into my wet boots and soggy yellow rain coat and sloshed out to my unmarked police car, a blue Chevrolet Impala. Someone thought it was amusing to assign me the parking spot in the furthest corner of the parking lot knowing I can't park to save my life. To add to the entertainment value, the parking lot is located in full panoramic view of the police station gym. Some wise guy put the treadmill in front of the window so my police colleagues could sweat it out on the treadmill while I sweat it out parking in my spot. I feel I do a good job if I park with less than a fifteen-point turn. Of course, the person assigned to the spot beside me contributes to the sport by parking as close to the line as possible thus making my task much more difficult. At least once a week, I bang or scrape something against my car. It's happened so many times that they have photocopied "Police Vehicle Incident" forms with my name on so that all I have to do is sign and date it and submit it to my supervisor. My chance of getting the new red SUV police car I requested is virtually nil. Five minutes later I was tucked in my rapidly steaming car. This was due to the rain and not due to my morning coffee that I'd left in the office. I was off in the morning traffic to meet Spencer and the sunbathing goddess.

Cookfield is a typical southern Ontario city and 300,000 people choose to live here and call it home. The city is split into four main districts. The downtown core is the centre hole in more ways than one. It's also the historical centre of the city and from that point the rest of the city developed. Cookfield is bordered to the north by the Sussex River. The industrial sector is located to the east. The western part of the city circles around the university and fades into the wealthiest part of the town. Finally, the southern most part of the city houses the ever-expanding suburbia.

The call I was going to was located in one of the nicer neighbourhoods in the downtown core bordering on the west. The address was easy to find since a small crowd had gathered around our lady who, as reported by the dispatcher, was lying naked on a beach towel on the front lawn of a house on one of Cookfield's busier downtown streets, oblivious to the people around her. She was a large woman weighing at least 250 pounds and was lying face down. Facing down wasn't a great view but it was better than the alternative. The "gentlemen" of our town, unwilling to miss any opportunity to act like the pigs that they were born to be, honked their car horns as they drove by and yelled, "Let it all hang out, Granny!" and "Way to hang your fanny, Granny!" Looking at Granny's fanny it appeared that Newton's theory of gravity was correct by observing her butt after eighty years of heavy downward plunging forces.

I parked carefully at the side of the road behind Spencer's cruiser, got out of my car into the torrential rain, and pushed my way to him through the crowd of fifteen or so fine citizens who apparently had nothing better to do than stand and stare in the rain.

"What's up, Spencer?"

"I just got here myself," he replied. "I thought that I'd let you have the honour of doing the investigation and show me how it is properly done."

"Liar!" I said. "And you're chicken shit!"

"Yeah, and you're the nurse so go do your stuff. I'll see if anyone knows her in the house."

He shuffled off yelling at the crowd to go home since this peep show was over.

Our sunbathing geriatric gal started to stir, threatening to roll from lying on her front to her back, much to the fear of the crowd that started to back up. Who could blame

them? I was ready to imitate Custer's Retreat
200-pound woman, give or take 50 pounds, wa⸝
I could stomach at 8:20 on a Tuesday morning. ̤
caffeinated stomach, might I add and I was starting to shake
from withdrawal.

I approached our lady cautiously, not wanting to make
her jump up. I wasn't sure how to start my introduction but
knew that a handshake was out of the question.

"Ma'am, I'm Chailey Smith from the police department."
Feeling badly for her predicament I begrudgingly took off
my raincoat and laid it on top of her. "You look cold, Ma'am.
I just wanted to help keep you warm."

"Thank you, dear," she replied with a smile. "The sun
is a little mild today, isn't it?" It was an observation that
missed me completely since my back was stinging from the
pelting rain. At that moment, Spencer returned to my side
with a very agitated man who looked terribly distraught but
resembled my lady.

"Mum, what are you doing out here? I've been looking
all over the house for you. This kind policeman told me
where you were. Come in out of the rain or you'll catch the
death of cold. Thank you officers for your help."

He carefully walked his mother into the house as she
muttered about how high the humidity level was today.
Mother and son carefully returned to the sanctity of their
home leaving the citizens of Cookfield in their wake. That
is they now had my police issue rain coat in their possession.
Cold, wet and fed up, I marched up the walkway and knocked
on the door. With the intensity of the rain increasing I
banged louder with no success. This mother and son duo
had locked the world out. No doubt she was getting a warm
cup of coffee given to her at this very moment.

Defeated, dejected and desperately wet, I headed back
to my car fearful that Noah and his ark were going to mow
me down since the rain was like a monsoon and driven

horizontally by the wind. Spencer pulled his car up beside mine and rolled down the window to talk to me.

"Careful, Smitty, you're going to catch a cold if you don't cover up. You should get a raincoat like that old lady had!"

I started my car, ran the heater high and tried to ignore the disgusting feeling of wet panties sticking to my butt and listened as Spencer gave me the goods on our lady.

"That is Gloria Jones. She is eighty-two years old and lives with her son, Norman. He told me that she has dementia and wanders at times. He was desperate when I found him and was terrified as to what had happened to her. She's been doing strange things lately. Last night she put the cat in the dryer saying that the rug had to be aired and Norman heard the poor thing screaming for help." A visual popped into my head of this lady manipulating the feline into the dryer. "The cat survived. Funny thing is, its name is Fluffy."

"Is Mrs. Jones being seen by a doctor?"

"Yes," Spence replied. "Today at 10:30."

"Good." Obviously Mrs. Jones was not doing very well and her family doctor needed to see her. "I'll call her son later on and see how the appointment went."

Spencer gave me her details including telephone number and date of birth. The radio came to life and Spencer was being sent to another call.

"Good job, Chailey," Spence added. "See you later." Spencer was one of my best supporters at the police department. After fourteen years on the job he knew about the many problems that older people encounter. He also understood on a personal level, since his own grandmother had dementia and had just moved into the nursing home beside my house.

I returned to the police station refusing to take on the challenge of my parking spot with a steamed up car and parked in Jody's spot instead. She obviously rated higher than I did as she had been assigned a spot two down from the main entrance. I didn't want to know what she had to do to gain that type of treatment. The guy who assigned parking spots was four foot ten and stunk like a dead groundhog. Thankfully Jody was the kind of gal and willing to do what I wasn't. At least I could benefit from the fruits of her labour with only a thirty-second run from my car to the front door.

Sergeant Frank Court was sitting in his usual spot at the front desk with a long line up in front of him of what appeared to be wet, disgruntled Cookfield citizens. He waved to me. "Hey, Smitty, You should get yourself a police rain coat. It would keep you dry on a day like this."

"Thanks!" I grunted and squished my way up to the second floor, pokey office that was assigned to our small "team". Flo looked in a darker mood than usual, which was difficult to imagine. Working with Flo was like living with a menopausal Darth Vader.

"Morning, Flo," I cautiously offered which was replied to with a grunt. It could have been worse. I sloshed my way over to my desk, peeled off my shoes and replaced them with another pair of sneakers. My toes were so wet they were pruney as if I had been in a warm bath for too long. If only... My pants and T-shirt would have to dry au naturel.

"Charlie 13 to dispatch - I am clear of that call," I called into my radio. The police department uses a phonetic alphabet to spell names. "A" is for "Alpha" and "B" is "Bravo". They use the first letter of my name, "C" for Chailey, hence "Charlie" is my call name. The unlucky "13" stuck after several incidents with my car during the first month of my employment. In comparison, Jody gets "Juliet" for the letter "J" and her number is a very pretty "22". I figure *that* number represents the number of police officers she slept with in the first month of her job.

"10-4 and thanks!" replied the dispatcher.

Yeah, thanks all right. So far my Tuesday morning was as cold as the cup of untouched coffee sitting on my desk. At least I had the chocolate chip muffin to enjoy.

I wrote up my brief report on Gloria Jones, put it in the filing pile and made a note on the board to call her son this afternoon to check up on her visit to the doctor. Dementia is a horrible illness that effects people's memory and some people become so disoriented that they misperceive things and people around them. Fluffy the cat could relate to that. The question the doctor had to answer was if the disease had progressed to the point that Gloria was unsafe at home and therefore needed placement in a supervised setting such as a nursing home. This was going to be a difficult decision for everyone. Well, everyone except for Fluffy who appeared to be on the endangered species list in the Jones household.

I called dispatch to clear myself from the call. My phone rang. It was Maggie Denton, one of the people I'd seen over the weekend, and she sounded scared.

"Someone is trying to kill me, Chailey. Help me!"

Chapter 2

Maggie sounded upset and breathless as if she'd been running.

"Chailey, I need to talk to you. I can't right now because I'm at work. I'm leaving the office soon and I'll call you from my house. I should be home in half an hour," she whispered. I could barely hear her.

"Are you okay, Maggie?"

"Yes, I think so, but I need to talk to you soon. Please."

"Okay, I'll come to your place or I'll meet you wherever you want." I gave her my cell phone number. "Call me if you need anything, Maggie."

"Thanks, Chailey," she whispered in a virtually inaudible voice. "I knew I could trust you." I heard her hang up the phone.

That was weird, I thought. Somehow I felt like I was in some spy movie. Of course, any movie I'm in will also have to star Mel Gibson and I hadn't seen him hanging around the office lately so this must be real. I wondered what was up with Maggie. I was beginning to believe she did have some emotional problems since Maggie sounded extremely distraught and mildly paranoid on the phone. Maggie was a woman who had called 911 repeatedly about prowlers trying to get through her door. Each time police responded to her home they found no one there. This was not an unusual outcome for such a call. Many times a suspect is gone upon the arrival of the police.

When the call came to Maggie's address for the fifth and final time on Friday, I was dispatched with Abby, the officer I was riding with, to the residence to see if we could assist in dealing with the situation. Cops are very pragmatic and use a concrete problem-solving approach. Their hypothesis is if there is no rational explanation then the answer is an irrational one so they call me, Queen of the Irrational!

Maggie lived in a small bungalow just on the border of downtown. A background check completed by Abby on our way over revealed that Maggie was squeaky clean. She'd never even had a traffic ticket. Hell, I get a parking ticket every other day in this stupid city. Over the years, my parking ticket payments alone had probably paid for one year of Abby's salary.

Two uniformed officers were in the house talking with Maggie when we arrived. Kevin Harrison was one of the officers and Ed Plzmitshatski was the other. Maggie had called the police four times over the previous two nights hearing someone trying to enter her premises through different doors and even the window. This typically happened around ten or eleven o'clock at night. That night she heard him call her name repeatedly. She didn't know who was doing this and could only provide a vague description of the person as tall and in dark clothing. There had been several reports of break-ins in the area in the past few weeks but these were the first reports ever by Maggie. They wanted me to talk with her to see if her fears were based on a mental disorder. In the meantime, the beat officers had promised to keep an eye on her house.

It was now Tuesday so I wondered what had happened over the weekend. The roads were busy this morning and as in any city, the wetter it is, the faster you drive! This psychopathic approach to driving had caught five idiots in a pile up downtown directly in my path and earned me a twenty-minute hold-up in traffic. It was well worth the wait to drive by and wave at the cop, Chris Long, who appeared wetter than the *Little Mermaid* and more grumpy than Flo, as he directed traffic in the torrential rain. I considered this payback for Chris after he'd kept me locked in a room with a corpse once telling me since I had found the person dead, I had to keep visual contact with the body until the coroner arrived three hours later. Jerk!

I finally arrived at Maggie's house forty-five minutes after she had called and parked in the driveway behind her Honda being very careful not to hit her car. If I hit a police cruiser my boss gets mad, but if I hit Joe Citizen's car he gets darn right nasty. I went to the front door and rang the bell with no immediate answer. I knew Maggie was home because her car was in the driveway. Perhaps she was in the basement or on the toilet. If she's anything like me, if I've got business to take care of in the bathroom the house could burn down around me and you still wouldn't get me off the throne. So I rang the bell again. And again. No matter how annoying I was there was no reply, which was somewhat curious. I couldn't see into the living room from the front porch because the curtains had been drawn shut. I opened the screen door, knocked hard on the door but still there was no response. I tried calling on the phone but the answering machine picked up the call. I checked the door but it was locked. Feeling frustrated and a little annoyed, I thought I'd try the back door knowing this would be a futile attempt. Maggie had a double lock on the door including a dead bolt and she also locked the screen door. She kept the back door locked up like Fort Knox since the prowler had been bothering her. On Friday she told me that she only used the front door because it was visible to her neighbours and that made her feel safer. The back yard appeared undisturbed and I banged on the screen door as loudly as possible without breaking the glass. I found the screen door unlocked, which surprised me after what Maggie had said. I became more than a little alarmed when her cat, Alfie, purred and walked around my ankles rubbing white fur all over my pant legs. Maggie *never* let Alfie out since he had some type of disorder that didn't allow him to mix with other felines. I tried the door handle and was surprised to find it turned in my hands. Once again, I heard the alarms going off in my head since the door should have been barred shut. I managed to convince myself that I was just being dramatic and there must be a perfectly logical explanation for the door being open. Maggie had sounded very upset on the phone and maybe in her hurry to do something else she had absent-mindedly left the door unlocked. I've done that myself and woken up in the morning to find the back door wide open and a kitchen filled with squirrels fighting over a doughnut and the dog food bowl. Having found both a possible and most probable answer, I opened the door slightly and called for Maggie. Once again, there was no response. Alfie rudely pushed his way through the door and I figured I might as well follow him to ensure that his safety otherwise it would have been break and enter.

The kitchen looked as it had on my previous visits. Martha Stewart had a strong influence in this house. It was tidy and clean with everything in its place, except for a mug on the table. It was half filled with what I presumed was tea since Maggie told me she never drank coffee. When she told me that I felt guilty since I can't start my day without a half-gallon of java to give me the edge I need to get through my day. I called out to Maggie, fearful I'd make her jump out of her skin if she hadn't heard me and ran into me. Still there was no answer.

I went into the living room. What I saw when I went around the corner just about made me jump out of my skin. I had finally found Maggie. She was half-sitting and half-lying on the couch and she was dead. At least I was pretty sure she was, based on the enormous hole in her right temple and the equally large amount of blood sprayed over the couch. Her eyes were wide open and I felt that she was looking right at me. I went over to Maggie feeling obligated as a nurse to check for a pulse, but I knew within three feet of approaching her that there was no chance that she was alive and nurse or not, I wasn't going to touch her. The gun in her right hand had completely extinguished any chance of her living through that experience and the pool of blood and brain matter on the couch and wall confirmed my suspicions. I grabbed my radio.

"Charlie 13 to Control," I said calmly into the radio.

"Go ahead, Charlie 13."

"Control, Charlie 13 needs back up at this address. I have a... a.... a..." Crap, I couldn't remember the official code number for a dead person and it was starting to upset me. Maggie was dead and I couldn't even remember a stupid code.

"Charlie13, what do you have?" I recognized Cindy's voice. She sounded calm, cool and collected. I bet she wasn't looking at a dead person right now.

"Dispatch, what is the code for a dead person?"

"Charlie 13 that would be a 10-85."

"Bingo! That's what I have." I finally got it out.

"Are you okay there, Charlie 13?"

"Er, yeah, sure. Could you send me some back up? Soon? Please?" I was starting to feel a little hysterical. And to be honest, I wasn't really sure what to do next.

I had automatically presumed that Maggie had shot herself. A wave of panic paralyzed me when I suddenly thought, if someone did this to Maggie then that person might still be here. I stood frozen to the spot and listened very, very intently. All I could hear was the clock ticking and the cat purring in the kitchen. I was surprised that I could hear anything over the loud thumping of my heartbeat. And then I heard a "pat, pat, pat". My first reflex was to think that it was footsteps but my brain told me, no, not footsteps but something dripping. Oh-my-God! It was blood dripping. Maggie's blood was dripping onto the floor. I backed up as fast as I could and ran out the back door.

By the time I got outside I could hear the comforting sound of a siren coming closer and closer. I felt like a damsel in distress waiting for my knight in shining armour to arrive on his trusty steed. Hell, I'd take the dead-groundhog-guy riding on Jody's back at this particular moment if it meant I wasn't alone anymore. I went out to the driveway as a cruiser screeched to a halt in front of the house. It was Kevin Harrison.

"You okay, Chailey?" he asked as he ran up the driveway.

"Yeah, I'm fine," I replied a little shakily.

Kevin called into his radio, "Everything is ten-four here. Chailey's okay." He then turned to me, "We heard you call in the death and that you were alright but then you didn't respond to the dispatcher after that."

I couldn't remember what happened to my radio. "I'm sorry. I had a radio but I don't know what I did with it. I think you'd better come in."

Kevin finally asked the obvious question. "Who died, Chailey?"

"It's Maggie. It looks like she killed herself. She shot herself."

I led him into the living room. As stupid as it sounds now, I hoped that I'd find Maggie alive and well and that I'd made a mistake of some kind. But there was no denying the facts; Maggie was very, very dead.

"There's a suicide note here," Kevin said. All of a sudden I felt completely overwhelmed. I couldn't believe this had happened. I'd spoken to this wonderful woman only an hour ago and now she was lying lifeless on the couch. I walked past him and out the back door. I sat on the back steps and did my stress reaction and vomited. Like most people I close my eyes when I ralph and when I opened my eyes, I was horrified to find a pair of police issue black boots, covered in my offering to the stress Gods. I looked up to see Kevin staring morbidly at his boots.

"You okay, Chailey?" he asked kindly.

"About as good as I can expect. Sorry about the boots, Kevin. I didn't know you were there."

"That's okay," he replied. "I would have been offended if you did it knowing it was me." He went over to the garden hose, rinsed off his boots and washed down the walkway destroying the evidence. If my cop buddies Neil and Zack were here they'd have surrounded the area with crime scene tape and had the forensic guys photograph it for future embarrassing moments such as the Christmas party. Kevin sat down beside me on the steps under a small verandah which protected us from the infernal rain.

"Chailey, this may not be very helpful right now but I'm going to say it anyway. We can't save everyone, no matter how much and hard we try – and I know that you tried to help Maggie. You are one of the hardest working people in this department who does a great job. I know that you are going to feel like you failed."

"Are you sure it's a suicide, Kevin? She told me someone was trying to kill her."

"We won't know for sure until the detectives investigate. It looks like Maggie killed herself."

"I know, Kevin, but Maggie was different. She showed no signs of being suicidal. I saw her three or four times and spoke to her at length. She offered me nothing to indicate this was what she planned or that she felt this depressed. I must have missed something. I just don't know what. She was frightened that something would happen to her and now this. What the hell is going on here?" I know I sounded like I was babbling but it felt right. Coherency seemed to beyond my capabilities at this moment.

"Here we go!" announced Kevin as we heard cars coming down the street fast. "If you ever need to talk, I'm here for you," he said as he squeezed my left hand.

"Thanks, Kevin," I called out to him as he went out to meet the patrol car. I needed to wash out my mouth since it was starting to taste like the armpit of a Turkish wrestler. I grabbed the hose, washed my mouth and headed back into the house.

Within minutes the calm tranquil atmosphere had been replaced with police cars, an ambulance and even a reporter who must have been listening to a police radio. I went back into the house and looked around. Maggie was a very neat housekeeper. Her house was incredibly clean and tidy with not even a scrap of paper out of place. The piano was covered with numerous photos of Maggie and her family. The walls were painted a pretty yellow and her luxurious, cream area rug had turned red from the blood.

The coroner had arrived and was examining the body. Members of the Crime Scene Unit were completing their gorey tasks of photographing the scene and collecting evidence. Unlike the beautiful men and women on the popular crime shows with blonde hair down to their asses and trendy clothes, these guys were wearing overalls and looked more like construction workers. They were measuring every detail and photographing each bit of evidence that would be required to support the coroner's conclusion. It certainly looked like a suicide. A note had been typed and left on the dining room table. I just didn't have the heart to read it. I was sure it was titled: *Chailey Failed Me!* There was a gun in her hand and the bullet hole in her temple looked genuine. The kitchen was clean and only one mug was left on the kitchen table. Alfie purred gently and walked around my legs with his tail swishing getting white fur all over my black jeans. I guess that I was the closest thing he had to a friend in the room. This pushed my cat allergy into high gear and I started sneezing. I noticed that his cat bowl was empty so I asked Bryan Black, one of the Forensic guys, if I could give the cat some milk. He threw me over a clean pair of gloves as he said, "Use these and go ahead!"

I opened the fridge door. Maggie's refrigerator looked better than my own. Okay, so she actually kept food in hers and didn't just use her fridge as a condiment holder. There was a half-eaten casserole, yogurt containers and lots of fruits and vegetables. I grabbed the 0% milk, a.k.a. milky-looking water, poured some into Alfie's bowl and then grabbed the cat food tin and scraped some of the "meat" into the other bowl. Alfie immediately forgot our newfound friendship to fill his stomach. Cats were finicky things and a bit like men that way. It doesn't matter what you are doing, if you sling a bit of food in his bowl, his attention is gone.

Kevin's detective prediction was wrong. Maggie's bad luck persisted and her case was going to be assigned to one of the police department's biggest pig-headed jerks. Detective Rick Simmons, or Dicky the Dick as he was known in the department was an embarrassment to all hard-working police officers. I'd dealt with him on a previous case with a woman, Hannah Jones, whose husband had been murdered. Word around the station was that this had been a relatively clear-cut case. My role with Hannah had been after the murder when she was feeling desolate and depressed and having thoughts of suicide. I had witnessed Dicky being rude and disrespectful to Hannah and treating her like she was an idiot. He did such a shoddy job on the case along with the not-so-bright Crown Attorney that the accused murderer was recently acquitted. Abby's boyfriend, Nick, was hired to replace the incompetent Crown Attorney and now the case is being appealed so this time justice may be served. Rick has only year one left until retirement so they let him stay on in a position that is unofficially supervised so he only partners up with skilled senior detectives. Tonight, he was working with Liam Fitzgerald, one of the department's best detectives who also happened to have a great ass.

"Smith, what's going on here?" Dicky demanded brusquely.

"Hi, Rick. I'm fine, thanks. How are you?" I answered sweetly. There's no way I was going to let him see how much he got under my skin.

I started to give him a brief summary of Maggie's case dating back to the first contact we had with her less than a week ago. He quickly and rudely cut me off.

"I know all about her. That cute chick cop with the cute boobs, what's her name, Abby Hartford, asked me to investigate after you saw her. It seemed pretty clear to me that she was a nut job and her suicide just confirms it. I guess you missed the boat on this one, Smith. How are you going to explain this one to your uncle, the Chief?"

He smiled his ratty smile. Dick is five-feet, four-inches tall and has the "Little Man" syndrome, meaning he needs to have a huge ego to make up for his diminutive size. He has short dark hair, big ears, black beady eyes and a massive nose that any alpine skier would salivate over the opportunity to ski down. He had a little moustache that reminded me of whiskers to complete his rat imitation. Now *his* ass was small and bony. His comments about the chief, my uncle, related to the fact that I'd complained about his treatment of Mrs. Jones and he had been disciplined for this. I knew he was baiting me and I was ready to bite. People around us had heard the exchange. I was blessed, or cursed, I'm never sure which, with the Smith temper. It means I don't get mad often but when I do, you'd better watch out because I'll bite your head off in a second. I was trying to restrain that temper now but I was quickly losing control.

I could hear a voice quietly whispering, "Don't do it, Chailey. Think of Maggie." It was like Obe-One Kenobe's voice to Luke Skywalker in *Star Wars*. I think it was Kevin but I couldn't be sure. It made me take a second to look at Maggie and remind me why we were here. It also gave me a moment to produce a good comeback.

"Where's your senior supervising detective, Simmons?" I'd give that a nine out of ten on a bitch scale. Simmons looked pissed. If there's one thing worse than being supervised when you think your shit doesn't stink, it is being reminded that you have a superior watching your every move. As far as I was concerned, the dead-groundhog parking lot guy was superior to this turd.

Simmons leaned towards me with his cheesy, garlicky breath and whispered, "You screwed up, Chailey. This woman is dead and she killed herself. You should have prevented that. You good as pulled the trigger yourself."

I figured that nobody heard him although people around us were straining to hear. If I complained, it would be my word against his and a complaint would go nowhere. So, I did the next best thing. I head butted him in the face. Hard enough to make his nose bleed, but not hard enough to break it. Hell, looking at the size of that honker you'd need a sledgehammer to put a dent in it. His nose started gushing blood.

I whipped my head back to avoid the geyser and said in my sweetest voice, "Oops! I tripped. I'm sorry Detective Simmons. Did I bang into you? Are you okay?"

"Fuck off, bitch!" he yelled just as Detective Liam Fitzgerald joined us.

"I don't know what the hell is going on here but can you two bickering children smarten up? Rick, get something on that and take it outside."

"There's a hose there if you need it," I offered, as a Good Samaritan should.

"Chailey, tell me what's going on here."

"Dick told me you guys knew all about Maggie."

"Well, I know nothing about her which is the way Rick likes it. That Son-of-a-Bitch does this to me all the time. He takes the cases as they come into the office before I can see them, "investigates" them and then tells me about them after he has closed the case. I'm sick to death of him and his antics. So start from the beginning."

I gave him a brief summary of our involvement with Maggie, from the panicky 911 calls about prowlers to her call today and my subsequent discovery of her body. I offered copies of my report which he wanted me to attach to my written statement. I told him that I didn't believe that Maggie was mentally ill, she had no risk factors for being suicidal and that, as strange as it may seem, there had to be some truth to her claims of a prowler. I also told him that Maggie had not expressed suicidal thoughts at any time.

"You realize that everything points towards suicide, don't you Chailey?"

"I know, Liam. Something isn't right here. I just can't quite put my finger on it."

"I need you to head back to the station to write up your report. If there is anything you think of, let me know." He was trying to be open to my opinions while also being mildly patronizing. I recognized that I was only a Mental Health

Worker and my opinion had little to no impact. At least he had listened and it was more than Dick had.

I gave him a sheet of paper with Maggie's mother's name and phone number and the number for her fiancé, Michael, who was in Mexico on a business trip. It is a tragedy for parents to bury their children. It's not part of the natural order of life. And as for Michael, he would have to bury Maggie along with his dreams of a life together.

I looked around the house one more time before I left. Everything was as it should be, neat and tidy, the way Maggie liked it. Except, of course, for Maggie who looked distinctly out of place lying on the couch with blood all over it. I'm pretty sure she wouldn't have liked that at all. She was definitely not a messy person.

I went out the front door so as to avoid another confrontation with the Dickhead. Kevin walked me out, either not trusting my ability to control myself or Dicky's homicidal tendencies. After what he said to me, I'd like to kick his skinny little butt however, knowing him he'd probably play dirty and shoot me and blame it on some punk.

Kevin walked me to my car and told me that he'd see me back at the station. He was being very kind but professional. To be honest, I had never really paid much attention to Kevin Harrison. Our paths had crossed periodically over the past two years. He'd always seemed so cross with me and walked around with a scowl on his face. Okay, so that's *probably* because I rear-ended him but that was a long time ago. He was really, really mad that day and got out of his car and asked me sarcastically if I had a driver's license because he couldn't believe that someone who drove as badly as I did would be given one. He looks like all the other cops. Tall, dark and handsome in that rugged sort of way. Today was the first time I had seen him smile.

I drove back to the station absent-mindedly and oblivious to the world around me. Dicky had reached a new low in his insults, however, his accusations kept ricocheting around my brain. Shit sticks! I had failed Maggie. I hadn't been able to keep her safe despite my reassurances to her that I would.

I was so distracted that I drove through a red light or that's what Spencer said I did after he pulled me over on Main Street in the rush hour traffic.

"What the hell is going on Chailey? You just about nailed someone going through the red."

I looked up at him and said that I was sorry as a tiny tear slipped out.

"There's no need to cry, Sweetie. I'm not going to give you a ticket. I just wanted to make sure you were okay." He was panicking. Tears are to be avoided at all times, especially those tears running down the faces of female friends.

"Honey, what happened?" It was his own fault. He shouldn't have asked. I gave him a full rendition of the events of the past few hours including what Dick the Dick said and how I head butted him. He listened as cars whizzed by and the rain piddled down.

"How about I drive you back to the station? You don't seem quite yourself."

"I'm okay," I sniffled.

"No, Chailey. I'll drive you. You've been a whole two days with no accidents and you're upset." He radioed to dispatch for a two-man car to meet him at this location.

"Are you the one creating the traffic mess, downtown, 666? People have been complaining," the controller snapped into the radio.

"Roger, Dispatch. Send me that unit and your traffic tie up will be over."

Obviously Spence wasn't having a good day, either. Perhaps he had helped someone kill herself today too.

"Spence, you won't tell anyone I had a meltdown, will you?"

"I'm honoured that mine was the shoulder you cried on," he replied solemnly.

The police wagon eventually arrived and Spencer went out to talk to Adrian and Simon, the two officers riding the wagon today. There appeared to be a small argument between the wagon guys and it looked like Simon lost as he stomped over to my car.

Once Spencer got back into the car, I asked him about the discussion.

"They were arguing about who was going to drive your car."

"Why would they do that?" I asked. "It's just my regular Impala."

"The guys think that you have bad car karma and they don't want to get it," he replied rather sheepishly.

"You're joking, right?"

"Actually, no I'm not. The guys in the Maintenance Department have a "Chailey Chart" tracking how many days you go accident-free. Your record is twenty-three days."

At least they weren't charting the number of days I'd been without sex. I'd be past the 1,000 mark by now!

Spencer dropped me off at the police station and I went up the stairs to the Squad Room to write my report. I felt completely done in. Thankfully there was no one around so I didn't have to go through all the gorey details. Cops like hearing about all the disgusting details. All I could see in my mind was Maggie lying on the couch with those wide eyes pleading for me to help her. It took me a few hours to write up my report and I had to call my boss, Ben, to update him on my failure for the day. He's a good guy. He told me to go home, relax and not to worry. Fat chance that was going to happen because as soon as I was back at the office the dispatchers sent me on another call.

Chapter 3

I was just about ready to grab a coffee from the Squad Room next door to my office and scoff down the chocolate chip muffin when the bloody radio came to life again.

"Dispatch to Charlie 13." Jody never gets this many calls in one week let alone one morning. Everyone knew that Jody does nothing around here so if they wanted the Mental Health Workers to do work it had to be done on my time. Jody doesn't work Monday mornings or Friday afternoons since they are too close to the weekend, which she *must* have off. All those men to bed and only two days on the weekend to do it in. When Jody does manage to shuffle into the office, she does one or two calls in a day and then disappears for the rest of the day to do her "paperwork". That's probably a euphemism for something else. I can't fathom why they keep her around here and figure that she must be more than just eye candy for the males in the station. When I find out what she has been using to blackmail her way into keeping this job, I am going to blow her out of the water. No doubt she did her fair share of sucking and blowing to get the job in the first place.

"Go ahead, Dispatch," I replied as I scoffed down half the muffin.

"You need to go to 1167 Queen Street North, apartment 1309. The officers responded to a neighbour trouble and need your expertise to resolve the situation." I was immediately suspicious when the dispatcher complimented me.

"10-4. I'm on my way." I prepared to leave by grabbing my police radio and fanny pack filled with all of my paraphernalia. As a civilian, I don't carry a gun but I do carry pepper spray for protection and have been taught self-defense techniques. The best form of self-defense I know is to run away – fast! I've been issued a bullet-proof Kevlar vest but don't like to wear it because it makes me look too busty. Policewomen's vests are designed with one pocket due to their smaller stature. Men get two pockets in the front. If luck has it that you are a big woman then you get the two-pocket vest and the daily advertisement that you exceed the police department's expected dimension for a woman. Jody only has one pocket and I have two pockets so vanity prevails and I refuse to wear mine. Instead I try to stay out of the way of guns and knives and hope for the best. It may not be the greatest solution but I'm not going to publicize to the whole world that I'm a double pocket, big-boobed girl. Along with the pepper spray, I carry a radio, note book, identification, pen knife, lipstick, toothbrush and toothpaste, gum, change for snacks, stickers for kids, *Vicks* for under my nose in stinky houses, a small cassette player and several *Mars* bars for emergencies. The idea of going on a call with no chocolate close at hand frightens me. Kevlar vest I'll do without but not chocolate. I figured that I could leave my bottle of water at the office for today.

A quick glimpse out of my small window revealed the rain had slowed to slightly less than hurricane force which meant that I needed to find some kind of protection from the elements. I looked around the office hoping to find a long-forgotten raincoat, black garbage bag or even a discarded tarp if I could find one. I lucked out and feasted my eyes on a beautiful yellow umbrella. Jody's umbrella! I needn't be surprised to realize that the princess had an umbrella that announces to the world, "See me!" She wasn't here and I was in need so I borrowed it from her and headed out the door.

"Flo, I'm going."

"I heard the dispatcher," she growled. That was all the warning I needed to leave the lioness alone.

"And I'm telling Jody you stole her umbrella!" Fine, I thought, you'd have to find her first.

"Actually I am borrowing it. Bye!" I added in as cheerful voice as possible.

"See ya' thief," Flo responded. You've got to admit, if crankiness was an Olympic sport, Flo would be a gold medal winner. I could hear her leaving a message on Jody's answering machine as I went down the hall.

Queen Street was part of our downtown core area and the person I was about to see lived in a high rise apartment. I quickly glimpsed up getting a face full of rain for my troubles and the water quickly trickled down my back into my underwear. Bloody rain! At least I didn't see anyone hanging off the balcony so I figured it must be something else. The dispatchers didn't give me any details except to say that the situation was "unusual". The last time they sent me on a call with a similar description was to assess a depressed clown who was threatening to drive his little clown car into the Sussex River.

There was no response from apartment 1309's buzzer so I hit the superintendent's button and told him I was police so he'd let me in. He popped his head out the door to see what was going on and looked thoroughly disappointed to see that it was only me. I took the elevator, which stunk of fried onions and disinfectant, up to the thirteenth floor and headed down the hall to the apartment. I didn't think that apartment or office buildings had thirteenth floors and I should have taken that as a sign of things to come. Hatshu and Burton were standing in the apartment hallway with smiles on their faces. This was going to be good.

"What's up guys?" I asked innocently.

"You are not going to believe this place, Chailey," said Hatshu. "We got a complaint that the guy who lives in this apartment plays his music loudly all night long. The neighbour got so frustrated that he came over today and a yelling match started. We were called to sort this out. We spoke to the neighbour and he just wants the loud music to stop. He told us the noisemaker's a freakazoid which seemed a little harsh at first. So, we went to talk to the neighbour making the noise and he appears to be, how shall I call him, a little out in space." Hatshu laughed at this. "As far as we can tell this guy is harmless but we wanted you to come and check him out."

So far so good, I thought. This was exactly what I was hired to do. If someone is threatening to kill himself then the police officer apprehends the person under the Mental Health Act and takes him to hospital. It's a slam dunk decision. This sounded a little more complex. They still hadn't got to the core of the problem.

"Come in and meet Walter Sptitzky, otherwise known as Z910 of the planet Belgrata."

He opened the door and I followed him into the brightest, strangest room I have ever been in. Walter had covered every surface with aluminum foil. He was sitting in a chair that looked like an old dentist chair. Walter himself was fully dressed the part. He was about five-feet, ten-inches tall and weighed about 170 pounds. There was little else to describe other than he was wearing a full body suit in emerald green capped off with a silver helmet and a silver athletic cup.

"The helmet and cup protect him from the earth's stinger rays," offered Hatshu.

The man looked like a Ninja Turtle in a WWF wrestling match.

"Hi, I'm Chailey Smith. I work with the Cookfield Police Department as a nurse. The officers asked me to come and talk to you. Make sure everything is okay." I wasn't sure if I should give the Vulcan greeting sign.

"Greetings, Earthling," he replied.

Pretty hokey beginning, I thought.

"Can I ask why you are dressed that way?"

"I am Z910 of the planet Belgrata. I wear the uniform of my planet. I must protect myself from the earthling rays."

"How long have you lived here?" I asked.

"I have been on earth for two hundred years. I was planted in the womb of my great, great, great grandmother. I have been accumulating knowledge and skills to help lead the planet Belgrata into the year 31,716."

"And why do you play the music so loud at night?" I inquired. He had a massive sound system that would have made *The Stones* proud. It, too, was covered in aluminum foil.

"The music confuses the Predlincans, members of the warring planet who look for me every night. I am waiting for the people from my planet to come and retrieve me."

I figured Z910 was willing to wait a while since he had a huge fifty-four inch television to help while away the time.

"Do you have food in the apartment?"

Hatshu answered. "He's got a fridge full of food."

Apparently our Belgratan was willing to eat earthling food and drink earthling liquids and couldn't be apprehended under the earthling Mental Health Act and taken to the hospital, which also happened to be located on earth.

"Where do you get your money from to pay for this apartment?"

"I inherited it from my parents."

I figured his parents must have been very proud of their son's achievements.

"What do you do if you need health care? Do you have a doctor?"

"I am protected from the diseases of your planet. I have, however, been injured before and have gone to the hospital."

"Do you feel in fear of anyone?"

"I fear no one," he answered in a serious tone.

"Do you feel that you want to protect yourself or hurt someone else?" I hoped he wasn't planning to use the Vulcan Death Grip on anyone.

"Of course not," he replied. "I protect myself and wait for my people to send for me."

As far as I could tell this guy was not in his right mind. The law says if a person is not hurting himself or others then he can't be taken to hospital against his will. It's not a crime to be crazy. Before we left him in his apartment, Officer Burton gave Walter a stern warning to keep the noise down. He threatened to contact the Predlincans himself and tell them where Walter, or Z910, lived if he didn't keep the peace. Not the most therapeutic approach but effective all the same.

I talked to the guys outside. They had been through the whole apartment and Walter had painted everything silver including the toilet and the bathtub. His bed was covered in one of those silver, emergency thermal blankets. The man was certainly delusional but not a harm to anyone. I thanked them for calling me and walked out into the monsoon rain to my car ready to head back to the office to close up shop for the night and go home.

All in all, a rough day for this Mental Health Worker. Not such a good day for Maggie. Nor Jody. I had left her umbrella Walter's apartment and was **not** going back to get it! Yeah, it was definitely time to go home.

Chapter 4

I had to work at my security guard job from eight to eleven tonight at "Blimpey's Bingo" and to be honest, I was glad for the distraction to keep my mind off Maggie. I had just enough time to eat and shower. I'm not much of a cook so the biggest decision of each day is picking which restaurant will have the privilege of preparing my dinner. My idea of preparing dinner was calling the take-out joint on my cell phone while driving home. My final choice was *Blimpey's*, my ever-present back up plan. Tonight I would eat healthy by having a veggie burger, fries and, of course a *Pepsi* to help maintain my caffeine level at it's required high level in order to function in my day. The added advantage of going to *Blimpey's* is that my meal is always free, compliments of the owner himself.

Blimpey was one of my high school buddies. He was a big guy and at least three-hundred pounds hung on his six-foot frame in high school. The kids ostracized him because of his size and called him Blimpey. They ridiculed me because I looked like Blimpey's little sister. We would hang out together at lunchtime, play euchre and plan how we were going to get back at the world. My plan of revenge was to become a cop and pursue each of the bullies through every legal angle available to me in the criminal justice system. I would sit with Blimpey and the other so-called-losers for hours, gleefully visualizing jerks like Joey DiTonolli on a darkened highway in a stolen car. I would chase him down in my big cruiser until I executed a perfect pit stop sending his car into a 360-degree turn and roll across a field five or six times finally landing on its roof. I'd run over, pull him out of his burning car and slap cuffs on him yelling "Punk, you are under arrest!" Okay, so "COPS" was new on television and I had nothing else to do on a Saturday night, e.g. like go on a date. I watched the show as if it was a training tape and learned how all the cop stuff was done. Well, I failed out of Police College and Joey made it to the big leagues as the manager at the town's largest grocery store. One more fantasy in my life was squashed forever like a bug. I know for a fact that Blimpey and I will never forget the pain of being tormented. I believe that is why I like my work so much. I help one of the most ostracized and stigmatized members of society; the mentally ill.

My shame continued on in Police College when I fell from grace due to my hoplophobia, otherwise known as a fear of guns. Simply put, when they put a gun in my hands, I threw up. It became so bad that I became dehydrated and had to be hospitalized. Pretty pathetic, huh?

In the end, Blimpey worked hard, went to university to get his business degree and opened *Blimpey's Barbecue Pit*. The restaurant was incredibly successful and now Blimpey's is a multi-million dollar, national chain of restaurants. The funny part is that Blimpey no longer looks like his name. While he was a student at university, the doctors discovered Blimpey had an abnormal thyroid, put him on medication and he slimmed down to a very sexy and un-blimplike 180 pounds. He is married to Mary-Anne, another member of our ostracized high school loser group. They have three children and live in a humungous mansion by the river.

Blimpey and I are soul mates and we have always been there for each other. When I quit Police College, I hid out at Blimpey's guest cottage for six weeks until I had the guts to go home. When I didn't have money for college, Blimpey gave me a scholarship to pay my way through nursing school. My plan to become a cop and put those bullies away in jail forever failed miserably. My family never really supported my dream. Women in my family became nurses or secretaries; male Smith's became firefighters or policemen. I was fascinated with the police and my brother, David, was equally enthralled with the fire department. When I was ten and David was thirteen, we'd take the bus downtown together. My brother would visit Dad at the fire station and I would go down the road to the cop shop to see my uncle. He was the Desk Sergeant at that time and would welcome me warmly, sit me up on the desk and go on with his job. Periodically he'd consult me for my opinion on some matter or another making me feel very important. I would sit there for hours propped up on that counter like the police department mascot. Eventually, my brother would be kicked out of the fire station because the crew had to respond to a fire or he was disturbing their nap.

As my brother got older, our visits tailed off because he had other things to do such as sports and date girls. As a teenager, I'd go downtown to "shop" and would always visit my father at the fire station and my uncle at the police station. By that time my uncle was rising upward through the police ranks but he'd always make time to come down to the reception desk and chat with me. My greatest disappointment was failing out of Police College and not fulfilling my lifelong dream. Okay, so the other dream was to lose my virginity to Brock Simpson, but he's in jail now for domestic violence so that was probably a good dream to squash. Life is good for me and I love my job. Mind you, if I could just eradicate Jody and my ex-husband from the face of the earth and complete my search for the future Mr. Chailey Smith, then I'd truly be in heaven.

I dropped by my local *Blimpey's* to pick up my dinner and headed home to 11 Grand Avenue. Home is a Victorian house built in Queen Victoria's Golden Jubilee year, 1897 and was called "Golden Manor" in her honour. The house is located on the border of the rich south and downtown and surrounded by other beautiful Victorian homes. It's a two-story house with a basement and an attic. I renovated each level into apartments and plan to rent them out until I can afford to live there alone and switch it back to a single-family home. At the rate I'm going, the house should be completely mine in 2050. I worked hard to ensure that the Victorian character was maintained. So far the income from my renters is paying for the mammoth renovations and my income continues to be diverted to my divorce lawyer. My grandparents willed me the house and money to my brother and cousins. Grandma and Grandad knew no one loved that house more than I did. Well, to be honest, nobody really wanted the place. It needed to be updated dramatically and was as old as the house in *Mary Poppins*.

I live on the ground floor, Martha, a seventy-five year old spinster, lives on the top floor and two young guys named Bart and Harold, live in the basement. There is a shared front hall and the large carpeted staircase takes you upstairs to Martha's one-bedroom apartment. Martha has lived in this apartment since I started renting them out. She's sort of adopted my six-year-old black Labrador, Randy, who now takes residence with her however I have maintained unlimited visitation rights. I also get the privilege of taking him to the vets - lucky me! He's caused such chaos and mayhem at the vet's that he's been banned from entering the office area and the vet comes out to see him in the back of the car. Martha worked all of her life as a waitress and she never married but according to her story, she was a dating legend and was never without a man.

Above Martha's place, at the very top level of the house is my attic retreat. My grandparents allowed me to hide and play in the room as a child and I have many happy memories from those days. Back then the room was dark, dusty and filled with junk – a true treasure trove to a nine-year-old girl with a vivid imagination. I cleaned it out, installed several skylights and now use this place as a retreat to relax and be by myself. Even Martha follows the rule and keeps out. Of course, it also a great place to make out at night with the stars shining in on you through the skylights. Talk about a vivid imagination. The closest I've ever come to having a guy kiss me up here is when my dog Randy sneaks in and gives me doggy-kisses.

I live on the first floor in a one-bedroom apartment. I am still in the process of renovating my apartment and I only just painted my bedroom and bought a new bed and bedding. I figured that using the linens from my marriage was giving me bad divorce vibes making me unlucky in the world of love.

Two guys, Bart and Harold, live downstairs in a two-bedroom apartment. They are around the age of twenty-five and are part-time university students, part-time *Blimpey's* employees and full-time potheads. Both guys have been in university for the past seven years and have so far have not established any expected D.O.G., or Date of Graduation. Between the two of them they have about eleven credits. I'm very anti-drugs and have made it clear to them that they do not use any on my property hence they have negotiated to use the neighbour's shed to pursue their hobby of "woodworking". They seem to be very hungry after these "woodworking" sessions. Bart and Harold are good guys and help both Martha and me a lot. In typical guy fashion if we give them something to eat as a reward they will do anything for us.

I made it to the "Bingo Palace" just in time. I enjoy my work there but find that the worst part of this job is when I have to call 911 for emergencies. The "Bingo Palace" has been held up twice in the past five years; both times when I was working. Each event involved crack addicts who wanted fast money for a quick fix. Arnie Banks, a sixty-nine-year old bingo regular tripped the first thief as he headed for the door and held him at knifepoint until the police arrived. They arrested the suspect and relieved Arnie from the responsibility of carrying a big, pointy eight-inch knife around that he had pulled out of his pocket. The second guy used a gun to hold up the cashier at the end of the night. The cashier was smart and gave him the money which promptly exploded with ink as the goof ball made his way out the door. Half-blinded, he begged the cops to take him to the hospital to wash out his eyes. Loser!

Of course, there are the 911 calls to the ambulance for every type of injury known to mankind. We regularly have angina calls caused by the excitement of the bingo game. Many times the bingo addict refuses to leave convinced that the angina will go away and their bingo numbers will come up. One guy waited so long that the big number did come up and he expired on the spot. The bingo caller didn't miss a beat and kept calling out the numbers.

Tonight turned out to be pretty uneventful. The only unruly person was drunk out of her gourd. It was one of our regulars and her water bottle was filled with gin. She was absolutely soused by the time the third card was called. She kept calling "Bingo" when she wasn't meant to. She was breaking a bingo commandment and was likely to start a riot so I hustled that little granny's butt out the door and sent her home by taxi.

I finally got home around 11:30 exhausted both mentally and physically. All night long I kept thinking about Maggie being dead. Deep in my heart I didn't believe she committed suicide. But who would kill her and why? All of this thinking was getting me nowhere. I was ready to settle down for the night however Randy was awaiting my return with a different idea and was in the living room with his leash in front of him. He likes a walk before bed so I put on his leash and walked him around the garden twice. He's so stupid he doesn't know the difference between a real and a fake job. Typical guy! Make all the right sounds and actions and they are completely fooled by us women.

Chapter 5

I must have been tired because I didn't wake up until ten the next morning. Either that or I was subconsciously hiding from the world. Yesterday had been one of the worst days of my life and I hoped that today would be a little better. I wandered out to the patio to drink my daily two gallon dose of coffee to kick start my day while I sat and read the paper. Technically, that would be *part* of the paper since Martha had taken the good bits, which left me with the Classified Ads and Sports. At least she had ripped out the horoscope for me to read and I was quickly disappointed to learn that money, fame and sex were not to be mine today. As a Mental Health Worker I feel obliged to review the gossip column to see how the other professionals deal out advice. I didn't have the heart to look in today's Obituary section.

The joy of working an afternoon shift is that you can sleep in for half the day and still have time to make money. I fantasize about being married and having sex all morning long. The longer I've been single, the greater the fantasy I have woven about marriage. Conversely, married people have a warped view of singlehood thinking we un-married ones date ten times a week, drive beautiful, fast cars, vacation every year in tropical resorts and have sex any time, any where. I wish it were true.

Martha dropped by to say that she was going to the podiatrist to have a corn removed. A little too much information for this early in the day. Oh, and by the way, could I please let Randy out for a pee? She then dashed out the door. Damn! That was code for Randy has done something disgusting in her apartment and since he was my dog, it was my privilege to clean it up. I wish she had told me this before I showered.

I grabbed my rubber gloves, black garbage bag and bottle of industrial cleaner and headed up to the dreaded surprise. Last time this happened, Martha had fed Randy a *Blimpey's* burger combo with a chocolate shake. Apparently it was the "Special of the Day". Yeah, that combination was real special! God only knows what she fed him today. Fortunately, the disaster was small and relatively inconsequential. Hey, maybe this day wasn't going to be so bad after all despite what my horoscope said.

I finally arrived at the station and stopped to chat with the Desk Sergeant for a few minutes. On afternoons, if I chat at the front desk, I miss Jody and Flo leaving and don't have to engage in witty dialogue with them. "Miss" might not be the appropriate word since I'd be happy never speak to the evil duo again. I found Abby in the Squad Room ready to start her shift. She's thirty-six, tall, blond and doesn't take shit from anyone. She's like a blond Xena.

"Sorry to hear about Maggie Denton. I heard it was a suicide. I was surprised to hear that she killed herself."

"Yeah, so they say. I know that it looked like a suicide but I don't believe it. With her complaints about the prowler I wonder if there may have been more to her death than a suicide. Liam Fitzgerald is on the case so he'll do a good job. Dicky stopped the investigation into the prowler case."

"What a jerk! I heard what you did to him. Way to go girl! I'll call Liam myself and let him know our concerns about the prowler. There was nothing that made me think that she was depressed. Mind you, it's a big step to say she was murdered."

"I've got to admit that it looked like a suicide but Maggie didn't reveal anything to us that would support that. Maybe Liam will listen to you more since you're a cop."

"You don't need me to tell you but don't let it eat you up. You did more than what was expected of you. You know that when people really want to kill themselves they don't tell anyone anything so that they are successful. Mind you, I really didn't think that Maggie fit into the suicidal category."

I grabbed a coffee, my sixth for the day, and returned to my office next door to read over the report I'd written on Maggie on the weekend. I thought through everything Maggie had said and done while Abby and I were with her on Friday night.

Maggie had told us that she was thirty-two-years old, single and had never married. Lucky her! She had worked as a legal secretary at the legal firm of *Bell and Peters* for the past eight years. She was engaged to Mr. Michael Brigham, one of the lawyers in the firm and met two years ago. Michael had left on Tuesday four days earlier, on a business trip to Mexico and was due to return in five days. She hadn't told him about the nightly intrusions since she didn't want him to worry. He had left a few messages on her phone since he had left but that was it.

Maggie denied having angry ex-lovers who wished her ill harm. Our beige-clad secretary looked like the kind of person who had no ex-lovers – period! She had made only a few friends since moving from Winnipeg to Cookfield, working long hours at the firm and had limited opportunities to make friends. She bought the house five years ago after saving hard and had few debts other than her mortgage. Sure, she didn't have to put her ex-scummy husband through medical school like other people I know. Maggie's mother and sister still lived in Winnipeg – her father had died several years ago from a heart attack. She called her mother and sister weekly and visited them yearly.

Maggie was basically normal and a little on the boring side. She had no history of mental illness nor did her family. She denied using any alcohol or drugs and told us that she was healthy. Maggie did admit that she was under some stress at work in regards to dealing with a case but was not able to divulge any information at this time. All that was unusual was her nightly persistent belief that someone was trying to break into her house and that night the person said, "We're going to get you!"

Abby looked around the house to check for security. The house was a bungalow with two well-sized bedrooms, a kitchen, dining room and living room. The windows were all strong, new with secure locks as were the doors. Even I could break through a door with a sharp knife if the lock was flimsy enough. The basement was unfinished and there were bars on the windows. Maggie was locked up tighter than a drum.

Abby also checked outside. The back garden was small with bushes surrounding the perimeter. Conceivably someone could hide in the bushes however the police would have checked this upon their arrival to her panicky 911 calls. Her windows were not very high off the ground so a tall person could potentially look in. Abby reviewed with Maggie some basic safety such as leaving her outside lights on, informing the neighbours that she was having difficulties so they could keep an out for problems, always carrying a cell phone and so on. She was starting to sound like a Boy Scout leader.

I gave Maggie my business card and asked her to call if she had any concerns. I reassured her that the police would continue to look into the situation. I also suggested that Maggie see her family doctor for a check up. I didn't want this paranoia to be caused by a missed medical condition such as a tumour, which can make a person hallucinate. When we got into the car I asked Abby what she thought of Maggie.

"Boring," she replied.

"No, I meant about her paranoia," I had persisted.

"Well, she seemed perfectly normal until she started talking about the person knocking on her windows. Then it sounded like she was crazy, especially when he talked to her. But it wasn't bizarre, just creepy."

I had agreed with her one hundred percent. Everything had sounded normal but her presentation was unusual. All in all, I thought that Maggie was genuine and that her experience was real. Abby had asked the dispatchers to let me know if there was another prowler call at the Denton residence so that I could see Maggie during one of these "episodes". We were to be given that opportunity an hour later in our shift.

It was 11:15 and Maggie had called in another prowler call. Abby drove like the bats out of hell to Maggie's house with the red lights flashing and sirens going. She knew I hated it when she does that. It just seems unnatural to go through a red traffic light and it feels like you're on a Disney ride with Robin Williams driving and the brakes are not working. My buddy Zack learned the hard way not to go too fast or stop too often with me in the car after I barfed all over the front seat of his cruiser. So it was over me too but I did make my point, don't mess with Chailey or she'll mess all over you.

We were the first to arrive and, surprisingly, we were in one piece. Maggie had locked the front door and wouldn't answer so it took a few minutes for her to respond.

The person who opened the door was a very different person from the prim, conservative, beige-dressed legal secretary we'd met earlier in the day. Maggie was extremely distraught, crying and shaking. Between sobs she told me she had prepared for bed at her usual time of eleven. Lights were out by 11:05. A few minutes later she heard someone unlocking her door and walking towards her bedroom. She tried to dial 911 but was stopped by the intruder who had lifted the telephone receiver in the living room making the phone unusable. It's the kind of thing I've had nightmares about myself. She yelled, "Go away!" but the footsteps came closer. She then heard a deep and unrecognizable male voice which said, "We're going to get you, Maggie Denton!" and then the footsteps retreated. When she was sure he was gone, Maggie finally got the courage to get out of bed to hang up the phone so that she could call 911. The intruder had left the house through the way he came in, the front door.

Abby had returned with Hatcher safely in tow and told us there was no suspect found on the premises or in the area. I quickly filled them in on what Maggie had told me. After twenty minutes, everything had settled and we left the house.

"What do you think, Chailey? Is it really happening or is this lady delusional and hallucinating?" Abby asked. I love it when cops use terms I've taught them and they reciprocate by teaching me how to break into locks and get out of handcuffs.

"I don't know, Abby. With no logical explanation it would make you think that she is delusional. She was terribly distraught. It just doesn't make sense."

"What shall we do? The cops are getting fed up with showing up at this address with all the bells and whistles going to find no one here."

"Perhaps I'll drop by and see her tomorrow evening and see how she's doing. I don't know how to explain it however my gut tells me that this is not part of a delusional system."

"Well, I'm going to forward this case to the detectives. They'll probably turn their noses up at it but that's okay. At least it will be investigated."

Or so we thought. And now Maggie was dead.

Chapter 6

Abby is a great cop and a good friend and I was glad it was her who had been with me on the call to see Maggie. Periodically, we work together on prostitution details. There's nothing more fun than wearing "ho" clothes. You have to leave your inhibitions and any sense of propriety at the door and emerge wearing clothes that are bright and tight. Short skirts barely covering your butt, fish-net stockings, bras that push your boobs so high you can barely see over the top, let alone breathe, and five pounds of makeup that makes a raccoon look pale. Not exactly the outfit you wear to Granny's 90th birthday party.

My job is to stand at the corner while Abby does all the deals with the "Johns". While she is off with the vice cops arresting the "John", another female cop takes her place to actively pursue deals. In the seven times I have done this, not one "John" has asked for me. I'm not sure if I should be offended about this or not. Abby is the best "prostitute" the department has and we are very proud of her achievements. At last year's department Christmas party, Abby got the award for "Best Ho of the Year" with a sex toy as a prize.

My award was "Most Damage to Cars" with a broken fender prize.

I am living vicariously through Abby's love life. She recently met a guy named Nick who is a new Crown Attorney in town. He's a "tough as nails" kind of guy who can put up with Abby's bullshit. At six-feet, four-inches tall, blond-haired, blue-eyed and handsome, he looks like he can hold his own physically against her. I figure that they must have great sex each night and by the smile on her face, he took the morning off to be with her.

Abby's new guy far exceeded any of our expectations. One night while drinking on the patio with Martha, we had a discussion about the "perfect guy". We each took pen to paper and wrote a list of our demands for a future spouse. Abby and I included traits like heterosexual, not too fat or thin, non-smoking, gainfully employed, single, no criminal history or STD and not too hairy. Nothing is worse than braiding a man's back hair. Of course, the man has to be intelligent, fun and love to laugh. Only those meeting these qualifications needed to apply for the future Mr. Chailey Smith Contest. Martha listed only two traits – breathing independently and some level of bladder control. I guess the longer you wait the less demanding you become. Mind you, after my ex-husband Adam, anyone looks good to me.

Abby's relationship with her new blond Adonis proved that there are single women in this city who are having great sex, unlike me who has been in a drought since my divorce. At work, no one wants to date the Chief's niece and dating a colleague can be disastrous when the relationship ends. I've been on one blind date a year since my break up and one of those ended with a call to "Crime Stoppers" and not one has extended to a second date. Drought! Hell, it feels like I live in the middle of the Sahara with no camel and an empty water can. I'm thinking of changing my name to Sandy!

When I work evenings I am not allowed to drive my car alone. I guess that is the department's way to save money on car insurance by keeping me off the road after six o'clock. If there are extra officers available, they will assign me to work with one officer and we do all of the mental health calls together. Some cops call it the "Nut Job", which I don't appreciate since I'm not sure if they are referring to the people we see or me! I was thrilled to hear Abby was riding with me tonight.

Abby called into dispatch to tell them we were ready for the night's first escapade. Lance Milton is a fifty-year old guy who has manic depression, which means he has periods of high endless energy and other times when he is unable to get out of bed for days or weeks on end. He was diagnosed with this disorder about ten years ago. Lance has always preferred to treat himself the good old-fashioned way with alcohol while giving his liver a run for its money at the same time. I have taken him to hospital twice while in a depressed state. He is typically depressed from fall to spring and spends his days lying in bed in a dirty hotel room with food and alcohol delivered to him.

When summer arrives, Lance also comes alive and he enters a manic state. It's at these times that he gets into trouble with the police, often for being drunk and disorderly and is regularly taken to the local alcohol detoxification centre. When he's high he brings back ladies of the night to frolic all night long in an apparently very loud manner.

This evening Lance had tripped on the sidewalk cutting open his face and was taken by ambulance to the hospital. He'd left the Emergency Room wearing a hospital gown and headed over to the bar across the road. The bartender called the police after seeing Lance's attire and thought that he had escaped from the hospital. A quick check with the Emergency Room revealed that Lance had been stitched up and released so the cops took him home and told him to go to bed.

The two officers who took Lance home directed the police dispatcher to send the Mental Health Nurse if there was another call to see Lance again in the evening. Apparently we were going to have our chance to see Lance since he didn't heed their advice and he was sighted walking downtown in his blue hospital gown. The citizens of Cookfield are very attentive and when someone walks down the street in a hospital gown, the 911 call-takers service hundreds of calls of the sighting. The police dispatcher guided us to the Town Square where we finally got a glimpse of a different version of a man in blue.

"I can see him, Dispatch," Abby announced into the mike.

And could we ever! Lance had discarded his blue hospital gown and was frolicking in the fountain under the watchful eye of Queen Victoria's statue. Upon closer inspection, we learned that Lance was using the fountain to bathe in and was currently washing his hair. A small crowd had gathered around the fountain. Some people were talking on their cell phones no doubt calling 911.

Abby parked the Impala and we got out and headed over to the growing crowd. We pushed our way into the front of the circle and I called out to Lance.

"Hey, Lance. It's me, Chailey! Shower time is over. We need to talk to you."

Lance looked up at me and yelled, "Fuck off!"

"Well, that wasn't called for," I replied indignantly.

I guess the cops weren't kidding earlier when they said that Lance was irritable since he's usually charming. Time for a cop presence, meaning it was Abby's turn.

"Lance, this is Officer Hartford. You need to get out now."

"You can fuck yourself, too!" he yelled back.

"That's not nice, Lance. This is your last chance. Out! Now!" yelled Abby over the loud splashing of the water. She sounded like my mother.

"Didn't you hear what he said, Pig. Go to hell! He's not harming anyone!"

I looked up to see who had said that. I had been so focussed on Lance that I hadn't realized that a crowd of fifty or so Cookfield citizens had gathered around us, and at least half of them looked like punks. The Town Square historically had been the centre of town where special events were celebrated such as welcoming the men home from war. History books always showed pretty pictures of men in hats and women in long dresses pushing perambulators. The Square of today is a hangout joint for punks and their pals – a magnet for anyone with no job and a bad attitude.

"Back off!" yelled Abby. "I'm a cop." She pulled out her badge. Lucky for them that it was only her badge because with the temper she has it could have been her gun.

"Call for back up," she told me, "Four units."

I grabbed my radio. "Charlie 13 to Dispatch. We need back up at the Town Square fountain. Four units." I had wanted to say fourteen but that would be overkill.

Some other punk kid yelled, "Get lost Big Tits! You too, Fat Ass!"

I wondered which one of us was which. I figured we could debate that later.

"Yeah! Fuck off you fat cows!"

Abby was transforming into her cop look – kinda' like how the *Incredible Hulk* changes from man to *Hulk*. Even Nick would be frightened of her now.

"Back up, Chailey, until we get help," Abby directed me.

I tried to walk backwards but couldn't. The crowd had pulled around behind us. I started to panic. Abby pulled out her police stick and yelled, "Back off!'

"Call for help, Chailey!" she yelled at me.

"Control, this Charlie 13. We need help NOW!"

I couldn't hear the dispatcher's reply because the fight started at that moment. Someone pushed Abby and she hit them in defense. The punks jumped after us and some of the good citizens helped us to fight back at the punks. I pushed two or three away and kicked a few. Next thing I knew, the Square was wailing with police sirens. Help was on its way and within seconds there was an all out brawl with the citizens of Cookfield on one side and the Police Blues on the other. I was terrified, so I did what I thought was the smart thing and waded into the fountain and stood under the water out of the way of the fight. At times like this, if you are not wearing a police uniform then you're one of the bad guys. The police presence expanded rapidly and they took over so the brawl came to an end fairly quickly. None of the good guys were hurt badly however more than half the cops looked like they had scraped themselves and a few eyes would be well bruised. I guess the police dispatchers expected the worst and had sent ambulances. I was terrified to see one thug had been knifed and paramedics were looking after the victim. That could have been us. I finally found Abby in the crowd and she looked like she was okay.

"You can come out now, Chailey," she yelled to me. I hadn't realized it but I was still hanging onto the fountain.

I sloshed my way out and once I was out of the spray, I could see that approximately twenty men and two females were handcuffed and lying on the ground. Police custody would be busy tonight processing this mess.

The Sergeant approached us. "You girls okay?" he asked. He'd always been a bit of a sexist. "What the hell happened? We heard you request for backup, Chailey, and we knew we needed to come quickly. You must have left the mike open cause we heard the guy calling Abby a "Fat Ass" and knew that she'd have something to say about that."

So he presumed that I was "Big Tits". Hmm, interesting!

"Sarge, she was great. We tried to back out of the situation but we were surrounded. That's when we called for the Cavalry," I explained excitedly. Okay, so the adrenaline was still flowing and I felt like I could kick James Bond's ass if he was here and pissed me off.

"I'm glad you're safe. Why were you here in the first place?"

"We came to pick up Lance Milton and see if he needed to go to hospital."

"Isn't that the guy in your car?"

Abby and I looked over in unison and there was Lance, dripping a little and waving at us with a big smile. The bugger had escaped the fight into the relative safety of our car. Now why didn't I think of hiding in there?

It took me a moment to see that Lance was unscathed but my car wasn't! Someone had smashed a large metal garbage can through the front windshield. Bastards! Now I was really pissed off. Abby went over to the car and told Lance to stay there or she'd whoop his ass, too. Lance stopped smiling at that point. We spent about twenty minutes helping to sort out the carnage of prisoners. A truck was called to tow away my wounded Impala. We remembered to extricate Lance before it left, although I was tempted to let them take him to the wrecker's yard as well.

As the prisoners stood up and were slowly transferred to the police wagon and cruisers, Abby watched the procedure very closely. She finally spied what she was looking for and yelled to the cops.

"Hey! Stop! I want to talk to that guy. Yeah. The punk in the blue shirt." She turned to me and said, "Come on Chailey. You deserve to get a piece of this action."

We went over to the guy who was now coupled between two cops. The average citizen might have thought that they were concerned that their suspect might escape. I had a sneaky suspicion that it was an intimidation tactic. Abby had everyone's attention, including mine when I realized the guy was the one who had told us to get lost and called us rude names that inaccurately described our body parts.

"Sir, I think there was something you were saying earlier which I couldn't hear properly over the fountain. Care to repeat it?"

The punk looked at the ground.

"Are you sure you don't want to share that with the class?"

He looked up at Abby and he gave her the dirtiest look I'd ever seen. I needed to remember that one for my ex-husband the next time I saw him in divorce court. The punk chose that moment to do the unthinkable. He horked on Abby's boots. Yuck! I was ready to spew myself. Abby's look was thunderous. Our Xena was pissed.

"Book him for assaulting police." She went to leave but turned back again. "And I'll remember you, punk!" she added.

"Is that a threat?"

"No," Abby replied with a smile. "It's a promise!"

I figured that the only way that this guy's life could get worse is if the Crown Attorney who prosecutes this punk lands up being Nick Coomber, Abby's new squeeze.

A few minutes later we were ready to go back to the police station to pick up another car so that we could take Lance to the hospital. I could hear someone call out to me on the police radio.

"Hey, Chailey, I'd vote for you to win the wet T-shirt contest."

Oh God! I looked down my front. Today was obviously *not* the day to wear a white T-shirt. I knew who the chicken-shit cop was who said that but wouldn't give his name. Abby was grinning. So was the Sergeant across the Square. So that's why he presumed I was Big Tits!

We spent a few minutes with Lance. He was definitely unwell talking a mile a minute and said that he wanted to go to the hospital. He certainly sounded delusional when he told me that he was God and that he shouldn't be treated this way. Hey, as a Mental Health Worker, I shouldn't be treated this way either. I'm sick and tired of having wet knickers every day.

We took Lance to the hospital and left him there in the capable hands of the nurses. We headed back to the station to complete the paperwork that went with arresting twenty goofs. Two hours later we were ready to grab some supper but were interrupted by a call from the Desk Sergeant to say that a Michael Brigham was in the reception area. I wondered why Maggie Denton's fiancé would be here to speak to me? And might I add, he was still supposed to be in Mexico.

Chapter 7

The advantage of having your office on the second floor is that you can look over the balcony to the reception area ahead of time and prepare your plan of attack based on the events occurring down in the hole. The Desk Sergeants had learned how to get people down to the reception area. For example, the Sergeant will call me and introduce the person to see me as a "hot, sexy guy". The Sergeant sits and watches the balcony for me as I take a quick peek at the "Hottie" and he then yells at me across the lobby by name so that I can't escape. Usually the "hot sexy guy" may actually have been one in 1955, last had his own teeth in 1972 and currently reeks like a brewery. In this case, I knew who Mr. Michael Brigham, Esquire, was immediately. He was approximately six-feet tall and was slim with dark brown curly hair with a nice matching dark tan. Michael was well-dressed wearing black Docker pants and a white golf T-shirt. Certainly he was a stark contrast to the hooligans in line to see the police at the desk. I went down the stairs and approached him, introduced myself and shook his hand. He had a strong handshake and he told me how pleased he was to finally meet me. His eyes were strikingly blue and he had a dimple on his chin.

"I am so sorry for your loss," I offered in a kind and sympathetic voice.

"Loss? What loss? Is everything alright with Margaret?" he asked anxiously.

Shit! "Mr. Brigham, we need to talk." I lead him into the Interview Room and asked him to sit. "Have the police not called you?" I asked.

"No," he replied. "I came straight from the airport to see you at the police station. Your messages had me concerned and I wanted to speak to you before I saw Margaret." Maggie had suggested I call Michael on Saturday and I had left a message for him to call me at his leisure. "What has happened to my Margaret?"

"I'm sorry to have to tell you this but Maggie died. She was found shot yesterday afternoon in an apparent suicide. The police are investigating her death. I am very, very sorry."

He put his head into his hands and started sobbing. I could hear him say, "Not my Margaret. Not my beautiful Margaret." It took him a few minutes to compose himself and I stayed quietly at the table not knowing what to do or say.

"Can I get you a drink of water or something?" Pathetic, but I couldn't think of anything else.

"No, thank you. I'm fine."

"I can arrange for someone to drive you home if you'd like," I offered.

"No, Ms. Smith. I'm fine. Just a little shocked. You said she shot herself with a gun. Where would she get a gun?"

"I don't know any details right now." I knew that it wasn't wise to share information. "Detective Liam Fitzgerald is leading the case along with Detective Rick Simmons. One of them will contact you directly. I gave him your phone number in Mexico since I didn't expect you to return for a few days." I sneezed. "Excuse me." Apparently my cat allergy was still activated.

"Bless you," he replied. "When I received your message and hadn't been able to connect directly with Margaret, I decided to return from my business trip early. Did you know her well?"

I explained how Maggie had reported the prowler calls with no suspect found. I also explained my role as a Mental Health Worker and why I was involved and that the outcome of my assessment was that she didn't present outwardly with any signs of mental illness.

"It's too bad you weren't able to get hold of me. I could have told you how Margaret has been becoming increasingly fearful of people hurting her. I really didn't want to go on this business trip but Margaret, God bless her, insisted I go."

"Maggie denied having any problems, Mr. Brigham."

"Well, of course she would, wouldn't she?" he snapped. "I'm sorry, Ms. Smith. I don't mean to sound angry, but I'm just devastated by this news. Margaret is dead and I can't believe it. We were engaged in September and we had a wonderful wedding planned for next fall. Does her mother know yet?"

"I'm not sure. I gave Mrs. Denton's number to the detectives so they could call her."

"You seemed to know Margaret well. Margaret was a wonderful person. She's very quiet and some would say mousy but I would disagree with them on that. You just had to get to know her better to realize all of her strengths. Margaret was my secretary and what an amazing secretary she was. We both worked long hours and we'd often sit at the conference room table and eat a take-out supper that she'd pick up for us. It took me three long years to ask her out and it took her two long months to tell me "yes". We shared similar interests such as traveling, classical music and bird watching. Life together was simple and enjoyable. Losing her is like having my heart cut out. It took me a lifetime to find the woman of my dreams and now she is gone. What will I do now?"

"What did you mean by Margaret was in fear for herself?"

"Margaret told me that someone at work had sent her a letter that made her feel uncomfortable. I asked to see it but she had already destroyed it. Margaret denied there were any threats. "I've upset someone, that's all" she said. And that was it. Margaret never mentioned the letter to you."

"No," I lied. "She called the police repeatedly about a prowler on her property but she denied she was having any other problems." I didn't want to give too much information.

"I'm here for support if you need it. I should add that one of the detectives will be calling you, Mr. Brigham. They will be able to provide any additional information about the investigation." I sneezed again.

Michael shook my hand and said, "Please, call me Michael. Thank you, Chailey, for all that you have done. It sounds like you have been a good friend to Margaret." He gave me his business card and got ready to leave. "Are you really sure that I can I call you if I have any questions or concerns?" he asked.

"Absolutely," I replied and reciprocated by giving him my business card. I walked him out to the reception area, past the hooligans of Cookfield who were en masse today in the reception area. Michael shook my hand again, smiled and walked out to his black BMW car parked at the side of the road.

I went back upstairs and headed back into the Squad Room to finish my report. Kevin Harrison showed up just as I did and we sat down with Abby who was completing her paper work.

"Hey, Chailey. Good job with Dickhead yesterday. He deserved a bloodied nose after what he said to you. One of the forensic guys overheard your little interaction. If I ever meet him in a dark alley he'll get more than a bloodied nose and it won't be from a head butt. Fitzgerald's pretty angry about Dicky stifling the initial report on the prowler and Maggie. He may land up reporting the Son-of-a-Bitch."

"Well I just had another strange experience. Maggie's boyfriend just came in to see me. I had to tell him about Maggie's death." It was the first time I had to break the news of someone's death other than telling my seven-year-old niece that my dog had eaten her hamster. It was pretty rough both times. I guess that it was rougher for Michael to get the news.

"What's he doing back? I thought that he was coming home in a few days. How did he take it?" asked Kevin.

"Pretty well, I guess. He seemed nice enough. He just didn't look like what I thought he would."

"What do you mean?"

"Well, he was very good looking. Very good looking actually and quite GQ'ish." I replied. "He was terribly distraught by learning that Maggie was dead. They had dated for two years and had met through work. She was his secretary and they worked long hours together and fell in love."

"I know what you mean. I'd have thought Maggie would have been more attracted to a mousy, quiet nice guy."

"I guess she wouldn't be dating a cop, huh?" I added with sarcasm. "Maybe I'm being too judgmental," I added thoughtfully.

"No, Chailey, trust your gut instinct. I always do."

"Yeah, but you guys are cops and I'm not," I tried to explain.

Both Abby and Kevin smiled. As we were talking he had gone over to the coffeepot and poured each of us a coffee. I was ready for some whisky to be put in mine the way my grandfather liked his. I'm sure that if I looked in Flo's bottom drawer I would find a bottle of something.

"Listen to yourself. You're a Mental Health Worker. You help us, the cops, to figure out what is going on with people. You're the expert. What you're missing are experiences to apply your observations to. He's defense a lawyer, isn't he? So, you probably haven't met a lot of lawyers. Trust me you will. For every good lawyer there is one who is not so good," replied Kevin who sounded like any seasoned, mildly cynical cop. He saw me smile. "Yeah, smart ass, just like cops."

"Don't get me wrong. He was genuinely distressed over the loss of his fiancee. My heart went out to him. Michael told me Margaret had received some kind of threatening letter at work. He never saw it but Maggie admitted it made her feel uncomfortable. She told me the same thing but said it was a joke."

"Kevin, want to join us for supper? We were just heading out to pick something up," offered Abby.

Or at least we thought we were. The dispatcher chose just that moment to call us over the air.

"Charlie Thirteen. We have "Bridget" on the Hardman Bridge threatening to jump. Please respond as soon as possible. I have two other units responding."

"Ten-four," I responded.

Due to many reasons, "Bridget" is a person who feels empty and abandoned. She deals with these feelings by threatening to end her life through suicide. "Bridget's" real name is Veronica, we just call her "Bridget" because her chosen poison is threatening to jump from a bridge. She's pretty industrious and uses all three bridges that cross the river. Sometimes she'll hitch hike. I can just imagine how a driver would feel when he's kind and offers a ride to this little lady to have her demand he stop the car half way across so that she can get out and start climbing the bridge railing. Other times she will take a taxi if she has money. The suicide threats are a cry for help and represent her constant dissatisfaction with life. The trouble with the bridge threats is that they are very public and the average Joe Citizen gets real nervous watching her on the edge thereby causing massive traffic tie-ups on the major routes entering and exiting the city. "Bridget's" attempts are usually timed at peak rush hour thereby enhancing the effect of the act. She's done this thirty-seven times this calendar year. If I'm working, I go out and talk to her, she tells me about today's stress, we agree that life sucks and she accepts a ride home ready to start the cycle over again the next day. She sees a counsellor weekly and the attempts have reduced from twice a night to twice a week. Her attempts in May aren't too bad weather-wise but when you are standing on that cold, windy bridge in the middle of February, it's an experience that you won't soon forget. There is *nothing* that can warm you up after those nights. Okay, almost nothing.

"Sorry Kevin, we've got to go," said Abby. "So much for dinner."

Abby did the red lights and siren thing trying to get us through the traffic. As we hurtled along at the speed of light she said something that took me completely by surprise.

"I could be wrong but I do believe Kevin Harrison likes you."

"I don't think so. Trust me, that's the most pleasant conversation we've ever had. He was being sympathetic to the poor little nurse."

"Wasn't it Kevin you rear-ended twice?"

"No. I rear-ended him only once. Okay, so I *backed* into his cruiser once as well."

"He's a nice guy," added Abby. "He played on my baseball team last year so I got to know him a bit better.

His ex-wife treated him like crap. One day she just got up and moved to BC with their kid."

I wish my ex-husband would move somewhere. China would be nice!

"That's a tough deal. He was really very sweet yesterday at a time when I really needed it. I kind of felt bad when I puked on his shoes."

"You didn't!"

"Oh yes I did!"

Abby had pushed her way through the traffic jam that had virtually ground to a halt, compliments of "Bridget". It was windy so "Bridget" only had one leg over the railing. She really didn't want to slip in the wind.

Abby pulled up the car beside her and I got out to talk to "Bridget" while Abby helped direct traffic. I never get too close to her in case she does accidentally slip and grabs onto me to help keep her up and we both land up in the drink.

"What's up, Veronica?"

"Go away, Chailey. I'm not talking to you," she yelled at me.

"Hey, I came all this way and this is all the thanks I get?"

"Thanks, Chailey. Now I'm jumping. I'm fed up. Nothing changes. It's the same shit, different day."

If that's a reason to jump then ninety-five percent of the people on the bridge should get out of their cars this very minute and jump. I think that phenomenon is called "life".

"What's made you so upset today?"

"My mother. She called me today and told me I was a failure. I hate her!"

Hell, another good reason for me to jump, too. My mother has been known to be a wee bit critical at times. She has never quite gotten over me divorcing a doctor.

"What do you think about what she said?" I asked.

"She's right. I'm a failure!" she sobbed.

"In everything, right?" I asked.

She paused for a moment. "No, not everything!" she snapped back at me.

"Then she's wrong, right?"

"Right, she's wrong," "Bridget" said.

Now I was getting confused whether I was getting it right.

"So why don't you come down and we can talk about how to deal with your mother when she talks to you like that. Because you're right. It's not fair when she does that and it makes you angry and it hurts." I figured that we should try to help her sort out how to deal with her mother since I still was trying to figure out my own and maybe I could get some tips.

"Okay," she quietly sobbed. Bridget made a huge deal of getting off the barricade needing the two male police officers who had arrived ahead of us to assist/half-carry her to the car. She definitely deserved an Oscar for that performance.

When she got into the car she was thrilled to see Abby. "How are you doing?" "Bridget" loved Abby.

"Great thanks, Veronica," she replied. I waited for Abby to tell "Bridget" that life was great because she was getting laid. Abby managed to avoid sharing that little detail.

"Where to, Veronica?" she asked.

"How about my friend Zelda's place. She made lasagna for dinner tonight and there are probably leftovers." Personally I was getting so hungry I was ready to have a piece of Zelda's lasagna myself. "Bridget" gave us directions to her friend's place that was, of course, on the other side of town. Forty-five minutes later we headed back to the "barn" meaning the police station and our own dinner. I don't know where the term "the barn" originated from however they keep animals in the barn so it seemed appropriate to call the police station that. It was just before midnight and I was so hungry I could have eaten a horse and chased the rider.

Abby and I headed to our local pub, *The Wellington* for a drink (or two) and some well-deserved dinner. By the time I got home it was nearly two o'clock and I was more than ready to hit the sack. Thankfully Randy wasn't in my apartment waiting for a walk which meant that Martha was not entertaining male company tonight. Instead I was greeted by the sound of someone snoring in my living room. Being a cautious person, I went into the living room with my baseball bat in the ready to swing position. I switched on the lights and Bart jumped about three feet off the couch and screamed.

I jumped higher and screamed at him, "What the hell are you doing here?"

"Harold has a lady friend visiting and didn't want me there. The door to the apartment was locked and there was a sock on the door hand which is the "sign" to stay out. I knew you wouldn't mind me sacking out here." I was distracted by the news about the female.

"A lady friend! Who is it? How long has he known her?" I wondered how Harold would generate enough energy to do the dirty deed. The guy's pulse rate is about thirty and he is permanently in sloth-speed.

Bart had no details. Too bad for him because I'd be sending him down first thing in the morning to do some investigative work and then reward him for good information with breakfast. It's the modern day version of hunting and gathering.

"Yeah, you can sleep there but cover yourself up with a blanket and no snoring. And next time, leave me a note. You scared the crap out of me."

"Good night, Chailey."

"Good night, Bart," I responded.

My final thought for the night as I settled into bed was that it's kind of pathetic and depressing when I realized that Bart knew where to go to sleep. He was guaranteed that he wouldn't be disturbing me with a sleepover date at my apartment.

Chapter 8

Thursday morning started like most others when I work afternoons - slowly and quietly. Today I arose at the respectable hour of eleven o'clock in the morning. As with each day, I grabbed the newspaper and headed to the most important section – the horoscope! Gemini, my zodiac sign, was looking pretty optimistic today and stated, "You will reach new heights today in your career. " I decided to break the morning routine of coffee and *Special K* and be a little adventurous meaning I'd have a pot of tea with toast. The weather had brightened considerably and the predicted high was eighteen degrees Celsius. I thought I'd celebrate with a walk down by the river with Randy. I phoned Martha to tell her about my plan and she promised to leave Randy in the yard with his leash since she was off to the Senior's Centre. It was Thursday and she teaches a line dancing class in the afternoon.

Bart was still snoozing on my couch. I couldn't hear any movement or noise from the basement so I surmised that the two lovebirds must be sleeping also. I'd have to get details about this "d'affaire de couer" later.

My Aunt Janice called. She's married to my uncle the Police Chief. It's very appropriate that she's married to a cop since she's an absolute pistol.

"How are you doing, Chailey?"

"Not bad, thanks. What can I do for you?"

"Well…" There was a long pause. "How has your uncle been doing recently?"

That was a strange question coming from her. "I don't see him much at work. Fine as far as I know. Why?"

"Well… It's just that he's not been home much recently and he seems a little distant."

"I'm sure he's fine, Auntie. You know that he is very busy with his job." I was feeling more than a little uncomfortable with this conversation.

"Would you mind just checking on him? Make sure that he's alright."

Right, the person who's the lowest person on the totem pole and only one up from the parking-lot-guy is going to check on the Chief of Police.

"Sure." I'd promise anything to her right now to get her off this topic.

"Thanks, honey. Bye." And then she hung up. No chit-chat. That was it. It felt quite strange and if my radar was correctly tuned in then my aunt thought that my uncle was having an affair. Hmm… A foolish thought since my uncle was a completely devoted man, or so I thought. Mind you, I thought that Adam was a faithful husband….. Perhaps I should be looking into this a little more despite my better judgment.

I put on my sweat pants, my favourite "Bad Boyz" T-shirt and running shoes. Okay, so these shoes have never run a step in their lives but walking shoes sounds so ancient and orthopaedic. The shower could wait until after we returned from the walk. Last time I went for a walk with Randy he ran after a duck dragging me through the weeds and duck muck. Obviously I should have let go of the leash but hindsight is always twenty/twenty. Someone once asked me if I'd ever said any words that I had regretted in hindsight. My response was, "Yeah. On my wedding day when I said, I do!"

Cookfield is blessed with many beautiful spots and the Riverbank Trail is definitely one of the jewels in that crown. The river is about a half a mile wide and there is a busy industrial port on the east side of the city where ships come in from Lake Ontario to unload their cargo to be transported elsewhere by truck or train. There are three bridges in Cookfield that cross the Sussex River. There is a lift bridge and two high level bridges named the Hardman Bridge and the Centennial Bridge, otherwise known as the *Marry me Mary* Bridge. They started calling it this about eighteen years ago after a man (we presumed) had climbed on top of the concrete overbridge and painted his marriage proposal across the concrete. The city had proposed painting over the message on many occasions, however, the plan had always leaked out to the press and there had been an outpouring of letters to support leaving the message alone. The citizens of Cookfield were a funny lot and they go nuts if someone wants to paint over a marriage proposal on the side of a bridge. But bring an important issue like homelessness or the plight of the mentally ill and two or three letters may trickle into the editor of the newspaper.

The city came to life again about six months ago when someone had spray painted over the *Marry me Mary* writing in big black ugly paint. The debate since that time has been if a hooligan did the damage or if Mary and her hubby were getting a divorce.

I drove to the western part of the river just past the Westview Harbour where the rich people park their pleasure craft. Houses overlooking the trail and the river were big, beautiful and expensive. Purchase offers start at one million bucks each.

I parked my car in the parking lot and Randy started panting up a storm becoming extremely excited. You'd think that he was in heat and not just going for a walk. I opened the front passenger door where he insists on sitting and he shot out like a bullet into the water chasing the Canada geese who were mighty pissed off at this black ball of fur intruding their peace. He caught one a few years ago and I had to wrestle it out of his mouth. It was a bad scene and involved a visit to the Emergency Room, a home visit by the SPCA to assess my pet-keeping abilities (or lack of such) and subsequent mandatory attendance for me and my four-legged friend in an obedience class at a cost of a mere $150! I started to walk down the trail trying to look as though I had nothing to do with the big, barking, black dog until I heard a lady scream and saw Randy running muddy and wet towards some lady in a white boating outfit.

I turned and used my meanest voice. "Randy! Come here!"

I think that it had a paradoxical effect on him and made Randy run faster to the nice lady in the white outfit. He pretended that he hadn't heard me at first and jumped up on the sailor once and then dutifully ran back to me as though he was being obedient. I was giving him a good tongue lashing when someone walked up to me and said, "You could never keep your men under control."

My head snapped up to see Adam, my ex-husband, standing in front of me. He had obviously been out jogging on the path and to be perfectly honest, he looked very sexy sweating slightly in his white shorts and T-shirt against his dark tan. You'd think that he'd know better than to tan himself since he is a plastic surgeon.

I met Adam when he was a first-year medical student and I had been in nursing for several years. In medical school there was a saying, "If you can't get a date, get a nurse!" My relationship with Adam was initially hot and fast. His knowledge of anatomy didn't just help him excel in medical school! Within a month he moved into my apartment and by the end of six months I was dipping into my cash reserves to pay for his medical school expenses. He proposed to me the night before I paid his second year tuition. I worked as many double shifts as I could to help keep our debt load down. After all, it only seemed fair since Adam was on call two or three nights in a row. He was very thoughtful and did things around the house like change the sheets after I worked nights. Adam suggested that we get married the second summer we were together. Once again, to help save money we had a small wedding in my grandparent's garden. We celebrated his graduation day with him getting a piece of paper with his medical degree. That night he gave me a piece of paper asking for a divorce decree.

"After being married to you, you'd think I'd stay away from dogs, wouldn't I? Once bitten, twice shy."

"I didn't know that you like to hang out in this rich part of town. Are you aware I just bought a house across the road? The big brown one over there." He pointed to a huge mother of a house which was absolutely magnificent.

"Mmm. Nice. You know what they say about men who compensate for small penises with big toys." I attempted to produce my most benign, innocuous look while trying to restrain my jealous streak. I made a mental note to do a drive-by tonight to case out the joint and get a better look at Adam's new digs. Thankfully Abby was working tonight and she owed me a favour after the Valentine's Day fiasco. "I'd heard that you'd bought something out here. My lawyer had it on your list of assets. Too bad you couldn't get a house on the water."

"I figure that's a good thing, don't you think, Chailey? That way I don't have to watch people making out."

I blushed at that one. Adam knew that I'd lost my virginity to Ricky Jamieson along this waterfront trail. I'd felt grass under my naked butt more than once when Adam and I did the dirty deed while on picnics by the river.

My lawyer had told me that Adam had bought a house in this area for close to a million dollars. Nothing but the best for our Adam! That's why he married me, right? I was happy that Adam was the new owner of a big expensive house. My lawyer loves these kind of purchases. Money can be hidden but property can't.

After Adam and I had split up, I hadn't pursued a divorce immediately and Adam was more than satisfied to leave our marital legal situation status quo. Personally I was waiting for him to start making the big bucks as a plastic surgeon. By the time he figured out my game plan, he'd already made his first half million. I just wanted to recoup the money I'd paid for his medical school. Apparently my divorce lawyer had bigger and better plans. She wanted a new BMW and Adam was going to pay for it. And soon! Our court date was set for next week. Olivia, my lawyer, was ready to rock 'n roll. I think that she had already ordered the car and looking at this house, she could order heated leather seats.

Randy chose this awkward moment in the conversation to join our pow wow. He ran over, shook the water and mud off himself onto us and jumped up on Adam with big muddy paws.

"At least Randy is happy to see you. See you in court next week. Oh, and Adam, bring your checkbook. Bye!"

I walked off with a big smile and a little wave. Who's screwing who, Adam? I wondered to myself. Things were looking a little brighter already. The birds sounded like they were singing with a little more joy and the sun felt warmer. I found a spot on the grass beside the trail and sat down to relax while Randy went berserk chasing the ripples in the water. I've always loved the river and have many wonderful memories of being with my family boating and picnicking along the Sussex River.

It was eventually time to head back so that I could have a shower and Randy could have his well deserved treat for placing two big black paw prints on Adam's beautiful white shirt. They looked like wonky nipples. By the time we drove home it was two-thirty and I needed to get a move on so that I could be at work on time.

I made it to the station just in time with only two minutes to spare. The evening shift was starting like many evenings do meaning that it was busy. As soon as I had walked in the door, thrown down my backpack and logged on the radio with the dispatcher, I was being sent to see Veronica/ "Bridget". She was as predictable as she was annoying. Tonight "Bridget" was on the lift bridge threatening to jump while causing a major traffic jam. The rush hour traffic is pretty horrendous at the best of times. With good weather predicted on nights like these everyone makes a mass exodus out of the city to go to better and more beautiful places than our fair city. Well, at least they were trying to. "Bridget's" current prank was tying up traffic so badly that Spencer, my partner for this call, and I had to park the car and walk half way across the bridge to get to her. Her antics were doubly effective when we realized there were three boats waiting for the lift bridge to go up. By the time we got to her I was hot and sweaty, not the good kind of hot and sweaty, and if I was honest, more than a little on the irritable side. I managed to negotiate "Bridget" down from her perch in two minutes, a personal best for me and we all trudged back to our abandoned cruiser. "Bridget" was not pleased with the walk but I figured it was a natural consequence for causing this rush hour mess.

Due to the "Bridget"-induced traffic jam, it took us a good forty minutes to drive over the bridge and back again. After the lengthy wait in traffic sucking in the car fumes and "Bridget" jabbering away happily in the back seat, I was ready to jump off the bridge myself. We drove by *Blimpey's*, picked up a take-out meal of a hamburger, fries and a Coke to help rebuild "Bridget's" depleted energy level from the bridge trek and deposited her at the front door of her apartment. A smile and wave were exchanged and Spencer and I headed off on our merry way.

Spencer dropped me off at the police station and I went up to my office to read the five million e-mails I get each day, of which half of them are identified as "Must Read". On my desk there was an envelope with a card inside which I opened. It was a "Thank you" card. I was a little mystified about its appearance since I was pretty sure that I hadn't done much recently to be thanked for. On the inside it read, "Dear BT," I presumed that was short form for Big Tits. "Next time we do a training session we'll get you to start a brawl for us to practice on. Best wishes, The Riot Squad." What a bunch of smart asses.

The next thing I knew there was another call to see "Bridget"/Veronica. Except, as the dispatcher added, we would now have to start calling her "Heidi" since she was high up on top of a crane. How the girl had enough time to eat that meal and hustle her butt over to the new office tower construction site where the crane was located was beyond me.

"She's specifically asked for you, Chailey. She won't talk to anyone but you so Sergeant Taylor has asked you to go to the site. Spencer will pick you up in front of the station. Good luck."

"10 - 4, Dispatch," I replied wearily.

I figured I could tell her to get down on the phone from my office just as easily as I could from the construction site. I guess I needed to talk to the officers on the scene. I headed down to the front of the station and out the door where Spencer was waiting for me.

"Well, we did such a great job with "Bridget" last time that we get to do it all over again. To the construction site and beyond," announced Spencer. He was doing his best *Buzz Lightyear* imitation. Badly, I might add and sounded more like Kermit the Frog on steroids.

It only took us a few minutes to get to the scene and quite the scene it was. Four cruisers and two big fire trucks, including the aerial truck, were parked underneath the crane. Things were looking up in more than one way since I *love* firefighters. I know that seems a little strange to say that I have a thing about men in uniforms since my father had been a firefighter and my brother David currently works for the Cookfield Fire Department. Freud would have a hey day with that one. Lucky me! My brother just happened to be here. He approached me along side Sergeant Taylor.

"Chailey, Veronica climbed up the crane about twenty minutes ago and is up at the top. She is threatening to jump. She said on the phone that she'll only speak to you."

I explained to him that our potential jumper had made these gestures to harm herself daily for many years however this was the first time she'd climbed up a crane as far as I could remember.

"If you give me the phone I'd be happy to talk to her."

"Er, didn't I mention this before? She will only talk to you in person," added the Sergeant.

"You're joking, right?" I asked.

By now a small crowd of cops and firefighters had gathered around our discussion. Apparently they had all heard about "Bridget's" demands and were curious to know what my response would be. The person leading the group was my brother who was grinning from ear to ear thinking that there was no way I'd do something that only a big, burly firefighter would do. I had suffered a lifetime of sexism in the Smith family in which the women did girly things like be nurses and the boys went out to do rough and tumble jobs like fire fighting and police enforcement. I just wasn't sure that this was the appropriate time or place to be proving my brawn.

Sergeant Taylor answered my question with a slight smirk on his face. "I wish I was kidding. Sorry!"

Not as sorry as I was. I guess my horoscope was right about reaching new heights in my career after all.

I could hear someone behind me ask what were they going to do now. I heard another voice announce, "I knew I'd win this bet!"

I turned around and asked, "What bet?"

A lot of uniformed men became very quiet at that precise moment.

"What bet, David?" I demanded to know. Now my brother started to blush a little.

"You bet that I wouldn't do this, didn't you? I haven't given my answer yet so you'd better hang onto your money, boys. Who put money on me going up there?"

There was complete silence and more than one guy looked down at the ground. At least Spencer was sweet enough to accept what he believed to be the losing wager and said, "I'll take that bet."

I made my announcement to the group. "Let's make it a real bet. If I go up, I win the money. If I don't, I will pay you double your money."

David yelled out, "You're on!" Since he was my brother everyone must have thought that he knew me well so they all agreed with him. Fools!

Spencer pulled me away from the crowd. "Are you sure you want to do this Chailey?"

"No, I don't *want* to do this but I have to. You saw my brother. Spencer, this Mama wants a new pair of shoes and that's what this Mama is going to get. I'll be fine. Veronica's up there and she's fine and so will I be. Have faith." We both knew that this was bravado talking but it served its purpose. "By the way, I wouldn't bet any money if I were you just in case."

I went over to tell Sergeant Taylor of my plan to go up. He provided me with directions such as not going near Bridget, to talk to her from a distance and to convince her to come down no matter what by promising her anything she wanted. David looked at me in a mocking manner and helped me get ready to ascend the crane. They gave me a radio that had open communication so I didn't need to push any buttons to transmit any message. I planned to have my fingers attached to the crane at all times. There wasn't much else to do. Except pray of course.

"You're all set to go. You're welcome to back out if you want," David offered hopefully.

"Not over your dead body," I replied, hoping to God that it wasn't my dead, mangled, squished, broken body we were actually talking about.

I put my shoulders back and walked over to the crane. It was about 150 feet tall and David had said that it was medium-sized. Usually men over-estimate size but who could blame them when the smallest size of condoms you can buy is described as "large".

"Good luck, Chailey," offered Spencer.

We all knew that there was no turning back now. Historically there has always been an interesting relationship between cops and firefighters. They really are like brothers. They share a sense of brotherhood by being in emergency response services and working together cooperatively twenty-four hours a day, seven days a week. Except that cops are awake twenty-four hours a day and the "hose monkeys", as the firefighters are so fondly referred to as, can sleep at night. But like brothers, there's always ongoing competitiveness. For example, firefighters have calendars and cops don't. Firefighters can work out on their down time to look good for the calendars; cops don't have down time. Cops are brave but firefighters are always perceived as being the bravest. With this kind of history, it left me to represent the police and I damn well had to climb up that crane if I said I was going to. Six or seven more cruisers had arrived at the construction site along with two more fire trucks. I guess the word was out that there was a little entertainment happening here.

At first, the climb seemed relatively easy. I looked up and just kept pumping those thighs up the stairs. It was just one big *Stairmaster*, right? Okay, so it only took five minutes before my leg muscles were screaming out in pain and I was only a third of the way up. If I was on the treadmill at the gym, the once or twice a year that I do attend, I would have stopped now and moved to something more leisurely, like the steam room. I was thankful it was a nice day and that it wasn't pissing down with rain as it usually did at this time of year.

"You okay, Chailey?" asked the Sergeant on the radio.

"Fine, thanks," I cheerfully replied.

About three quarters of the way up I stopped. "Shit!" I yelled.

"What's the matter, Chailey."

"This freaking thing sways! A lot!! Nobody told me this bloody thing blows around in the wind like a pendulum." The wind must have picked up at that point or I had just hit the right height to fully appreciate the true crane experience.

David came on the radio. "Chailey, it sways even more at the top. The bet is off unless you go to the top."

"Go to hell, David!" I yelled and started walked up tentatively. It took me another fifteen minutes to get to the top and I sat down firmly on the top step. The crane was swaying real well now and I was definitely feeling light headed so I put my head between my knees to make sure I didn't faint. Stupidly, I didn't close my eyes and had a bird's eye view of the ground 150 feet below. I started babbling, "Oh-my-God! Oh-my-God!" and then I puked. What a surprise!

The Sergeant was yelling, "What's wrong Chailey?"

"Nothing, Sarge, nothing," I managed to squeak out. I wanted to add, "Don't look up now!" but it seemed a little late for that.

At least I now knew not to look down.

Veronica was sitting on the floor of the crane operator's box. I wondered how she got in but figured that the crane guy probably thought, who'd be foolish enough to climb here so why bother to lock the door? Obviously he didn't know Veronica.

"Veronica, you okay in there?"

"Yeah, sort of," squeaked this little voice. "I was too scared to come down and too embarrassed to ask anyone to come and get me so I asked for you. I hope that's okay?"

"Yeah. Fine. Great." All I could think was that Jody would never have agreed to this. She'd be down at the bottom of the crane flirting with the firefighters.

"Veronica, you are coming out. And now!"

"No, Chailey. I'm too scared," she whimpered.

So here I was up at the top some huge crane that was blowing in the breeze like a kid on a swing and she thought that she was going to stay where she was. Veronica was coming out if I had to drag her out by her hair yelling and screaming.

"Yeah, it's fine for you all safe and sound in that cab while you leave me out here with my butt blowing in the wind. Get the hell out of that door. Now, Veronica, before I have to climb in there and drag your sorry little ass out. DO YOU UNDERSTAND?" I yelled.

"Okay! Okay! Don't get bitchy!" she yelled back.

"You ain't seen bitchy yet, honey!" I screamed. "Now, kneel on the floor and I'll open the door."

I reached up and opened it up. "Now you are going to back out the door and I'll guide your feet onto the stairs. When you get half way down, I'll ask one of the cute firefighters to meet you and guide you the rest of the way. Okay, honey?"

Veronica was able to follow my directions and gradually started to head down the stairs backwards.

Fifteen minutes later I heard the Sergeant on the radio, "You can come down now, Chailey. Veronica is safely on the ground."

Great. My turn to descend. Do you think that I could move? Not an inch. I felt like I was frozen stuck to the stairs like shit to a blanket. You could have put Mel Gibson naked at the bottom of the crane and I still wouldn't have been able to move a muscle.

"Chailey, did you hear? Veronica is safe and you can head down now," Sergeant Taylor called into the radio.

"Sure," I replied. "I'm just enjoying the view," I lied. I would have probably enjoyed it if my eyes weren't closed shut. That just made the swaying worse.

David came on the radio. "Hey, Chailey, you chicken shit. You can come down now or do you need me to come and get you?"

That was enough to get my ass in gear. I'm pretty sure that the view of my butt slowly descending down the stairs was not a pleasant sight to the large crowd that had gathered at the base of the crane and I was probably causing a solar eclipse.

I arrived on terra firma alive and well with no shattered vertebrae or broken bones. I resisted the urge to do the Pope thing and kiss the ground; I'd save that for a private moment later.

Spencer, the Sergeant and David met me at the bottom of the ladder. I could tell that David was in a snit; he hated to be bested by his sister. Sergeant Taylor told me what a great job I'd done and Spencer winked at me.

"Here's your money, Chailey," David said as he gave me a huge wad of bills. "More than five hundred bucks. Well done! You earned it. I still can't believe you did that."

I took half the wad and gave it back to David. "Here, put it in the girl's education account for me."

David smiled. "Thanks Chailey. You're a doll."

The crowd of firefighters, cops and ambulance crews started to dissipate now that the main event was over. They were probably little disappointed that no one was gorged or maimed and would have to go to the streets of Cookfield for that entertainment. Perhaps they might be lucky and there would be a multi-vehicle car crash to make their day! Apparently Veronica had been taken to hospital by ambulance for a psychiatric assessment. I was ready for one myself after my climb to the top of that rickety old meccanno set.

I told the Sergeant that I'd write a brief report and send it to him. I was pretty sure that Veronica would stick to bridge jumping from now on and that we'd have at least a twenty-four hour reprieve from her antics.

"Chailey, I can't believe that you did that."

"Me neither," I replied hoping to God that I hadn't pooped my panties and I would know for sure once I sat down. "What I can't believe is how many people thought I couldn't do it. Look at all of this money." I still had about three hundred dollars sitting in my sweaty hands.

"Well, when everyone heard on the radio what was going on they called in their bets."

Unbelievable, I thought. Bloody unbelievable.

"Spence, did you bet for or against me?" I asked.

"Never ask questions that you don't want to know the answer to, Chailey," he replied with a smile.

We headed back to the station and I went up to my office to write my report. I stopped by the snack machine on my way by and bought a *Mars* bar. I figured that I'd done enough exercise today that would allow me to eat a *Mars* bar a day, not have to go to the gym for six months and still not gain an ounce. I knew that I was going to have one sore ass tomorrow. I then called Abby on her cell phone.

"Abby, I need you to do a drive by with me to see Adam's new house. It's over by the marina and it's absolutely beautiful from the brief look I had. It's just I don't want him seeing me gawk at it."

"Sure, no problem. I'll pick you up at home just after midnight after my shift is done. I'll bring the eggs." I could hear yelling in the background so she must have been on a call.

"No! No eggs!" I told her. "This is not another Valentine's Day fiasco."

The yelling in the background increased.

"You're no fun. See you at midnight," and she hung up. Yeah, no fun but I've never been arrested. At least not yet!

Chapter 9

I wanted to review my notes on Maggie Denton. I continued to have this uneasy feeling about her death and needed to do something about it. I tentatively opened the drawer to my desk to look for the Denton notes. My trepidation related to an incident about two months ago when I had a nasty run-in with Neil Bentley and Zack Shortman, the department's pranksters. Neil and Zack were always participating in the infinite game of one-up-man-ship. Zack had been on the force for twenty years or so and Neil had only five years on the job so Zack took it upon himself to teach Neil everything he knew. We'd work in pairs to get the third person or work as a threesome against some poor unsuspecting victim.

You name it, we've done it. Put Neil's new car for sale in the paper for $1,000, announced a garage sale at Zack's for 7 a.m. on a Saturday morning. Of course the tables have been turned on me more times that I care to remember. I'd once broken the rule of the police department by foolishly letting them know what my fears are. Rule number eighteen of the Unofficial Police Department Survival Guide - never show your weaknesses! Hence, I regretted the day when we were chatting and I revealed one of my phobias. The next afternoon I came to work, opened my drawer and two snakes were slithering inside. I have never screamed so loudly in my life and believe me, snakes have ears. Those buggers slithered out of that desk drawer as quickly as their little tails could shake them. The snakes disappeared unfortunately in the direction of the Squad Room, which was directly adjacent to my office. Apparently I wasn't the only one with ophidiophobia, or snake phobia, because I could hear yells and screams from the Squad Room. So much for being big, brave cops! Despite the attempts of two brave officers to shoot the snakes, the reptiles escaped and I had to send a general e-mail to the whole department to keep an eye out for the MIAS – "Missing in Action Snakes". For weeks after, the department smart asses would leave rubber snakes, live turtles, dead snake skins and any other reptilian-like products in my desk on a daily basis. I knew that it was Neil and Zack who'd left the slithering twins in my desk because they were the first ones to respond to my hysterical calls and had grins on their faces. I taught them a lesson that night. I took the car keys to their personal cars, drove them with Abby's help out to "The Snake House", a store on the main drag downtown and returned to the station to place each of their keys in a two-litre pop bottle which I then put into the freezer. They'd be nicely frozen solid by the time the two of them finished their night shift. Bastards!

One of the better tricks they'd pulled on me was making me believe that someone had been murdered in my office and kept me out of it for a week. The first day started off with Crime Scene Tape across the door and the outline in chalk of a person slumped over the desk. They even got the detectives involved interviewing me wanting to know where I had been the night before. Yes, they even had me in a line up. When they fingerprinted me I knew something was up.

I was more than relieved not to find any nasties in my drawer tonight. There really wasn't much in my notes to review. I had reread Kevin Harrison and Abby's reports and there were no facts there that I hadn't read before. I made a quick call and learned that Liam was not only in but he was available to talk to me so I headed up stairs to the Detective's Office. We sat at his desk.

"I wanted to let you know some things that I have been thinking about that I believe are unusual in regards to Maggie Denton."

"You know the coroner has ruled Maggie's death as a suicide?"

"I figured he would," I replied, realizing I was about to lose all my credibility in the next few minutes. "I'm not a cop and don't profess to be one but I do know that Maggie wasn't a straight forward case." It was time to suck up to him. "I know that you're a good detective and want to cross the "t"s and dot the "i"s before you close a case."

"Okay, I'll listen." He must be married because he knew when to concede to a female and just listen so she'll have her say and leave you alone.

Over the past few days I'd had a lot of time to think about Maggie and what had happened. There were several missing pieces to the puzzle and to be honest, nothing added up. I planned to put the pieces together for Liam to see if he could come up with a better picture than I had.

I took my time and carefully laid out my thoughts. It was a pretty big accomplishment for an airhead like me. I started by telling Liam how events had been out of character for Maggie. She never used her back door especially since the prowler had shown up but the day she died it was not only unlocked but open; she never let the cat outside but Alfie was in the garden upon our arrival. Someone must have let him out. Maggie was meticulous - she would *never* have left a cup of tea half drunk on the table like that. I got a raised eyebrow on that observation.

"Liam, I'm telling you, something wasn't right. She didn't even drink tea with milk and that mug had milk in it. She stopped about a week prior. Maggie told me. Alright, so it sounds like nothing but she left her fridge with a half-finished casserole inside. She loved Alfie and would not have left his cat bowls empty. Finally, she was a woman of tradition. I believe that she would have handwritten a suicide not, not typed it. Somebody wanted us to believe she wrote it. And the prowler. One night the prowler actually entered her house to frighten her. I believe that it was because she found out something at work. She admitted that there were some problems there but wouldn't tell me any details. I think that she was getting close to an issue and that someone wanted to shut her up. Okay, so this isn't overwhelming evidence but I think it means something."

"Chailey, I appreciate you feel that this is evidence but it's inconclusive. When you have some hard facts, it will give more credibility to what you have now. I'm sorry, it's just not enough. I will leave the file open. Come and see me in a week and we'll discuss it then."

"Thanks, Liam." I felt like a kid when I asked for something from my mother and she'd reply, "I'll think about it." We all knew she meant "no", just like Liam had.

The radio dispatcher called me. "Charlie 13. The Desk Sergeant wants to talk to you. Can you go down and see him?"

"No problem, Dispatch," I replied.

I walked down the back stairs to the front reception area. I should have known something was up because Sergeant Jim MacPherson, or Mack for short, was tonight's Desk Sergeant and he looked happy which is quite unusual for him. He's a Scot and is usually a cranky old son-of-a-bitch who has a permanent scowl on his face, a quick temper and a nasty comeback for everything. He was a crusty as a bowl of week old porridge hence everyone called him Sergeant Crusty behind his back. Tonight he had a smirk on his face. I looked around and had no doubt whom the person Crusty had called about. Sitting on a chair, a vinyl one thankfully, was a man who looked like he was in his early thirties with short red hair and very blue eyes. Oh, didn't I mention this, he was also buck naked, or should I be clearer and say, *butt* naked. What was amazing was that people were ignoring him and walking around like he wasn't even there.

"Hey, Sarge, what's up?" Perhaps not the most appropriate question at that moment, however, he got my point.

"The gentleman over there would like to talk to someone about people being after him. He came here for protection. They have been taking his clothes as well as his thoughts and dreams. They placed a microchip in his teeth to control his behaviours. I thought you'd be the best person to help him. I've assigned Carter here to help you."

Poor Carter! He was a new recruit and already blushing. So Crusty had the joy of making the Mental Health Worker *and* the new recruit squirm. A double hit as far as he was concerned.

"Carter, this is Chailey. She'll talk with this guy and you can help take his statement. Just to warn you, if you ever see Chailey driving, stay away from her or she's likely to shove her car up your arse." With his Scottish burr MacPherson rolled his r's and made "arse" into a three-syllable word.

"Nice introduction, Sarge," I replied in a sarcastic tone. "Accurate, but nice!"

"Before you ask, Lassie, he refused the offer of a blanket or clothes. He said that his nudity was his proof of his rights being denied."

"Jim, can you call up to the dispatchers and ask them to log me on this call?"

"They know already, Lass. It was them who suggested I call you."

Okay, so it's not just my imagination, there is a conspiracy against me and they are *all* in on it. The whole lot of them! As I said before any naked calls become property of the Mental Health Worker.

I shook hands with Carter and suggested that we speak to the man right where he was. There was no need for him to move in any way unnecessarily and I planned to make this interview short and sweet. I also suggested that we stand around him to block the view from the public. The viewing public tonight consisted of a bunch of gawking policemen. For some reason the reception area was a particularly busy place tonight and it was virtually swarming with officers with six or seven extra cops hanging around the desk. They're like vultures – any action happening and they have to witness it live from the front row. There was only one person present seeking help from the police and that was our chap wearing his birthday suit.

To add to my misery, Zack and Neil were front and centre, grinning from ear to ear like two Cheshire cats.

"Chailey, how are you doing? Got any good calls tonight?" asked Zack.

I gave them the biggest "fuck you" look I could muster and walked over with my head held high to our good citizen in need. Okay, so my head was held unusually high and I made sure that I maintained eye contact the whole time. On the way over I whispered to Carter, "I want to be clear about this. I'll interview the guy but if there's a scuffle, he's all yours. Come on, let's get this over and done with."

Sergeant MacPherson shouted across the reception area. "Sir, this is the young lady I told you would come and talk to you. She'll take real good care of you." He gave our nudist a smile and a wink and then made himself busy with some important task. Carter looked terrified and frightened. I wasn't sure if he was more scared of me or our man sliding on the vinyl chair.

"Hi, my name is Chailey. I'm a nurse with the Cookfield Police Department. This is Constable Carter. The Sergeant told us a little about what has happened to you." I launched right into my spiel hoping that he wouldn't want a handshake. I had filled my hands with a pen, paper and clipboard to thwart any efforts for hand-to-hand contact however, Carter was unfortunately less prepared and empty-handed. I hoped it would stay that way and figured that Carter would have to learn the hard way not to shake hands. The reception area went unusually quiet. No doubt that was so that everyone could hear our conversation. So much for confidentiality and professionalism!

"What is your name, sir?" I asked.

"My name is Willie."

"Do you have a last name?"

I swear to God that he replied, "No, Kailey, I'm just a Willie."

I could hear the Sergeant just about choke when Crusty heard Willie's answer along with a smattering of similar chokes and giggles around me. I have to admit, it took every ounce of professionalism to continue on. Momentarily I had my suspicions that this was a hoax. If it had been a joke, they would have had the guy in an Interview Room and it would have been much later at night to ensure that the big wigs had left the station.

This situation reminded me of my initiation. Who could forget that little incident? Younger, more naive and only on the job for a month, I had been sent to a call by the dispatcher to see a man who was apparently delusional and the police present requested the Mental Health Worker's input. I was happy to attend since my role was new and this type of call was exactly what I'd been hired to do. Zack had been assigned to take me to the scene to meet the other officers currently attending the call. He drove me to an apartment building that looked well-kept and moderately expensive to rent. There were more than ten cops present and Zack told me they were there in case the guy became too much to handle. It made me more than a little nervous to think that they needed this much muscle to keep one guy under control. I was pleasantly surprised to meet a mild mannered man sitting in a chair in the tastefully decorated living room. One of the police officers told me that they wanted a mental health assessment because the man kept telling the police he had a special mission to fulfill in life but wouldn't tell them what it was. He was a young looking guy in his early twenties and to be quite honest, he was a tall, dark, handsome hunk with a delightful little dimple on his well-tanned chin. Well, I started my interview by asking him what his name was and he replied, "Gorgeous George." I thought it was a little strange however I proceeded to ask him about his special mission in life at which point he jumped up out of his chair and yelled, "THIS!" I expected all the cops to jump on top of him and haul his cute little butt down onto the ground. Instead, the room was suddenly filled with loud music and Gorgeous started dancing. Once he started gyrating his hips and stripping off his shirt I *finally* realized that this was a setup. Gorgeous was a stripper! Somehow I stifled my urge to flee and run like the wind and put up with the twenty-minute show which ended with Gorgeous naked and me sitting on his lap. I managed to wrestle my way out of George's grasp and whispered to Zack that if he didn't get me out of there then I was going to call my uncle. Zack finally relented and made excuses for us to leave and walked me down to his cruiser and drove me back to the station. He smiled from ear to ear telling me what a great job I'd done by not running away. He must have repeated that ten times. It was like driving with ALF. He was too busy enjoying himself to notice that I had grabbed his police hat and thrown it out the window just as we drove over the Burton Bridge that goes over the train tracks.

"Next goes your lunch bag and then your police radio," I threatened.

"Not my lunch!" he yelled. I guess he didn't care about the three thousand dollar police radio.

"Hey, where's my hat?"

"Drive back a block, stop at the side of the road and look over the edge," I told him.

"You didn't?" he asked incredulously.

"Oh, I did. The purpose of my initiation was to see if I had balls. Well I do!"

The next day I met Neil for the first time who sidled up beside me and asked if I wanted to get back at Zack. The friendship was set in stone from that moment on. I passed my initiation and periodically someone will hum the Stripper song when they pass by me or they'll e-mail me a picture from that horrific night. I swear I could hear some bozo humming the Stripper song now and if I had the time and opportunity, I would have ripped his vocal cords out with my bare hands.

I asked Willie why he had come to the police station this evening and he told me that he had been kidnapped from his home in the middle of the night by a band of thugs and taken to a room with a white light. They had taken his clothes and wouldn't let him leave. He had been there for a week frightened and scared. His thoughts were being ripped away from him. He didn't want his thoughts to leave. That seemed to me like a strange way to describe somebody's thoughts.

"Do your thoughts talk to you?" I asked.

"Oh yes! It's Thelma and Louise. They talk to me all the time. Louise is my girlfriend. She makes me feel soooo good!"

I quickly became aware of how good Louise made him feel through the movement in his lap. That was it! Enough was enough. I quietly growled to Carter, "Stay here," as I stomped through the crowd to the Sergeant's desk, grabbed the blanket that was sitting on the counter, brought it back to Willie and threw it on his lap.

"Department policy!" I announced, "Policy 69 only comes into effect at ten o'clock. Everyone's privates must be covered in some manner. Contravening it means that you must leave the building. Now I'm going to turn my back and you will use the blanket to cover yourself up. Do you understand?" I added. "Carter, you don't get to turn." Both men nodded sheepishly and I turned around to find ten cops grinning from ear to ear.

It took about a minute and I finally heard Carter mumble, "Err, you can turn around now, Chailey." I wondered how this guy got through police college when he blushed at the drop of a hat. The man was as red as a beet.

Willie was sitting with the blanket around him snug as a bug in a rug.

I continued on with the interview. "What about Thelma? What does she say to you?" I asked.

"Thelma makes me do bad things like hit people."

"Have you ever done that?" I prodded.

"Well, I did hit my apartment superintendent Jane the other day. Thelma told me that Jane was going to kick me out right then and there if I didn't stop her."

Quite obviously this man was mentally ill, he met the criteria that allowed the police to take him to hospital and he needed to be in hospital to keep others safe from him. He was doing what the voices told him to which was not safe.

"Can you please excuse us for a moment, Willie?" I took Carter aside and asked him his opinion. He concurred with my assessment. The weird thing was that Willie's story sounded oddly familiar.

"Go and tell Mack what we've decided and find out who's going to take him to hospital. Tell Mack that I want Shortman and Bentley assigned to this one. Okay?"

"Okay, Chailey," he replied eagerly. Recruits hate dealing with mental health calls since they really don't know what to do so he was more than happy to allow me make the decisions and boss him around. I'm pretty good at that.

Carter returned a few minutes later and gave me a note. "Mack asked me to give this to you." It was a pink message slip dated for today and timed for 9:50 p.m., the time that I had started the interview with Willie. The Cookfield Psychiatric Hospital had called and was missing a Mr. William Dickens. That would be our Willie! It only took me a moment to realize that this interview could have been stopped at any time but Mack had let me sweat it out.

I approached Willie and broke the news that his gig was up and that we now knew that he had left the hospital unauthorized. Sadly he had to return. People were worried about him and were looking for him. He looked despondent. No wonder his story of persecution had been familiar to me. If he had hit his superintendent then the police would no doubt have been called to pick him up and take him to the hospital where he was required to take medication that would stop the voices, or thoughts as he referred to them.

"Willie, you know that it's Thelma's voice that is making you hurt people. You don't want to hurt people, do you"

"No," he replied. "I'm glad that Thelma is gone but I miss Louise. She brought excitement to my life."

"How about we drive you up to the hospital. Would you like a coffee or something along the way? How about a *Blimpey's* takeout meal?"

Carter came over to Willie and me to tell us that Zack Shortman and Neil Bentley would drive us up to the psychiatric hospital and that they were on their way over to pick us up in front of the station. Carter provided escort duty and walked the two of us out to the cruiser.

I helped Willie into the back seat of the police car ensuring that his blanket stayed tucked around his body and I climbed in beside him.

"We're going to *Blimpey's* first," I announced. Thank God I had an open account at the joint or I'd be broke by now.

Zack was our chauffeur and drove us over to the closest *Blimpey's* drive-through where we ordered four super-sized meals fondly known as "Blimpey Blasters". I told Zack to take the long way to the hospital so that we would have enough time to consume our meals. We kept the chatter light which was easy with Zack and Neil in the front seat. We finally arrived at the hospital and walked Willie in. I knew from experience that he'd be kept on the locked end of the unit under close observation for the next few days and made a mental note to myself to call the ward tomorrow and talk to Willie's nurse.

We settled ourselves back in the car with me in the back seat again. I hate that spot. You can't get out unless someone lets you out and you look like a convicted felon. I told Neil he'd have to sit in the back but even I knew that would look dumb with a uniformed officer in the back seat and a civilian female in the front. Dumb and suspicious looking!

"That was really nice what you did for Willie," said Zack. "You know, getting him something to eat and not rushing him back to the hospital. You treated him respectfully. I guess that it's what he wanted. Someone to treat him like a person." Wow, an insightful police officer!

We were approaching the police station and I looked at my watch.

"Oh no! It's eleven thirty! I've got to get going!" I blurted out.

"What? Are you frightened you'll turn into a pumpkin at midnight?" asked Zack.

"No!" I replied. I sounded more defensive than I had planned to. "And if that's a comment about my butt, you're going to get smacked. That is, once I get out of here."

"So where are you off to, Chailey? A hot date? Is it already that time in the decade?" asked Neil.

"NO! Now shut up, smart ass, and let me out of the car." I was sitting in the back meaning that someone had to let me out from the outside.

"Now, now, Chailey," Neil admonished me. "Is that any way to talk to a friendly police officer?"

"No. And if I were talking to a friendly police officer I'd probably talk nicer. But I'm not. So let me freaking out!"

"Hey, what's the rush, Trailer Trash Mouth." Neil had passed the police station and was slowly driving away and slowly increasing my blood pressure. I was heading towards a stroke.

"Someone's picking me up from home at midnight. Let! Me! Out!" I punctuated each word with a bang on the window. Perhaps I do have control issues after all.

"Just tell us what you're up to and we'll let you out, Chailey," offered Zack.

I could see the police station fading into the distance.

I thought about it for a minute. They were my buddies and it didn't matter if they knew what we were doing. Zack and Neil were both working nights and couldn't join us so who really cared. I decided to take the plunge.

"Okay. Abby's picking me up after her shift ends at midnight. We're going to drive by Adam's new million-dollar home. It's no big deal. And if you're nice to me, I'll tell you about it tomorrow."

"Are you going to trash the place?" asked Zack excitedly. I could see the gleam in his eyes.

"No, I told you, I just want to drive by without him seeing me gawk at his new digs."

Neil had circled around the block and pulled up in front of the station. Zack jumped out of the car and opened my door.

"Thanks for the *Blimpey's* meal and good job with Willie. Have fun tonight. See ya!"

He jumped back into the car and we exchanged smiles and waves. It seemed just a little too cordial and easy but at that point, I didn't care and was too late to worry.

I headed back into the station and quickly updated Mack that Willie was safe and sound in the hospital. I ran up the stairs, grabbed my backpack and called into dispatch to tell them that I was done for the night.

I made it home in record time and was in the door by five after midnight. There was no sign of Bart except he'd left all the lights on. I headed into the bedroom to put on my black jeans and sweater. I felt a little better by looking stealthy. Alright, so I have a big butt which isn't particularly stealthy looking but I figured that I'd try camouflaging it just a little. They say that you can never go wrong with basic black and it works well for every situation; that includes a midnight drive by of your ex-husband's house.

I went into the bathroom to brush my teeth and just about had a coronary when I found Bart in my bathtub. We both shrieked, him louder than me.

"What the hell are you doing in there?"

"Er, having a bath Chailey," he replied.

Okay, ask an obvious question get an obvious answer.

"I can get out if you want?" He looked as if he was going to stand up. I'd seen enough naked men tonight to last a lifetime.

"No! Stay there! When can you go home again?" I asked in a rather exasperated way. If I had to have a man staying in my apartment I'd rather it be someone whom I want to share my bed with. Bart certainly did not fit that profile.

"Lorelei's here in town, Chailey. That's who Harold has downstairs."

"Damn! Not Lorelei! What the hell is she doing here?" Lorelei was Harold's one and only love. She is a decade older than him, a flower child and also a fellow pothead. She moved to California several years ago to join a commune and broke Harold's heart when she left him behind. She comes back to town every now and then at which time she and Harold hide in the basement screwing like proverbial rabbits twenty-four/seven. Bart is person non grata at times like this.

"Please tell me she's leaving soon, Bart. I love you like a brother but I need my space. And you need some clean clothes."

I suddenly realized that the delicious smell in the bathroom was coming from the bubbles and I saw the empty *Alfred Sung* bubble bath bottle lying on the floor.

"You used all of my bubble bath liquid. Do you know how much that bottle cost me? Fifty stinking bucks! That should last for twenty baths or more and you emptied it. It was full!" I could hear myself becoming hysterical over bubble bath.

I stormed out of the bathroom and slammed the door. All I could hear beyond the throbbing of blood in my ears was a muffled voice from the bathroom, "Chailey, I haven't been in here for long. I could get out and you could use the bath water after me."

I gave up at that point. "It's okay, Bart. The thought is appreciated but I'm heading out. You enjoy that bath. I'll see you in the morning."

"Good night," he called. Let's hope that it is, I thought, as I prepared to leave for a drive-by of my ex-husband's house in the middle of the night.

Chapter 10

Abby rang the bell and I went to meet her at the front door. "Hey girl! You look hot in black. What's that delicious smell?"

"That would be Bart having a bath in my *Sung* bubble bath liquid."

"If I were you I wouldn't let him use it. I'd be keeping that for myself. That stuff is expensive!"

"Really?" I replied in a mildly exasperated manner. Apparently I do look dumber than I am.

Abby had parked outside of the house and I followed her down the darkened path. It wasn't until I got to the car that I realized that it was not her regular Toyota Rav 4. I loved her Rav 4 and lusted for my own.

"Did you get a new car, Abby?" I hadn't remembered her telling me anything about buying a new vehicle, and I was pretty sure if she was going to buy a BMW, that she would have told me ahead of time. Knowing her she'd have to borrow money off me as well.

"No," she replied, "it's Nick's!"

"You mean to tell me that you are using the Assistant Crown Attorney's car to do a drive-by of my ex-husband's house?"

"Yeah!" she replied triumphantly. "This car fits into Adam's neighbourhood and if there's any trouble, who's going to accuse him of doing anything?"

"First of all, why do you think that there may be trouble? And secondly, does he know *why* you asked to borrow his car?"

"Well, no, not really…"

"I don't even want to know if you asked him to use it!" I walked over to the passenger side of the car and got in and put on my seat belt. I just about wet myself when I heard a chorus of, "Hi Chailey!" from the back seat. I whipped my head around to find the "Dynamic Duo" of Zack and Neil in the back seat. With the life I lead and the friends I have, I figure I'm going to need a cardiac specialist real soon.

Abby had seated herself in the front seat of the sleek black car. "What the hell are they doing here, Abby?"

"They were both off at midnight and asked to come. I didn't think that you'd mind. Well, you wouldn't mind too much. You told me not to bring eggs. You didn't say anything about not bringing the eggheads." She smiled at that one.

"This isn't funny Abby!" I growled. "You know these bozos aren't safe to take anywhere. They go over the edge no matter what they do. It's dangerous!"

"Ladies, and I use the term loosely, the bozos you're talking about are right here. We can hear you talking about us," announced Zack righteously.

"Then get out!" I snapped. That shut him up.

Abby started up the car and drove off heading in a northerly direction.

"We're taking these guys home where they belong," I announced.

"But my wife said that I could stay out and play," said Neil cheerfully.

"So did mine!" announced Zack equally as cheerful. If I were their wives I would let them stay out every night to prevent them causing chaos when they finally arrived home. I love their wives because they have to be saints to put up with the shit that they deal with daily. That and be heavily medicated!

"They promised to behave themselves, Chailey," offered Abby.

"And if we aren't then we told her she could spank us!" Neil added cheekily.

"Come on, Chailey. They won't get out of the car and you'll behave yourselves, won't you boys? We're only driving by. They've promised to buy as much beer and wings as we want afterwards. Right guys?"

Both replied eagerly that they would. Mmm, I thought, all the beer and wings we could eat and drink. I could feel a hangover coming on already.

"Okay. Everyone stays in the car and behaves. Right?" I announced this to a car of cheers. "Er, you guys don't have your guns with you or anything, do you?"

"Of course not, Chailey. *That* would be against the law."

"Yeah, and so are half the pranks you two get up to."

"I'm offended by your implications. No, we don't have our guns with us," Zack answered. "Any way, Abby wouldn't let us bring them," he added rather sheepishly.

"Need I remind you people about the burnt shed? I believe two officers sitting in this car are responsible for burning down my shed," I announced.

"You're never going to let that one go, are you?" asked Zack sarcastically.

"Forget it? It happened a month ago! Randy still stinks like soot every time he goes out for a pee in the garden!"

"We didn't mean to do it," offered Neil. "It was an accident."

Zack and Neil were assigned to the beat that my house is located in. They dropped by the house to say "hi", except I wasn't home. Just as they were leaving, they noticed Bart and Harold walking down the garden path in a rather sneaky and suspicious manner. Following their police instincts, Zack and Neil followed discreetly at a distance and quickly learned that Harold and Bart were using the shed to smoke some pot. The two cops knew that I didn't allow this activity on the property so they decided to teach the potheads a lesson by performing a mock raid on the shed. The cop raiders yelled, "Police! Open up! This is a raid!" and beat the hell out of the shed by banging on the walls and windows. Bart and Harold just about shit their pants and in the wake of their fear, hid their stash under a bunch of junk in the shed before heading outside to face the music. The cops gave the druggies a hard time but used their discretion and let Bart and Harold off with a warning. Unfortunately, in Bart and Harold's rush to escape the shed they had not stubbed out their joints properly and in the middle of the dress down by Zack and Neil, the shed started burning. It took only minutes for the dry old shed to burn down to the ground. Of course, I had returned home in the middle of this fiasco. I had just finished work and followed a pair of fire trucks rushing to a fire. Unfortunately I followed the fire department to my house and a smoldering pile of wood, ironically called my potting shed, and four men who looked mighty ashamed of themselves. I believe that it is the first time in my life that I have actually been speechless. The four men threw themselves at my feet begging for mercy. I let them stew for a few days or so and allowed them to buy and build a new shed for the garden this summer.

"The less said about that the better. Let's get going then. Adam's at the hospital tonight."

"And how would you know that little fact, Officer Shortman?" I asked.

"Well, I called my sister-in-law who works on the switchboard at the hospital and she checked his schedule. She paged him just before midnight to see if he was still there."

"Abby, I told you they were trouble."

"You're welcome!" Zack added snottily.

"Suck it up, Chailey. Consider it a road trip," announced Abby.

As we were driving I heard the unmistakable and distinct sound of the clink of a beer bottle. "Please don't tell me that's what I think I heard?" I pleaded.

"Hey, it's a road trip! Relax, Chailey! We promised you all the beer you wanted."

"Put it away!" I growled. "Any more noise from the two of you in the back seat and I'm taking you home." Wow, it sounded like my mother was in the car threatening my brother and me on a car trip. Before long I'd be grabbing my umbrella and smacking the two of them. The only thing stopping me was that those two would enjoy it.

Abby put on some tunes that sounded real good on the state-of-the-art hi-fi stereo system. In my car the only music you can hear is the soundtrack from *Beauty and the Beast* since the tape has been stuck in the tape player for the past two years. The guys were on a roll and got us laughing. I directed Abby out to Adam's place as best as I could remember. The roads were pretty empty especially as we headed to the north shore through the more upscale neighbourhoods. They were all monster homes out in this part of town and it was particularly difficult to see in the dark. It was easy to locate Adam's house through his car being in the driveway.

"He's at the hospital, is he? Good detective work, officer!" I added sarcastically. All of a sudden this whole idea seemed like a bad one. We drove down what I call "Million Dollar Drive" and Abby swung the car around to come back again slowing as she approached Adam's house.

The second pass gave us a chance to really look at Adam's new mansion. There was a huge window above the massive entrance hall which looked like it belonged on Cinderella's castle. The window allowed a view of the circular staircase and fifteen-foot long chandelier. There were two wings to the house and I figured that the house had at least six bedrooms. The front garden was large, at least seventy-five feet deep and was beautifully landscaped with professionally pruned bushes, numerous ornamental trees and manicured lawns that were similar to the putting greens at the Master's Golf Tournament in Augusta, Georgia. Despite having a three-car garage, Adam had left his BMW in the driveway. There were lights on throughout the house however the California shutters and fitted curtains maintained the occupants' privacy. In other words, the house was magnificent in every way I had ever dreamed of.

Abby must have noticed my look of wonderment or perhaps it as the drool dripping down my face and said, "Chailey, the house wouldn't suit you. And think of all those toilets to clean. You're too down to earth for that monstrosity."

"I know Abby but it really is beautiful." I didn't want to add that if I owned a house like that I would have someone clean those toilets for me.

"Yeah, about as beautiful as a tank," she added.

Abby had slowed enough that the guys thought that it was a good time to jump out and walk casually up to the house as I watched in horror.

I quickly rolled down the window. "Where do you think you two are going? Get back into the car!" I hissed as loudly as I could.

"I thought I saw a prowler in the back. You wouldn't want to put Adam's home at risk?"

I didn't care if his house burned to a cinder, I just didn't want to be in the vicinity when it happened.

"You know there's no prowler," I persisted. "Please get in before anyone sees you."

"No can do!" announced Zack as he walked up the driveway as though he owned the place. "I'm a police officer sworn to protect and to serve!"

"Yeah, me too!" called Neil.

I gave up at that point and glared at Abby with my meanest premenstrual glare.

"Don't look at me as though this is my fault," retorted Abby. "You let them come!"

"Drive away!" I growled at her.

"You're kidding, right?" she answered. "You want to leave these two here alone? It's up to you!"

Damn, she was right. "Okay, stop the car and you go and get them."

"I'm not leaving you here alone. I don't trust you. You'll leave without us." She was right about that, too. "Abby, pleeeease, go and get them," I begged her. I had lost sight of the guys who had disappeared through the gate into the back garden.

"Okay, we'll give them five minutes and then I'll go and get them." Abby pulled the car to the side of the road and turned off the engine and the lights.

"Do you think that they have video surveillance cameras?" I asked Abby.

"Chailey, stop worrying. Those guys won't get into trouble, I promise you."

"Yeah, you also promised me that they would stay in the car." I was definitely starting to sound whiney.

It was at that moment that a police cruiser pulled up behind us. We couldn't tell who the cop was with the car's lights shining into our back window. The officer got out and rapped on Abby's driver side window.

"Hey, Abby. How are you doing? Is that you Chailey?" Thank God it was our good buddy Pete McNeil. "What brings you ladies into this part of town at this time of night? I was checking the neighbourhood and saw your car looking a little suspicious."

Unfortunately I lack the skills to lie and anyone who claims to know me is aware of this character flaw. Of course, the lack of lying ability is not in any way related to being virtuous and moralistic. There are times when I want to lie and I just can't do it right and I become all tongue-tied and stutter and basically make an ass out of myself. It's definitely a handicap in my job. I'm not saying that all cops lie, but the best cops know how to say a little white lie. For example, let's say I'm on a call with a cop and we decide that a person needs to go to hospital. And let's also say that the person doesn't want to go and we know that they may go berserk when we tell them that they have no choice. That is the appropriate time to use a little white lie to tell them that we are waiting for something or another before we tell them of our decision. Of course, in reality we would be waiting for back up to help me and the one little cop stay alive and avoid being pulverized. Even in moments like that I just can't do it. I mumble and stutter and by the time I'm finished with my ten-minute rambling explanation, I've agitated the person to greater heights. And if not being able to lie is a deficit, then my ability to help in a brawl is a damn right handicap. So, I always let others take the lead at moments like that to avoid brawls. I had always marveled at Adam's ability to lie in more ways than one by fibbing to me about sleeping with someone and then actually *lying* with the person and doing the dirty deed.

I decided to come clean and tell the truth. "Hey Pete. How are you doing? We're just drove by this house to have a look at it. It's my ex-husband's new place. Zack and Neil are in the back doing who knows what."

"Fine Chailey! If you don't want to tell me the truth, that's fine."

Abby stepped in at this point. "Don't listen to her and her stories. My boyfriend Nick was thinking of buying a house. Chailey and I were going to *The Wellington* for a drink and thought that we'd have a look at these beautiful homes first so that we can give Nick some advice." She didn't miss a beat. She's a good liar, our Abby.

"See Chailey, was that so hard to tell me the truth? You know you shouldn't lie to the friendly police officer! Which house do you like? They're a little rich for my blood but to each their own."

No kidding! The three of us could combine our annual salaries and we'd still not have enough money to buy the garage. As he was talking I could see Zack and Neil coming out of the back yard through the gate. Thankfully they had the smarts to hide back in the shadows.

"Bonnie said that you guys are going out this Saturday. Have a good night and make sure you take bail money." The way tonight was going I might need the bail money this evening.

"I know how you lot are when you get together," he added with a chuckle. I could hear his radio calling "481". "Gotta go now. Take care guys."

"See ya, Pete," called Abby.

"Stay safe," I added.

"Well, you're cool as a cucumber. Hope I have you with me in an emergency," added Abby sarcastically.

"I'm sorry. You know I can't lie."

Zack and Neil had returned to the car and slipped into the back seat. "I can lie," stated Neil. "You look nice tonight, Chailey!"

"Very funny," I replied. "Get the hell out of here, Abby."

Abby sped off and I spent the next ten minutes berating everyone in the car. Neil and Zack just sat in the back seat smirking and replying, "Yes, Chailey!" and "We're sorry, Chailey!" obediently like the two liars they were. The car had barely stopped before I was out of the door and headed into the pub. By the time the crime trio came in I was sucking back my first beer. The trio sat down and Zack said, "I'm really sorry Chailey. We didn't mean to upset you. Are we forgiven?"

"Paint my driveway for me next week and I'll think about it," I growled.

We spent the rest of the night drinking and eating ourselves to oblivion. The guys wisely waited until I was half drunk before they finally told us what happened at the house earlier. Dr. Adam Chartwell was home and finishing off the night by shagging his current partner in the living room. Believing that the gigantic backyard afforded them plenty of privacy, they didn't bother to close the curtains. Apparently Adam has some kinky sexual fetishes and the guys gave us explicit details of the action that unveiled in front of them. I couldn't believe that they actually stood and watched all of this happen. I was horrified to learn that Neil and Zack came prepared for the garden raid and left a little package in Adam's pool floating around. Of course I would have been even more disturbed if I hadn't been half in the bag. Thankfully last call was at two o'clock and we all went home by cab.

Chapter 11

The next morning I woke up with a really bad headache. Okay, so it was a hangover and I felt like crap. I took a couple of ibuprofen and stayed in bed as late as I could finally getting up around two in the afternoon feeling much better. I slept so soundly that I even didn't wake to answer the ringing telephone. There was a very angry message on my answering machine from Adam demanding to know why the day after he tells me where his house is, he wakes up to find three lumps of shit floating around in his pool. I deleted that message really fast. I skipped brunch and dropped by the local coffee shop on my way into work for a large, black coffee to wash down another couple of pills and finally shuffled into the station.

I usually start my Friday shift at three in the afternoon so that Jody and I can meet with Ben, a Sergeant and our supervisor. Today he was busy and cancelled our meeting which left me sitting at my desk trying to plan my next assault on the dynamic duo, Zack and Neil. I was still pretty pissed off with them after last night. So far, the prank involved hiring naked call girls. I just hadn't figured out what they were going to do

I had to put the naked call girl prank planning on the back burner for now because the dispatcher was calling for me over the radio. Noah Drake was a forty-three year old man who had started the day off married and had received the bad news at breakfast that his wife of nine years, eleven months was leaving him for another man. According to his wife, Noah had taken this news relatively well. In retrospect she now believes that he kept his anger under control because his two young sons were present. Mr. and Mrs. Drake had headed off to their respective jobs with the agreement that they would negotiate conditions of the separation this evening. Unfortunately, Mr. Drake had a change of heart around two o'clock in the afternoon when he called his wife from his job at the steel mill and told her to "fuck off", called his parents to tell them that he loved them and goodbye and marched off to the top of the building ready to jump. Thankfully his foreman had noticed his slightly odd behaviour and tried to talk to Noah and got punched in the face for his troubles.

By the time I arrived the police negotiator had been talking with Noah for forty-five minutes with no success. They wanted me to talk to him and see if I'd be any more successful. I was met at the door by one of the workers who escorted me up to the top of the building. It was one hell of a long way up there! Considering the amount of stair climbing I had been doing for work lately my ass should be tiny and I should be able to fit into a size two. Of course, it was a windy day to make things a little more hazardous. I joined the group of six coppers who were standing at a distance from Noah who was standing extremely close to the edge. He was obviously very distraught as evidenced by his tearful face and pacing. This was no "Bridget" sitting on the bridge for attention – this was a man who felt he had lost everything and couldn't live this life any longer.

I got a quick run down from Steve Robinson, the police negotiator. In a nutshell, Noah didn't want to talk to the negotiator and was just working up the nerve to jump. Steve thought that the presence of a female non-cop might be beneficial.

To be perfectly honest, I was shitting bricks. Let's face it, I hadn't exactly been on the top of my game recently with Maggie killing herself after I saw and assessed her *three* times.

"Chailey, talk to him. Now!" commanded Steve.

So I did. I just talked to him. If there's one thing I know how to do, it's talk.

"Noah. I'm Chailey Smith. I'm a nurse who works for the Cookfield Police Department. I come and see people who are emotionally stressed and I know you are under a tremendous amount of stress. What has happened to you is unfair. You didn't deserve it. I'm not saying your wife is wrong or bad, it's just that the whole scenario sucks. And you are no doubt feeling incredibly overwhelmed by this. I know I felt angry and hurt and betrayed when my husband left me."

Now that caught his attention. He started to look at me as I talked to him and he slowly walked towards me. Now he locked eyes with me.

"You're probably wondering how a person gets through this. How did I do it? I don't really know. I just did. You take each day one at a time until it stops hurting a little and you lean on friends and family until you finally feel that you can manage again. And you will. You have to. Noah, you have two little boys who need your help to get through this."

As he listened several police officers had crept up behind him and finally reached a point that they were able to tackle him to the rooftop safely.

When they had Noah standing I walked over and told him that he would be okay and gave him a hug. I rarely do that but I felt he needed it. Maybe I did, too. He was crying but not resisting the police. I hoped that one day soon he would be happy to be alive again.

"Well done Chailey," said Steve.

"Thanks!"

I walked away and headed towards the stairs. I felt terrible and I didn't know why. I just felt like crap.

****

By the time I got back into my car and scoffed down a *Mars* bar, I decided it was time to climb out of this pity pit and do something productive. I was relatively close to the lawyer's office where Maggie and Michael worked and thought that it was a good opportunity to talk with Maggie's coworkers. Liam had told me if I had any additional information that I should let him know and I wasn't going to gather any sitting on my size 14 butt in my car.

It was a new office building in the downtown core area and was big, square and glass and I hated the look of it. The law firm filled one floor of the office block and was a sea of glass and chrome. The walls to every room were made of glass with a frosted finish at the four-foot level to provide a moderate degree of privacy. Rather an important feature for a lawyer's office, you'd think. I guess there was no slap and tickle going on behind closed doors in this establishment.

The receptionist was a petite, pretty brunette who looked a little like Jennifer Lopez. She had perfect hair, dazzling white teeth and beautifully manicured nails. Her desk was glass and spotless with a sophisticated phone that looked like it had been lifted off the Star Trek Enterprise. Let's face it, she was no Flo!

I hadn't thought through how I was going to get in and quickly realized that "Hi, I'm here to snoop around Maggie Denton's desk," was not the most innocuous or effective opening.

"I'm Chailey Smith. I was wondering if Michael Brigham is available?"

"Do you have an appointment, Ms. Smith?" Miss Perfect-Hair-and-Teeth asked.

"Err, no but I'm sure he will consider speaking to me."

The receptionist gave me "You should now better than to disturb the very busy Mr. Michael Brigham" look. I suddenly became very conscious of my rough look and tried to smooth down my porcupine imitation hair compliments of the wind on top of the warehouse.

"I'll check with his secretary, Kerrie."

She probably thought I was some criminal looking for a defense lawyer. I must have made her nervous because a security guard quietly emerged from a side door and stared at me as if I was pond scum.

"Mr. Brigham will be engaged for the next hour but would be pleased to see you after if you would like to wait."

"That would be delightful," and gave her a big victorious smile. Bitch!

Within seconds, a tall, slim, blond dressed in a business suit appeared. She introduced herself as Bronwyn and gave a realistic impression of a museum guide as she quickly provided an overview of the law firm as we walked through the massive office complex. Michael worked in Criminal Law however the firm also provided law services in Corporate and Business, Personal Injury and Family. I'd keep that in mind for the future. Every employee could see daylight but no one could touch it. The glass surroundings made me feel like I was in a round room looking for a corner. Bronwyn took me to a waiting area for the defense lawyers. I guess this is where all the criminals sat. Opposite the waiting corral was a large twenty-foot square area in which three secretaries sat. Behind each secretary was a door to an office presumably where the lawyers were kept. Bronwyn had spoken to the beautiful, tall, leggy blond on the left so I presumed that was Michael's new secretary, Kerrie. She was as different to Maggie as I was to Jody. I grabbed a cup of remarkably fresh coffee from the pot on the cupboard and snagged a chocolate chip muffin. Knowing my luck that would probably be my dinner for the night. I pretended to read the *Financial Times* while I surreptitiously observed the secretaries.

Michael's secretary was no doubt new so she wouldn't know much about Maggie. The secretary opposite me looked like she was in her late fifties and only days away from a cardiac arrest looking at the pallor of her skin and pained look on her face. The secretary on my right was probably my best bet as the one whom Maggie talked to the most. She appeared close in age to Maggie and had the same matronly look to her. No ring on her finger and only a picture of her little poodle dog confirmed my suspicions. It took me a few minutes but I finally came up with a plan. At least I hoped that it would work. I quietly called the law firm and asked for Kerrie. I then whispered in as deep voice as I could muster, " Meet me in the regular spot," and then hung up. I hoped at the last second she didn't re-dial the number nor have call display! Unbelievably, within three minutes she approached the poodle owner and pointed to her head like she was having pain and hurried off somewhere. I waited thirty seconds and approached my prey.

"Hi!" I gave her my biggest friendliest nurse's smile. I don't use it often. "I'm Chailey Smith. I don't mean to be nosy but I noticed that secretary who just left looked like she was in pain. I'm a nurse. Can I help in any way?"

"Isn't that kind of you. I think she's okay. She told me that she had a very bad headache and needed a few minutes to help relieve the pain." Well, that was one way of putting it, I thought.

"I'm here to see Michael Brigham. I'm the nurse who spoke with Maggie Denton a few times and I just wanted to make sure Michael was okay." I could see tears start to brim in her eyes. "I'm sorry, I didn't mean to upset you. It was awful what happened to Maggie. I only met her a few times and I thought she was wonderful. You must have known her well."

"Yes, she was. I miss her terribly. She didn't deserve to have this happen to her." For a second I had the feeling she wasn't talking about suicide. She quickly recovered and added, "You are very kind to check on Mr. Brigham. He seems to be recovering and came straight back to work. He says it's his therapy. I'm Julia by the way."

"Julia, I just noticed the time and I'm going to be unable to stay to wait for Mr. Brigham after all. If I leave my card would you mind letting him know that I dropped by to say hello."

"No problem, Miss Smith."

"Please, call me Chailey. I don't like to tell too many people but I'm looking further into Maggie's death. I find it hard to believe that she killed herself." Julia's head went down to her desk. Apparently I had hit a nerve. "It was a pleasure to meet you Julia. Thank you for passing on that message to Mr. Brigham and once again, give him my regrets."

I scribbled, "Sorry to have missed you. Hope all is well. Chailey." on the back of my business card.

"Bye, Chailey."

I left the office wishing I had left a trail of birdseed on my way in. Finally I found my way out of the glass maze feeling that I had done a reasonable job of making contact with someone who may know a little more about Maggie and her work life. If Julia needed to get hold of me she knew how. I had given her two business cards instead of just one.

Just as I pushed the elevator button, I heard Michael's voice behind me.

"Chailey, don't go. I'm glad to have caught you. There's someone I'd like you to meet."

We quickly arrived back at his office proving he must be smart because he could find his way through the maze. I was introduced to a woman who was in her early fifties with short dark curly hair and very slim. Her looks made her neither pretty nor ugly.

"This is Nadine Hopkins. She heads our Security Division here at the law firm. She asked to meet with me in light of Maggie's suicide and has some pretty disturbing information. I thought as a representative of the police you should hear this."

Michael looked slightly ashen and rough. He hadn't exactly had an easy few days and based on the serious look on Nadine's face, his week wasn't getting any better.

"I can't take the place of an investigating officer but I am happy to take information back to the detectives. They may want to follow-up."

"Trust me, they will."

Curiosity may have killed the cat but I was more than willing to take a chance.

"The Security Department of this law firm was in the middle of an investigation of Margaret Denton when she killed herself. Ms. Denton has been misappropriating funds into her bank account. So far, $25,000 has been located.

I can tell you little else due to the sensitive nature of this case."

And Maggie looked like such a nice girl.

"Did she know you were investigating her?"

"We wonder if she became aware of our investigation since she was reportedly increasingly secretive and con-communicative. Our hypothesis is she felt guilty and killed herself."

"That's quite an interesting theory. You need to contact Detective Fitzgerald about this news."

"I've put a call in for him to call me," she responded.

Our meeting had come to a natural conclusion. Michael walked me to the elevator.

"Did you know anything about this Michael?"

"Nothing. This is another shock." Admittedly he looked slightly pale.

Poor Michael! Little did we know but there were a few more shocks coming his way.

Chapter 12

The dispatchers do their best to send me to calls that look like they involve someone who is emotionally disturbed but many times they are wrong. We would later rate the last call on Friday evening as fitting into this category and the call went south fast.

Daniel Smith (no relation) was a guy in his forties who lived above a ratty, disreputable bar in downtown Cookfield. Daniel had schizophrenia and was always off his medications and therefore always unwell. The long periods of psychosis were interrupted regularly with month-long hospitalizations. When he became unmedicated and unwell, Daniel would stop eating because he thought the food was poisoned. He would eventually become so unwell that he would be paranoid about other people trying to get him so he would threaten to hurt them and earn himself a four-week stint at the "Hilton-On-The-Hill", our local psychiatric hospital. In this dumpy hotel, poisoned food was a natural byproduct of being exposed to this environment. One could get salmonella poisoning by breathing in the air and a pee in the bathroom would ultimately reward you with a sexually transmitted disease. When hospitalized, Daniel was the model patient by taking his medications and eating properly. He would celebrate his return home by stopping his medications and starting the cycle over again. Daniel had never hurt anyone however when he was ill he could act very aggressively and look pretty frightening at these times.

Tonight's call was for exactly that reason. The bartender had called to say that Daniel had threatened to cut the throat of his neighbour. This was a little extreme, even for Daniel who we figured must have been off his medications for a while. Tim Doyle, a veteran cop of seventeen years, picked me up from the station to take me on the call. We had worked together many, many times and I felt that he was one of the best cops around. Daniel Smith lived in Tim's regular beat so Tim also knew him well and we had been to see Daniel together repeatedly. On several occasions we had taken him to hospital. It was a quick drive from the station to the *Rose and Crown Hotel*. It's hard to get into the hotel since only the residents have a key to get in through the massive, steel door and the only other way to get in is to have the bartender let you in. He's kind of like the hotel bouncer. The many full-time "guests" of the hotel have limited expectations of the hotel and they are not disappointed. All they want is to have a roof over their heads and no one to hassle them. There is a communal bathroom on each floor. The bar downstairs allows them easy access to cheap beer and a short distance to stumble home at the end of a good night of stiff drinking. The hotel had added some sport to the "trip" home in the form of a long, narrow, steep and uneven staircase. Many a drunk had taken a tumble down them and sadly one guy died a few months ago from a fall.

The *Rose and Crown* also provides the opportunity for a tumble in other ways by renting out the rooms by the hour to vendors of the world's oldest profession, prostitution. All in all, the *Rose and Crown* was a busy place of business.

Tonight was especially busy with it being a Friday night and the beginning of the month. The monthly social service checks had been cashed and the money was burning a hole in everyone's pocket.

Daniel lived on the hotel's second floor. He must have moved rooms since the last time I visited. For many years he lived in room 13, but the police dispatcher had directed us to his new room 17. It was only seven o'clock in the evening and the hotel was already loud sounding like there were several fun parties going on. Lucky ducks!

Tim knocked on Daniel's door. There was no answer but we could hear some shuffling from the other side of the door. Tim knocked again, this time loudly.

"Daniel, open up. It's the police. We can hear you in there," he yelled through the door.

The door at the end of the hall opened and we heard someone say, "Hey man. I'm here!" We were thrown off guard because it was Daniel and he wasn't where we expected him – that is, in front of us. At that moment, the door to room 17 opened and a tall black man stood in front of us. He was holding some type of a gun in his hand. I watched in horror as I saw the gun fire at Tim throwing him back against the wall.

"No!" I screamed.

The man leaped out and grabbed me, pulling me into the room and slamming the door shut. He threw me up against the door and then onto my face on the bed. I felt stunned as he grabbed me by my hair yelling at me, "Shut the fuck up, bitch. Shut up!"

I didn't realize it but the person I could hear screaming was me.

"You shot him!" I yelled at the guy.

"Yeah, I know and I'll shoot you too if you don't shut up." He grabbed me by my hair and put the barrel of the gun to my temple. It was effective. I stopped screaming.

"Shut up bitch-cop or you'll get a piece of what your pig partner just tasted." His breath stunk of alcohol and he smelt of sweat and bad body odour. He certainly had my attention and I shut up. It was just that my brain kept screaming, "Tim! What about Tim!"

The guy threw me onto my face, pushed my head into the mattress making it hard to breathe and roughly frisked my body for weapons. He grabbed my radio and smashed it to bits against the wall. So much for my plan to push the emergency button. Next my fanny pack was savagely ripped off my waist. He looked through it and took the pepper spray and cell phone and put them into his pocket. I knew it wouldn't have really helped much but it was my only lifeline and all that I had as a defense.

He pulled me up by my hair again and yelled into my face.

"Your gun, bitch. Where's your gun?"

Somehow I managed to stammer out, "I don't have one. I'm not a cop."

"Lying bitch cop!" he screamed back. And then the unthinkable happened. I heard the click of the gun as he cocked it and placed it against my temple again. It was as if time had stopped in its tracks.

"Last chance, bitch. Where is your gun?"

"I told you. I'm not a cop. I just work with the cops. I'm a nurse. I'm telling you the truth. Please believe me." I pleaded with him.

I could feel his breath on my neck making every hair stand on end. It probably only took a moment but it felt like a lifetime before he finally answered.

"You'd better not be lying, bitch. I'll kill you if you are." He threw me back on the bed and then hit me across my face with his fist. I landed up against the wall. I was completely terrified and close to losing control.

"Stay still," he hissed. The guy took some string from somewhere and roughly tied my hands behind me and sat me up on the bed.

It was at this moment that the hysteria really took over. I knew that I had been trained for moments like this but I just couldn't think of what to do. Rule number one was, was... what the hell was it? All I could think of was "stop, drop and roll" but I knew that wasn't right.

My brain kept kicking back to Tim. Are you okay, Tim? Please let him be okay, I pleaded to God. It was the same God who appeared to have temporarily lost his sanity and let this madness happen.

I told myself to think. Rule number one – stay calm. Yeah, that was it. Stay calm. Okay! Okay! Stay calm, I told myself. Take a deep breath, I told myself. It's not a rule but it's a good idea. Take a another deep breath, I thought. So I did. Then another.. And another.. And another.. Fuck, now I was hyperventilating.

"Calm down!" yelled the gunman shaking the gun in my face. Christ! Even the criminal knew the rules! "And stop looking at me!"

Okay, I thought, focus on something, anything. The guy was agitated and kept waving the gun around. It was a Glock. It was the same type that the cops used. Cops have Glocks. Hey, that rhymes. I watched him walk back and forth with it, back and forth until... I vomited. Hey, I can't help it if I have a gun phobia!

"What the fuck is wrong with you? You're not lying, are you? You are some chicken-shit nurse, aren't you?" Finally, something this crazed gunman and I could agree upon.

"I'm sorry!" I replied and tried to trample the vomit into the carpet. Man, I thought, the maid will be mad when she does her monthly visit to clean this room. At least it was something to do while I waited for fate to take its toll on me.

Back to the rules. Rule number one – stay calm. Okay, rule number two, no vomiting. Okay. I was getting somewhere with this. Yeah! Rule number three, no crapping my pants. Tim, rule number four is no dying. I plan to follow that rule to the letter. Okay, this rule thing was happening. Rule number five.. Yeah! Let's make that no shooting, Mr. Gunman. Okay so I was getting hysterical again. Focus, Chailey, focus.

I know, look for clues, Chailey, I told myself. You always wanted to be a cop so here's your chance. I looked around the room. It was a typical *Rose and Crown* room. The green institutional paint was peeling off the walls. What a coincidence, my brain thought. I once read that they use green in hospitals so that blood doesn't show up on the walls. They also used it in the KGB dungeons for the same reason. That was probably why the owners of this establishment did it too. Move onto your next observation, Sherlock, I told myself. The bed was filthy and looked like it hadn't been changed since 1975. That made the bile rise up in my throat since I'd put my face into that. Remember rule number two, Chailey – thou shalt not vomit! Great! Now I was quoting Shakespeare. I didn't really know that was what Shakespeare had written but I know if he had been here, that is what he would have said. The room was a disaster. It looked like the guy had been here for a few days. Empty takeout food containers were littered everywhere and there were lots of beer cans all over. I knew that this guy was dangerous. He was even more dangerous with alcohol driving his rage.

Finally, a sane thought hit me. I knew if I waited long enough some sanity would creep into that little head of mine. I had seen this man's face before. But where? The back of a milk carton? *America's Most Wanted*? Then I remembered. I'd seen his picture when I went to get coffee from the Squad Room. His face was on one of those police department "wanted" sheets. He was the guy who had done the bank robbery a few days ago. He had shot a security guard who was still in critical condition last time I heard an update on his condition, the hospital gave him fifty-fifty odds of survival. This guy was a cold-blooded killer. He'd kill me and not think twice about it. I hoped that Tim was okay and vowed to make sure that he didn't kill any more victims. It was this revelation that sobered me up. I just needed to figure out what the hell I was going to do.

I noticed that the noise outside the hotel room had abated. They had probably evacuated everyone from the building. I bet that had been a popular move on a Friday night. No doubt half the people in the hotel didn't blink an eyelid when they heard the sound of a gunshot. Maybe Tim was okay, after all. I know that if he could, he would have called the code for "Officer down!" It was the call no officer ever wanted to hear. When it is broadcast, every officer drops whatever he or she is doing and rushes to the scene. I figured by now that the police would have cordoned off the area to make sure that this bad guy didn't get way. I hadn't heard any sirens but that didn't mean much since we were at the back of the building. The guy had picked a good room since it was on a middle floor with no ladders or fire escapes close by and no way anyone could easily access the room from the roof unless they were Spiderman. Admittedly, I wasn't very focussed on the outside since I could still hear my heart beating so loudly that I thought "Gunman", my name for my captor, could hear it and I'd be yelled at for making too much noise. I figured the police would not let this guy leave this building alive. He'd shot a security guard and a cop and was mad enough to do it again.

To be honest, I didn't know a lot about hostage-taking stuff. My role in hostage-taking and barricade calls had been limited to providing information on the suspect as needed and giving support to the victims afterwards. That, and getting coffee for everyone on the scene. There were several negotiators in the police department who were specifically trained to deal with these situations. I knew them all. I wondered if it made a difference to them if they knew the person they were negotiating for? I made a note to myself that *if* I made it out of this alive that I would make it a point to be nice to those negotiators for future reference. Maybe drop off doughnuts every now and then... Only a week earlier I had received an e-mail from my boss recommending me to be trained as a negotiator. Coincidence, I think not. Too little, too late, I would say on that score. One thing I knew for sure was that as a hostage I shouldn't piss him off. I pretty well had that part of the plan figured out. I also knew not to eat the food that they send in – that's if they every got around to sending any take-out food in. I'd have to wing the rest of it the best that I could. Hey! I came up with the rules *and* I hadn't been shot so far. Fighting this hysteria was getting more and more difficult. So what the hell would be the next step, I wondered.

We must have been thinking of the same thing because he said, "Get ready to go. You're my shield. I'm going to get out of this stinking city with your help. If I die, you die!" Not quite the attitude I was hoping for.

"Gunman" started to prepare to leave and he appeared to be going through a checklist. Checking his weapons was number one. I didn't realize that he had two other guns until he pulled them out to ensure they were loaded. I just about broke rule number three when I saw that he had a sawn-off shotgun. A very sharp looking, long knife was also checked and put back in a sheath. It looked too big to be legal however I figured that now was not the time to bring that up. He then dressed himself by putting on a bulletproof vest and a jacket over top. Great! I was obviously the *only* person in a three-block radius not wearing a Kevlar vest!

This was the first chance I'd to get a proper look at the thug since he was so preoccupied with dressing like Rambo that he didn't appear to notice me staring at him. He must have been at least a few inches over six-feet tall with a shaved head. The guy was huge – at least weighing 260 pounds and relatively good looking. In any other situation he may have been cute. A hostage situation was not one of those situations.

"Like what you see?" he sneered.

Toughest question I'd been asked tonight.

He laughed at my hesitation. "If we'd had a little more time, I'd teach you a lesson or two." and then laughed.

Oh please, will you O' Great One? Who did he think he was?

"Gunman" stood and paced obviously waiting for the right time.

Waiting was the hardest part. I had noticed that there wasn't a phone in the room so nobody could call us. He had my cell phone but it was turned off. I really didn't think that "Gunman" wanted to negotiate a release and that he would leave when he was good and ready. My thoughts would become morbid at times and I began to seriously debate as to how my mother would dress me for my funeral. I know that if my father had been around he'd make me wear that stupid wedding dress again. My Dad had complained severely about the cost of the dress and my pragmatic mother would realize that this was the only chance she'd have to make me wear it again. She had loved the way I looked on my wedding day to that jerk-off, Adam. Damn, with no divorce agreement I hoped that he didn't get the house and my money. Well, that would be if I had any money. I had planned to drain him dry of money in divorce court. I hoped that they'd do my makeup well because I wouldn't want to be pale in a white dress. And the veil. Would they use the veil? And what about the picture for my obituary? I hoped to God that she didn't use my driver's license photo. It seemed that my humour had not left me quite yet. It was quite possibly the only thing keeping my sanity.

I couldn't think about the things that were really important. Like never seeing my nieces again or missing their graduations and weddings. Or how my mother would handle this all. Thank the saints that she was visiting her brother in England this month. I couldn't imagine who would look after my house because I hadn't had the children I had planned to leave the Golden Manor to. And then I wondered about how everything would play out when I left this disgusting room. Now that was what made me really, really frightened. I finally allowed myself to cry, not out loud but silently with my head down and I let the tears roll freely.

The gunman appeared to be getting quite agitated and I was getting worried. He took out the cell phone and gave it to me.

"Dial the police and get the negotiator on the line," he demanded.

I knew that the final phase of his plan was finally here. At least he had a plan. All I had were stupid rules. I took the phone in shaky hands. For some reason I couldn't remember the police department's phone number. All I could think of was 911 so I dialed that.

"911. Do you need police, ambulance or fire?"

"Hi." I replied. "Actually, I need to speak to someone in charge of the hostage-taking at *The Rose and Crown*." As if there were other hostage takings in the city. "This is Chailey Smith." I added.

"Chailey, are you okay?" asked Ian the dispatcher. I could hear yells in the background saying that it was me.

Apparently people were aware of our little incident and that someone had alerted the police department.

"Yeah. As good as can be expected." I answered.

"Are they listening to this call?" Ian asked. I knew that he was trying to get as much information as possible in case our call was terminated.

"Er, no. That's negative." Negative, what kind of police crap was I talking?

"Is there more than one person."

"Unh-uh." Skip the police talk, I thought.

"Does he have more than one gun?"

"Yes. One's enough but three's a crowd." Now I was talking in rhymes.

"Who the fuck are you talking to?" asked the "Gunman".

"It's the police dispatcher. They are trying to patch me through. It takes a few minutes."

"Shut the fuck up " he yelled. "You only talk when I tell you to."

"Okay, okay." I replied.

"Chailey, listen, we are doing everything to get you out of there. Stay calm and do everything he tells you. Okay, honey. I'm going to patch you through now. Remember everything is being taped so if there is any information you can give to help us, just add it. We'll figure it out later." God bless, Ian, and every other police dispatcher across the world.

"This is Brian Davies, negotiator for the Cookfield Police Department. Who am I speaking to?" he asked. The Goddamn Easter Bunny is what I wanted to reply.

"It's me. Chailey Smith"

"I told you not talk unless I tell you, bitch!" screamed "Gunman". He hit me across my mouth, I screamed and the phone flew out of my hands.

"Pick it up!" he demanded. The gun was in his hand and pointed at my head.

I bent down and picked it up. My hands were trembling so much that I could barely hold the phone. I was whimpering and couldn't calm down.

"Tell them I'm in control and nobody does anything unless I tell them to. Especially you, Bitch."

It took me a moment to be able to talk. I knew that the negotiator needed to make a connection with "Gunman", but that was not going to happen.

"This is Chailey. The gunman wants you to follow what he says. Okay?"

"Okay, Chailey. Stay as calm as you can." How come everyone knows rule number one? "We are going to get you out of there safely. Will the gunman talk to me directly on the phone? Cough once for yes." I stayed quiet.

"Gunman" looked at me and said, "Tell them I want a plain SUV and I want it in ten minutes at the front of the building. If I don't get what I want, you get hurt."

I swallowed hard at that. I think that I was past fear and just working on auto-pilot.

""Gunman" told me that he wants a plain SUV in front of the building in ten minutes, or, or he'll..."

"Tell him," yelled "Gunman".

"Or, he'll hurt me." I started to cry. Finally I was going to get my police SUV and probably die in it too. If it had green seats, I wasn't getting in.

"Gunman" grabbed the phone and effectively turned it off by smashing it against the wall. He pulled out the knife, cut the cord on my wrists and told me to stand up. My foot was stuck to the dried vomit on the floor and I stumbled.

"Get up," yelled "Gunman". "Pick up that bag over there." He pointed at a large back pack, which looked full. I went to grab it and just about wrenched my back. The bag must have weighed a billion pounds.

"Pick it up or I'll give you another beating," threatened "Gunman".

I figured that fear and adrenaline were kicking in. I grabbed the handles, put them on my shoulders and yanked the bag onto my back. Hell, I could have carried the *Titanic* on my back at that moment. He put a similar bag on his back.

"Good girl!" snarled "Gunman". This guy was really getting on my nerves.

He pushed me in front of him and motioned for me to open the door. He told me to be quiet and not to say a word no matter what anyone said to me. All I had to do was to carry the bag down to the car and everything would be fine. Yeah, right, I thought. Everything was fucking hunky-dory so far.

I pulled open the door and I saw some motion down each end of the hall. It was the SWAT guys and they were fully dressed in their combat gear with rifles pointed at me.

"Tell them to back up," murmured "Gunman" in my ear. So much for the vow of silence he wanted me to take.

"Back up!" I yelled. Unbelievably they listened to me and backed up.

"Gunman" grabbed me by the hair, put the barrel of the gun to my temple and pushed me ahead. We moved down the hall and somehow I made it down the rickety stairs without falling and killing myself. Apparently that was the "Gunman's" job. We stopped outside of the front entrance door. In the middle of the road was a big, black shiny SUV. I hoped to God that the truck had some kind of monitor on it to trail us, that way they would be able to find my body. Come to think of it, the truck looked a lot like my uncle's.

"What is going to happen is we are going to the passenger side of the truck. You are going to put the bag in the back door and then you are going to get in the front passenger side and shuffle over to the driver's side."

Driver's side! I can't drive without a gun at my head let alone driving with some crazed gunman with a gun. I can't do the OJ Simpson thing.

"I can't drive!" I pleaded.

"Don't tell me you can't drive. I know you can. You have a driver's license. I saw it in your pouch." I wondered what he thought of the picture. He pulled harder on my hair. "You drive, bitch."

I pushed open the door and "Gunman" stopped me short on the steps.

"Show time!" he whispered in my ear.

It was night time but the area was flooded with lights. The red and white lights from the cruisers flashed through the night. I knew that there must have been officers surrounding us everywhere and that every weapon was pointed at "Gunman". Except for one and that was the one pointed at my head. I wondered if my buddies were out there. He pushed me out and I stumbled on the step but regained my footing. "Gunman" generously helped out by yanking me back onto my feet by my hair.

We walked slowly out to the car. "Gunman" was very nervous and I could smell his sweat and fear, or maybe it was mine. We got to the far side of the truck. As I opened up the back door, "Gunman" grabbed the bag to put it in the door but kept the gun up. He knew that I was terrified and that I would do everything he wanted me to. At least he thought he did. It was my one and only chance. I dropped down and rolled under the car. Stop, drop and roll! I knew it was a rule.

There was a hail of gunfire and I saw Gunman drop to the ground. I rolled out of the other side of the truck, got up and ran as fast as I could to the nearest cruiser. Someone grabbed me and hurried me to the relative dark behind the cars. I sat shaking on the ground and desperately pleaded with the officer to tell me if Tim was okay.

"Yeah, honey, he's fine. And so will you be."

Chapter 13

To be honest, I don't remember a lot of details after that. I had heard the officer yell, "I've got her. She's okay!" I wondered whom he was talking about. I think that I passed out at that time because next thing I knew I was lying on a gurney in an ambulance with someone taking my blood pressure.

We were moving and I could see two police cruisers following us. My only viable thought was, Stop, drop and roll! That's what you do in a fire. Well, he fired his gun, didn't he?

They took me to the Cookfield General Hospital and I was immediately seen by the Emergency Room doctor. Apparently people can be seen immediately and I noted that for future reference. Mercifully my doctor was Bryan Fields, one of the best physicians in the Emergency Room, who attended me along with Sally the nurse who dealt with me in a very professional manner. One of my greatest fears working in the medical world is that I'd pass out in the middle of street and come around with my clothes ripped off, EKG monitors on and my colleagues standing in a circle around me. Based on that fear, I quickly checked that my clothes were all on.

Dr. Fields stitched the cuts above my eye and my top lip. I had prayed that I didn't need any plastic surgery and if I did, that Adam wasn't on call. He'd do quite the job, I'm sure. I'd have 6-6-6 stitched across my forehead! Sally cleaned my bruises and cuts and took me to have a shower in the doctor's lounge. I tentatively checked my underwear hoping that I hadn't broken rule number three and pooped in my panties. Thank God I hadn't. She gave me greens to put on so that I could try to feel human again. Abby came in to sit with me and we chatted a little. The doctor gave me some medication for the pain and something to help me sleep and made me stay for a couple of hours for observation. Unbelievably I snoozed for a while before the doctor came back to tell me I could go home but he wanted to see me the next day.

My memory remains fuzzy but what I do remember is that Pete drove me home. At the hospital they told me I should go to a friend or relatives but I refused. I wanted to go to the safest place in the world and that was my house. I don't know what time I eventually got home but I'm pretty sure that it was close to dawn. It felt like a lifetime had passed since I had left home earlier that day and in many ways it had. Martha and the boys were sitting on the stairs when I got back. I hugged each of them and then Pete. He told me he'd stay – I told him that it was okay. Randy followed me up the stairs and I turned right and continued up to the attic. I lay down on my back on the futon and pulled my grandmother's quilt over me while Randy settled down quietly at the end of my bed. I was exhausted but not enough to make me to sleep. I looked up into the sky and did one of the simplest but most enjoyable tasks that people have done since the beginning of mankind and started counting the stars. It was the most wonderful thing that I have done in a long, long time. Sleep was a long time in coming but when it finally did, it was blissful.

****

The next morning I got up slowly since every muscle in my body ached. I felt like a Mack truck had hit me going at eighty miles an hour and then backed up to roll over me again. I carefully climbed down the stairs in order to avoid stepping on Bart and Harold who had slept on the landing outside of the attic door. God bless them! I left them there knowing how badly they needed their sleep and quietly slipped down the stairs to the ground floor. It was already ten in the morning. I looked outside and in front of the house was Pete in his cruiser. About one-hundred feet down the road blocking the entrance to the road was another cruiser with what looked like Kevin Harrison sitting in the front seat. A girl could start to like this type of attention. I let myself into my apartment and made a beeline for the bathroom for the longest shower of my life. I purposefully avoided looking in the mirror figuring I looked bruised. Pruney, but almost feeling refreshed, I got out, put on my jeans and a sweatshirt, quickly brushed my hair and headed out the front door. I left a note on my door telling Martha and the guys I was okay and that I'd be back later.

I walked up to Pete's cruiser.

"Hey, Chailey. How are you doing?" he asked.

"You know what, Pete. You may not believe it but I really am okay. Let's say I take you and your buddy over there out for some breakfast. My treat."

"Sounds good to me," he replied. Pete radioed over to Kevin to follow him and also radioed to the police dispatcher that he was leaving this location with Chailey Smith. Sandy was the dispatcher.

"You tell that girl that we are so proud of her. We love you, Chailey." Her voice cracked with emotion. There was a chorus of "10-4"s and "Way to go, Chailey!" which made tears well in my eyes. I hadn't had this much adulation since my initiation. I hoped everybody remembered those sentiments next time I backed into their car. Pete squeezed my hand and added, "It's going to be okay."

"I know," I replied. "It's just a little difficult." That was possibly the biggest understatement of the year.

We drove over to my favourite restaurant, *Blimpey's* and I ordered the Hungry Man's Breakfast. What can I say? Stress makes me barf and it also makes me hungry. I guess it's part of the same cycle, isn't it? At first the small talk was stilted and polite and reminded me that life had changed in a major way last night. As we got more comfortable with being together again and drank copious amounts of coffee, Pete and Kevin brought me up to date on the details of last night's events from outside of Room 17 of the *Rose and Crown*.

As I had witnessed, Tim had been shot at close range but had survived compliments of his Kevlar, bulletproof vest, which had done its job and absorbed the bullet. He'd been thrown back against the wall by the impact of the bullet at such a close range and had been knocked unconscious. The gunman had been in too much of a hurry to grab me to make sure that he had killed Tim and if he had, we'd have been preparing for a police funeral today. Apparently God had regained his senses and listened to my prayer.

The real Daniel Smith had been quite a hero. The gunman had overheard Daniel using his name and started to use it himself. It was actually the gunman who had threatened to kill the neighbour, not our Daniel Smith, who had witnessed the shooting from the door to his room. He ran back into his room and hid under his bed until he was sure it was safe and the shooting was over. He deserved a medal for bravery to have spent five seconds under a bed in that disgusting hotel let alone five minutes. Daniel had finally gathered the courage to peek out into the hall and saw Tim stirring as he began to regain consciousness. Daniel had crawled down the hall Commando-style and dragged Tim down the hall into his room. Apparently Daniel had been so scared that he broke rule number three and shit his pants. Poor Daniel! By then Tim was fully conscious and called the "Police Officer down" over the air. Tim had quickly recognized the gunman as being the bank robber, Reece Slater. Within minutes, the entire building was evacuated and surrounded, Tim had been taken to the hospital for observation and both the SWAT and Negotiating Teams had been called in. My uncle, the Police Chief, had also arrived on the scene as well as many other high-ranking officers. Taking a police officer hostage is considered to be one of the gravest sins in the police world. I guess that taking me hostage was a pretty close second.

The biggest mistake that Slater had made was being out in the open. At that point every sniper present had his or her rifle trained on him. He really didn't have a chance and I believe that he knew that. Apparently my actions helped to save my life. If I had gone into the car then the takedown would have been extremely dangerous and injuries would have been serious. That was a nice way of saying we'd probably have been shot. I told them about my rules and they laughed when I told them about "Stop! Drop! And roll!" And then I told them everything else. My fears and the terrible sense of loneliness. Both were present during the entire stand off and they told me about their feelings of helplessness as they watched everything unfold. Every police officer present had offered to take on the detail of "guarding me". Pete was one of my best friends and Kevin Harrison had been a pretty good pal over the last few days. They were under strict instructions by the Chief of Police to keep me safe and to prevent reporters having any access to me. I was to go nowhere without them today or at any time over the weekend. I hoped I could at least go to the bathroom alone. Perhaps by the beginning of next week things would settle down and we could return to normality.

Good luck on that one since life was not all that normal before all this happened.

I knew that there would be a lot happening today and we finally got around to talking about this. I would have to make a statement to the detectives and the province-wide Special Police Investigations Unit, or SPIU, who would be meeting with me today. SPIU investigates any police shootings. Finally, I would have to call my family and tell them I was okay. Pete told me that my uncle had done that for me already. There was one more thing that I needed to do before I did anything else.

We traipsed out to the cruiser and I went with Pete who drove us to the Cookfield General Hospital. I wanted to see Tim to make sure he was okay. We parked out front and Kevin and Pete walked with me between them through the main entrance of the hospital. Apparently they were taking this guarding thing to heart. We took the elevator up to the third floor of the hospital and turned left outside of the elevators to go to the Short Stay Unit. There was a police officer in the hall and I presumed he was guarding Tim's room. The officer was Jamie Swider. He's been with the police department for about ten years and is called "Bear" simply because he is six-feet, eight-inches tall and about weighs 250 pounds. He's also tame as a teddy bear and the sweetest guy in the world. When he saw me come down the hall, a big smile came over his face and he reached down to hug me. Man, it felt good.

I could hear his voice crack a little as he said, "Thank God you're safe Chailey."

He held me for a few more seconds while he tried to compose himself while I did the same. We chatted for a few minutes under the stares of the nurses and the other patients. I could hear someone say, "Is that the girl who was taken hostage?" Apparently, Kevin heard it too and put his bulky frame in front of the person and asked the nurses if they could clear the hall – something to do with "official police business". Seeing Tim was going to be difficult. Somewhere in my heart I felt that I had failed him by leaving him out there. He was my partner and I wasn't there to help him when I should have been.

Pete had gone in to get Cindy, Tim's wife who came out to see me. We knew each other relatively well and she embraced me warmly, told me that she was thankful that I was safe and to go in. Tim was anxious to see me. Somehow Kevin recognized my reticence and whispered in my ear, "It really will be okay. Go on in. We'll wait for you out here." He squeezed my hand and I felt that familiar tightening of my stomach. Kevin Harrison was having an effect on me and when everything settled down, we needed to have a chat.

I gathered up my courage, put on a smile and pushed through the door. I hadn't expected it but Tim was standing waiting for me. He looked like he normally did. There were no big holes in him. No big bruises or bandages or casts. All of his appendages were attached. It was just plain, old Tim with his big goofy smile. He grabbed me and hugged me. An incredible feeling of relief washed over me at that moment and then I cried. Tears flooded down my cheeks as I held onto Tim and sobbed. I felt Tim crying too and realized that at that moment he was probably as relieved to see me as I was to see him. Eventually Tim regained his senses and sat me down on the bed with his arm around me. I didn't realize it but Tim felt incredibly guilty by what had happened to me.

We sat talking for a while and the rest of the gang came in. Apparently Tim was being discharged as soon as the doctor came to see him.

As I got up to leave the room I was shocked to look in the mirror and see what was looking back. Having had such a long shower the mirror had fogged up in the bathroom and I had left the house quickly and as was typical for me, I didn't bother to stop and preen myself in front of a mirror. Big mistake! I looked like I had bounced around ten rounds with Mike Tyson. My left eye was swollen with a Harry Potter-like cut just above it. At least my puffed-up eye was a nice match for my swollen lip.

"Why didn't you say something, Pete?" I asked him.

"About what?" he replied. "You usually look pretty hellish in the morning and I just thought it was a particularly bad morning."

He ducked as I threw a punch at him. At least things were getting back to some level of normality. He gave me his black "Police" baseball cap that he had been carrying around in his pocket.

"Actually, I thought that you were just being brave so I didn't say anything. I think you look beautiful."

Well, the time had come for me to confess my sins to the higher ups in the police department so we got ready to return to the police station and do the official police business crap. I gave Tim another big hug and took the opportunity to peak in the mirror to see his butt through the back of his hospital gown. No such luck! He was wearing cute little plaid boxer shorts. I felt like the weight of the world had been lifted off my shoulders having seen Tim alive and well. Actually, he looked a lot better than I did. We left Tim and Cindy sitting together on the bed holding hands. They were probably thanking the Gods that Tim was safe and trying to avoid thinking about the unimaginable outcome if Tim had been shot and died. I was insightful enough to know that it was going to take me some time to work through the guilt associated with Tim.

Pete called my uncle to tell him that we were heading over so that he could meet us there. On the way out of the hospital I headed over to the Gift Shop to grab a few *Mars* bars, courage for the upcoming interviews. If I had been shocked to see my appearance in the mirror, I was even more stunned to see a picture of myself on the front pages of the "Cookfield Chronicle", our town's daily newspaper. A reporter had taken a long-distance picture of Gunman and me standing beside the car while he pointed the gun at my head. I stopped dead in my tracks and Kevin and Pete ran into me. I pointed at the papers and did the only thing that I could; I bought all thirty of them, made my "guards" carry them out to the car and then dropped them off in the dumpster at the police station. I wanted to set fire to them but Pete said "No!" There was some issue about thirty papers causing a major fire. See! I was dealing with this well. Out of sight, out of mind. Denial is a somewhat healthy defense mechanism, isn't it?

The remainder of the day was spent at the police station. We entered through the back door so that I could minimize the number of people I'd have to talk to. A bit of a coward's way out but I was comfortable with that. There were reporters at the front of the station whom I wanted to avoid. My uncle was present during the two interviews. He had brought along a lawyer to the Special Police Investigations Unit, or SPIU, interview. The "brief" sat beside me and poked me every time we got to a touchy subject. The first time he did this I yelped, but I quickly learned to cover my reactions and responded to those questions in a way that would make any defense lawyer salivate. They asked the obvious questions about how the events unfolded and my actions. I decided that I didn't like their tone at one point so I did what seemed to come naturally to me in my current sub-hysterical state - I cried. Between fainting and crying, hysteria was going to be my middle name. Freud would have been proud of me! There were some dark looks exchanged across the table between my uncle, the lawyer and the SPIU guys and the interview ended fairly quickly after that.

The second interview was conducted in the relative comfort of the Chief's office. The two detectives, John Brown and Dave Applegate, were investigating the armed robbery committed by Slater and they were the guys conducting this interview. I knew them fairly well since we had all played baseball together on a team the previous year in the police league. My uncle had dropped the lawyer and we sat in the Chief's office drinking coffee in a more relaxed atmosphere. I basically started my story from entering the doors of the *Rose and Crown* to my final desperate attempt for freedom. Man, that sounds dramatic. I included all the details figuring that I might help them understand why I did what I did. They let me talk which I do well at the best of times and they periodically asked questions. There was overall agreement that I had done a great job "considering the situation". I wasn't really sure what that meant! My statement was to be typed and then I could sign it. The detectives reassured me that there would be little else happening until the trial.

"Trial!" I shrieked.

"Yes, the trial."

"Didn't you know? Slater survived. He has been charged with second degree murder," John Brown blurted out.

I didn't hear much after that because I had my head between my knees while I tried not to embarrass myself by fainting. My uncle got up, stepped away from my chair and told the others not to touch me. He knew all about my Achilles Heel stomach. It took me a few minutes to recover as I listened to a series of apologies for not having told me earlier.

"He is in custody, right?" I asked, trying to dampen my sarcastic tone.

"Yes. He is currently being treated for his wounds at Cookfield General. And he'll stay there. No need to worry, Chailey."

Right! And I'm Santa Claus!

"There is something else you need to know, Chailey. The man he shot during the robbery died last night."

Whompf! It felt like someone had punched me in the stomach. How could that man die and Slater live? As far as I was concerned this interview was over and I left. Pete and Kevin were outside the door awaiting their guard duties and looked clean and refreshed. Obviously they'd spent their time more wisely than I had. At least they smelt better.

"So, did you two know that Slater was alive?"

Both nodded yes. Apparently I was the only knob in town who didn't know this minor detail. Don't get me wrong, I don't want anyone dead. It's just that I didn't expect the "Gunman" to be alive.

I stomped away pissed off at the world. In some ways, it felt good to be mad. Pete and Kevin sheepishly followed me out the back exit of the police station. I went over to a cruiser and got in. I was absolutely seething with rage. How dare they not tell me Slater was alive? I could see Kevin and Pete debating over some issue. They were probably doing "Hot Potato" to see who was going to take the wild cat. I could imagine the conversation – keep all sharp objects and things that go "bang" away from her, if necessary cuff and hog-tie her. Chicken shit cops, is all I could say! Pete obviously lost the toss and got into the car dejectedly. At least he had the decency to look ashamed of himself.

"Chailey, we didn't want to upset you. When we had breakfast this morning that Son-of-a-Bitch was still in surgery. I'm no happier than you are that he's alive. And I swear to God that every man and woman in this police department will ensure that the bastard will never, ever touch you again." He looked furious.

Sure, take the wind out of my sails. Obviously Pete believed that a good offense is a good defense.

"And the security guard dying. I didn't know about that either until you were meeting with the last group. So don't shit on me."

"So what now?" I asked a little sheepishly.

"First, we get out of this car because it isn't ours and I think that Zack wants to get to work." Hah! That was an oxymoron if I'd ever heard one. I looked out the window and Zack was smiling at me. "And then we go to the hospital and then to my house."

"Pete, I'm sorry"

"Not as sorry as I am, Chailey. As a police officer you fight to keep people safe. Slater lives, the security guard dies and you had to go through the shit that you did. It's not right. And I'm sorry that I sounded so angry with you. It's the last thing you deserve."

We got out, chatted for a few minutes with Zack who lightened the mood with several Barney jokes in deference to my current facial shade and then headed over to the Cookfield Hospital again. I felt like I had run a marathon. Fat chance I'd ever actually run a marathon but I was pretty sure that this is how it would feel if I did. We dropped by the Emergency Room and saw Dr. Fields who quickly checked me out. He suggested that I might want to talk to a counselor. I reassured him after living thirty-plus years with my mother and family, a gun wielding, hostage-taking lunatic was not going to scrape my psyche. In many ways, it was an extraordinary phenomenon. Everyone made the presumption that this was the worst thing that could ever happen to me. They were wrong. Losing my father to cancer was much worse. Dr. Fields told me to go home and get some rest. He wanted to give me a medical slip to be away from work but we negotiated for light duties. Basically I'd be doing the job that Jody does every day.

"Honey! You look like hell," Bonny told me as she answered the door. "But I am so thrilled to see you!" She had tears in her eyes and so did I.

The guys had made themselves comfortable and had beers for us all and we sat in the family room until dinner was served. My anger was starting to ebb a little. We finished the evening off with a few good games of euchre. Kevin was my partner and he quickly realized why Bonny and Pete didn't want to be my partner since I'm an amazingly bad euchre player. I learned that Kevin had just returned from a three-day trip to visit his four-year-old son, Jake, in British Columbia. They had separated two years ago and Kevin stated that he was gradually learning to adjust to this new life. He saw his son once a month and he had to travel to BC to see him.

Kevin added an apology. "Remember when you rear-ended my cruiser a few years ago and I went postal on you? I need to apologize. My wife left me that day and your little accident just about finished me off. Sorry."

"No problem," I replied. I tried to make him feel a little better by telling him about the lousy deal I had with my ex-husband.

For some reason I thought Kevin was married but just didn't wear a wedding band. Many men don't wear a ring, a fact that has always been a bit of a mystery to me. Virtually every married woman I know wears a wedding band so why different rules for the guys? Most husbands who don't wear one have some wimpy "reason" like they work with machinery and are fearful their fingers might get hooked in the machine. My ex-husband's excuse was that as a doctor he didn't want a ring to spread infection. Sure, he didn't want anyone to think that he was married and cramp his extracurricular, sexual activities.

Kevin was reasonably handsome and that was probably another reason why I never paid attention to him. I shy away from good-looking guys for several reasons. My marriage and separation had left me pretty emotionally bruised. Adam, who was considered to be sexy and handsome, had ridiculed me in front of my colleagues at the hospital. I was the last one to know what was going on and that's pretty embarrassing when your husband has tupped a good thirty or so women in the hospital where you work. So, in my mind, good-looking guys equaled scum. I'd eaten my way through my separation and gained a good thirty pounds that I have never quite shed. Okay, so I have only dropped half of those pounds and I feel like an unstuffed Thanksgiving turkey most of the time. My self esteem was not particularly boosted by my dearth of a dating life since one blind date a year didn't exactly count as the love life of a wild and crazy single girl. So I had never really paid attention to the guy and essentially knew nothing about him.

By eleven o'clock, the exhaustion caught up with me and I rudely fell asleep on the couch oblivious to everyone around me. Next thing I knew, it was three o'clock in the morning and I woke up covered in a warm blanket and my head on a pillow. I checked under the blanket to make sure I was still dressed. The excessive drooling from my swollen lip had caused me to wake up in a puddle of spit. Real sexy! I hoped that my snoring hadn't woken anyone up.

Kevin had pulled point duty and was sitting in the recliner watching the movie, *Star Wars.* He must have seen me stir, or heard the snoring stop.

"You okay, Chailey?" he asked.

"Wime wokay," I tried to reply. My lip wasn't moving the way it should. I felt like I had been to the dentist and had my lip frozen.

He came over to the couch and handed me a couple of pills and a glass of water. "I thought that you might want some Tylenol."

Wow! A thoughtful man and I believed that was an oxymoron. Of course my opinion is that most men were morons to begin with.

The reality was that my body and face felt like it had kissed the front of a fast moving train. The stitches in my lip really stung and I figured that the river of wet, slimy saliva that had poured over my lip onto my pillow was the cause of this discomfort.

"Don't you ever sleep?" I asked. The guy was like Batman. Did you ever notice that Batman never slept? Nor did his butler, come to think of it.

"Yeah. Sometimes. I don't mind staying up for this duty. Pete will be down in a few minutes to switch duties."

Kevin sat leaning against the couch looking towards the fireplace. The fire flickered making his eyes look more silver than grey and highlighting the silver streaks in his hair. He was a pretty good-looking dude for being in his late thirties. At least that's what I thought in my drug-induced haze.

"Kevin."

"Yeah?"

"Will you talk to me, please?" I felt lonely for some reason even though he was right beside me.

"About what?" he asked cautiously.

"Anything! Everything! Just not about the you-know-what."

"Sure," he replied. I think he understood what I needed. I eventually fell asleep to the murmur of his voice as he told me about his life. That he'd gone to university on a rugby scholarship with the goal of becoming a lawyer. He graduated with an honours degree but was fed up with school so he applied to the Cookfield Police Service much to the dismay of his father. He married two years later. He'd met his wife, Gillian, through a friend. In retrospect, he felt that he married her because people get married. Why else would you marry a viper?

Good question, I thought, since I married a dog!

Kevin likes hot sauce on everything, *Lord of the Rings* and *Happy Gilmour*, rugby, beer, *U2* and opera. He likes his family, adores his son and his idea of relaxation is sitting on a beach quickly followed by sitting on the porch of his family's cottage in Muskoka drinking beer watching the sun set.

The Tylenol #3's and sleeping pills worked well and I slept until three the following afternoon. I was ready to go home to my own bed and pillow. That is, after a huge brunch of pancakes, bacon, sausage and eggs washed down by the obligatory gallon of coffee.

Within an hour of being home my patio was being filled with friendly visitors. It appeared that everyone and his brother were dropping by this evening. It was like a "Post Hostage-Taking Open House" and I was pretty sure that it was the first of its kind. Tim and Cindy, Bonny, Abby, Spencer, Zack, Neil, my brother and his wife and of course, the Golden Manor crowd were there. Even some of the old fogies from next door dropped by. Loralei and Harold gave a guest appearance emerging from the love nest for a few minutes of fresh air. Each person brought some food for me, mostly in the form of casseroles, which I promptly placed in the freezer for future consumption. The seniors from next door brought cookies, juice and those little containers of apple sauce that I love, probably stolen from the snack table. Blimpey and his wife finally saved the day and brought a huge box of food from his restaurant.

It felt good to have my friends and family around me and to be doing something productive, even if it was running plates and beer and napkins to and from the kitchen to the patio. It was about as domesticated as I get. At one point I stopped in the kitchen and looked out the side window into the night just enjoying the momentary sound of silence.

"A penny for your thoughts?" I heard Kevin ask from beside me. I didn't realize that he had followed me in.

"I was just thinking how nice peace and quiet can be," I replied wistfully.

"Do you want me to ask everyone to leave?" he offered in his ever-present protective role.

"No. It's great having them here," I replied realizing that I was smiling.

"How about me?" he asked quietly.

"How about me what?" I asked back. I've always been a little thick in these matters and realized belatedly what he meant.

His point was made clearer when he bent down and whispered, "How about this?"

And then he kissed me lightly on the lips. He hesitated slightly, and then kissed me again deeper.

"Mmmm.. This is good," I replied.

"I know that this is not really the right place or time but I've wanted to do that for a long time."

"Do what?" I asked cheekily.

"This!" Kevin kissed me again more deeply than before.

"Holy Shit!" shrieked Martha.

Kevin just about bit my lip off when he jumped.

Unfortunately Martha had come into the kitchen unbeknownst to us and was completely shocked to see us kissing. Even more unfortunate was the fact that she had screamed making everyone run for the kitchen thinking something was wrong including Pete who was drawing his weapon.

Martha had enough savvy to try to cover up her faux-pas and Kevin got busy looking for something in some drawer leaving me to face Martha and the patio gang.

"Sorry, guys. I thought I saw a snake. Actually, I think that it was Kevin's gun in the dark." Nice job, Martha!

Kevin chuckled and headed out the door and I could distinctly hear him whisper under his breath, "That was my pistol!"

Martha closed the door after him and gave me a high five with a "Way to go girl!" It's pretty sad when a seventy-five year old is excited to see you making out. She'll probably be on the phone to my mother in a minute.

To make matters worse, Martha added, "You slay me, girl. Three years without a date and you get beaten up and look like a ton of bricks has hit you in the face and then you get kissed by a Hottie like that. What is with you?"

What was with me was that Kevin kissed me, and I liked that Hottie a lot.

Chapter 14

It was Monday morning and I decided to get back on the proverbial horse, which started me thinking about Kevin. I had woken up at eight with that familiar daily feeling of stiffness and soreness and I wondered if it would ever go away. This was one weary horse rider. The Mack truck that had hit me today had only been going forty miles per hour. Randy had been assigned to me to keep me company as my sleeping partner and had slept on my bedroom floor. It meant that I woke up to kisses – that is wet doggy-breath kisses. Of course, I still hadn't quite had the joy of looking in the mirror to see what shade the bruises had turned today and I can tell you, I wasn't too happy to find a "Frankenstein-beats-up-Barney" look staring back at me in the mirror when I did finally gain the courage to look. My bruises had turned to purple and my face was still too sore to put on makeup. I frightened myself when I looked in the mirror.

They say that every good day starts with a cup of coffee. The way I was feeling I needed at least triple that amount. With guests in the house, namely Abby and Bart, I felt obliged to cook a few pounds of bacon and a couple of eggs and left a mountain of bacon for them to scrap over whenever they managed to drag their butts out of bed. I ate on the patio enjoying the warm sunshine and fresh air. I continued to wear Pete's baseball cap in an effort to be a little more inconspicuous.

This morning I planned to attend Maggie's funeral. To be honest, I'm not a big lover of funerals, which I think confirms my normalcy.

Interestingly, the last funeral I attended was for a horse. My niece Chloe had called me one day to report that one of the horses had died at the stables where she took lessons and they were having a funeral service. Chloe added that her mother said since I insisted on paying for these God-damn riding lessons then I could God-damn well take her to the God-damn funeral. Out of the mouths of babes! Chloe's mother must have been having a God-damn bad day to say that. Christine is married to my brother David. She, like all other good Smith women, is a nurse. I presumed that Christine must be on nights based on her grumpy comments. My twin nieces, Chloe and Claire, are nine years old. They are fraternal twins and as different as any two girls could be. Claire has dark hair and eyes and is into fashion and music. Chloe is blond-haired and blue-eyed and loves sports and horseback riding. What they do share in common is intelligence and a brilliant sense of humour – of course, those would be family traits they inherited from their Auntie Chailey!

The horse funeral turned out to be merely a memorial service which was a good thing since I wasn't sure if they made horse caskets, and if they did, they'd have to dig one helluva a big hole. The biggest question of that day was what to wear. I ruled out the black business suit, which was lucky, because I didn't even own one. Instead, I opted for clean black jeans with cowboy boots and a sweater. It was one of the most moving but certainly the smelliest memorial services I'd ever attended.

Picking what to wear to this funeral was also a bit of a challenge. I owned two black dresses – one for nightclubbing and the other for formal events such as funerals and divorce court. But what to do about the face? A tentative attempt at applying face paint revealed my face was too sensitive. I considered a hat with a veil but felt that was a little too much of a "grandmother-meets-Madonna" look. My final option was Michael Jackson's approach with sunglasses and bangs brushed in front of my face. I only planned to stay for the service and if I sat in the back of the church I figured no one would notice me.

I wasn't even sure why I was going to begin with. This was the first funeral I'd been to since becoming a Mental Health Worker. Over the years as a psychiatric nurse I'd lost several patients including a few from suicide and others from natural causes. The last few were from neglect. It sucks to be mentally ill in more ways than one.

Just as tragic is the vulnerability of mentally ill people to the low-life snakes of society. No, I'm not talking about Adam but other people who prey on those who are less able to make good, safe decisions in their lives. I personally know two females with schizophrenia whom had been murdered by abusive male partners.

Suicide is not unexpected in our field of work however it is never, ever easy to accept. When a patient of yours commits suicide, it makes you feel like you have failed the person. Your job is to help keep the person safe however that is not always possible. The mother of a son who had killed himself wrote in an article that suicide was a way to end constant enduring emotional pain. I still didn't understand why Maggie had killed herself. Perhaps she did it to end her own emotional turmoil. My doubts about Maggie's death continued to plague me and I realized that attending

Maggie's funeral was one way of coming to terms with her loss. Or at least try to!

It took me a while but I finally found a pair of navy blue nylons with no runs or holes. The change of nylons meant that I had to change to my blue suit, which included a short skirt so if I dropped anything it was going to stay there. It was my "job interview" suit, hence the short skirt.

The nylons were half way on when the doorbell rang. You'd think with all the people in the house somebody would be able to answer the door who isn't half dressed. But no, the honour was left for me. I ran down the hall with only one leg in and the other leg of the nylons trailing behind to which Randy had attached himself.

It was Kevin.

"Hi Kevin. It's great to see you." And was it ever! Kevin was wearing a dark suit with a white shirt and blue tie and he looked hot. "Come on in."

He walked past me down the hall towards the apartment door and the rear view was just as good as the front. The three of us went into the dining room and I asked him, "What are you doing here? Don't get me wrong, it's great to see you."

"I guessed that you would be going to Maggie's funeral and thought that you might appreciate some company."

"Thanks. That's very kind of you. I was going to finish getting dressed and was going to have a coffee before I left. Do you want one?" I offered.

"I'd love one. Do you want me to make it while you're finishing up?"

Man, this guy was so thoughtful. I'd have to make sure that he wasn't a woman in drag.

"That would be great. I just like mine with cream. Let's drink it on the patio. Grab yourself a bacon sandwich if you want. The bread's on the counter and the bacon is on the stove. I'll be right out. I'll let Abby know we're leaving soon. She slept over."

Randy decided that the game needed to be moved up a notch and started pulling so hard on the nylons that I had to hang onto the door to keep standing. Bloody dog! I didn't care if they were soggy from the doggy spit; I just didn't want them ripped. Too late as I heard the crotch rip. I took them off and threw them at him.

"Fine! Have them! I don't need them!"

Randy dropped the stocking as soon as I gave it to him. It wasn't a pulling game anymore so it didn't interest him. He disappeared off into the kitchen.

I headed into the living room where Abby had slept over on the pullout couch since she had indulged a little too much in the liquor the night before. I swear if my bed had as many visitors as that couch did, I'd have a very busy and satisfying love life.

"Abby, I'm heading out in about half an hour. My room is free."

"Hmpf!" was the reply from the pile of comforter and blond hair. The mountain stood and shuffled out the door, through the dining room and into my bedroom. It was by no means a pleasant sight.

"Remember it's Bridge Day. "Whiteheads" at noon!" I called out to her.

"Hmpf," she grunted again as she slammed my bedroom door shut.

Kevin was standing in the dining room. "Was that Hartford? Man, she looks rough!"

We heard a muffled, "Fuck you!" through the door. I guess Abby had heard him.

"Trust me, she's ugly in more ways than one in the morning. The couch is free," I called to Bart who had also slept in the living room. I needed to talk to Harold to tell him that Bart needed to come home at some point. Bart was smelling pretty ripe and Harold had to at least give the guy some clean clothes.

I dragged Randy out to the garden to do his business, which takes a good ten minutes because he has to smell every inch of the garden before he can select an unused square for today's duty. He started coughing up a big, blue, bacon-smelling slimy ball onto the grass. Yuck! The blue part was one half of the nylons he had chewed and swallowed.

"Is this throwing up thing a family trait?" asked Kevin. He had followed behind me out to the garden.

"Well, he does this kind of thing all of the time, I'm afraid. I guess I won't be wearing those nylons again, huh?"

"Guess not," agreed Kevin looking a little green around the gills. "By the way, there was no bacon on the counter."

At least we knew what had happened to the missing bacon.

"You have a beautiful garden, Chailey." The garden was about three hundred feet deep and two hundred feet wide and filled with large garden beds and big trees at the bottom. There was a greenhouse for growing seedlings and had a large vegetable patch.

"Thanks. Martha and I both love to garden so we spend hours out here working on it. I have lots of fond memories from being in this garden. My grandfather had been a champion gardener and I have tried to keep it looking as spectacular as he did. Bart and Harold use to help out but they are banned from the garden. They asked to use a little plot of land and grew big beautiful green leafy plants. It took me a while to realize that they had a grow operation here. I sprayed the marijuana plants with weed killer and they died right in front of their eyes. Nice bonfire we had that night with lots and lots of snacks for the munchies. Of course that was nothing compared to the fire we had in the shed a month ago compliments of my tenants and Neil and Zack."

I told Kevin about how my father had stood in the greenhouse with my grandfather and asked for permission to marry my mother. I purposely failed to mention to Kevin that the garden was where Adam and I had our wedding.

Kevin told me about the farm he grew up on in a town about half an hour out of Cookfield. His parents continue to live there. He was the second of three boys and the children were expected to help out on the farm.

"Chailey, I wanted to let you know that Fitzgerald called me yesterday. Maggie's death continues to be deemed a suicide and he's closing the case. He'll call you later to tell you personally. It sounds like he tried to keep an open mind. If it was a murder, the facts pointing to that are small. I've never worked in major crimes so my knowledge is pretty limited."

"Thanks for telling me. But don't feel sorry for me. It's Maggie who I feel the worst for. I'll call him later. Just out of curiosity, what do you know about murders, Kevin?"

"Every murder involves a motive, a means and opportunity. And what's interesting is that most people can't stay quiet about what they did."

"No one has stepped up to the plate to confess yet. So let's start with motive. Why would someone kill a person?"

"Lots of reasons, of course. Money, love, revenge, anger. In your line of work, people kill because they are motivated by their crazy thoughts. Sometimes people are murdered by mistake such as a rape that goes wrong. Sometimes a person does it just for the joy of hurting someone else."

"Maggie wasn't part of some weird love triangle and she obviously wasn't having any affair since Michael was her first real relationship according to her. People like her wait to have their cherry picked by Mr. Right and she waited until her mid-thirties. That's pretty impressive."

Personally I spent every minute of my teens lusting for Brock Simpson to pluck my cherry.

"At first she appeared financially sound. Liam said they'd checked out her accounts and she was stable." Heck, the last time I was considered to be financially solvent my income was my allowance subsidized by a newspaper route. Money management is not my forte and I'm appalled to think that someone would actually look into my accounts should I meet an unfortunate and unexpected early demise.

"According to the Security Supervisor at the law office, they have evidence that Maggie was stealing relatively large amounts of company money. So far they have located $25,000. Why would she steal money? She was marrying Michael in less than a year and he looks pretty loaded."

"Twenty-five grand is a drop in the bucket relative to other thefts but it would have made her life much easier. I've met gamblers who are ten times that amount in debt."

"She told me she had no worries about money. Now I know why. I wonder if she felt guilty about this?"

"If she lied to you about this, Chailey, I wonder what else she lied about?"

"There was no sexual assault. The theory of a "crazy" person as you so aptly stated is a possibility. She was being stalked by someone and he did enter the house and threaten her."

"Perhaps she was the crazy one, Chailey. We never did find any concrete evidence of a person on her premises. Yes, there were other prowler calls in the neighbourhood, but not the same as Maggie described them. What about her work? You spoke with Michael and her coworkers."

"Yeah. Briefly. There really is nothing to be told from them. As far as I know her co-workers didn't know about the theft. I'm hoping one girl may call me. Michael told me little other than to say she was fearful people wanted to hurt her but didn't know why."

"Opportunity is another issue. Someone must have known she was at home since she normally worked in the middle of the day."

"That would suggest her coworkers since she left the office and went directly home."

"What about the prowler theory? Maybe Maggie went home and she disturbed the prowler."

"Chailey, there were no signs of forced entry."

"But the prowler may have accessed the home before with a key. Remember when Maggie told us the person came into the house and said her name."

"We have no proof of that either. It brings up another question. Was Maggie mentally unbalanced? Perhaps those were hallucinations she was having."

"Hallucinations or not, my final question is "means". Where would a mild-mannered upstanding citizen like Maggie get a gun? Admittedly, I can't see Maggie buying a gun from some shady character in the north end of town. Where do you buy a gun, Kevin?"

"Pretty well anywhere. You've just got to ask the right low life."

"I'll talk with Liam and see what he can tell me about the gun."

We sat quietly on the patio enjoying our coffee and chatting. I think that this was the most relaxed I had been in days. Of course, if my grandfather had been looking down from heaven at this particular moment he would have freaked out because Randy was currently lying in the pond having a drink of water. This is a regular practice for the dog without a brain. My favourite magnolia tree, the one planted the year my parents were married, was currently in bloom and dominated the garden with its large, tulip-shaped blossoms.

As with any moment, the peace and tranquility was eventually destroyed by the ringing of the telephone. I had brought the portable phone outside knowing that if the phone rang inside the house, no one would answer it.

"Hi Chailey, this is Michael Brigham. I hope you don't mind me calling you. I need to speak to you about something. Do you have any time to talk to me?"

"Uh. Hi Michael." I gave Kevin one of those looks that says, "Guess who's calling me?" "Uh, sure. Do you want to do this over the phone or do you want to meet with me?"

"I'd prefer to meet with you."

"Actually, I'm planning to go to the funeral, Mr. Brigham. What would be a good time for you?"

"Please remember to call me Michael. Could I take you out for dinner? I would love to treat you as my guest."

"Dinner?" I looked over at Kevin who shook his head from side to side in a "no" pattern. My sentiments exactly. "Uh, I'm sorry, I already have plans for dinner. Perhaps we could meet for coffee later."

"Great!" replied Michael. "Just name the place and time."

"How about we meet at *Causing A Stir* at the corner of King and Queen Streets. It's a small coffee shop where we can talk. Is seven o'clock alright for you?"

"Thank you, Ms. Smith. I'll see you in a little bit at the funeral then. Thank you again for agreeing to meet with me."

I hung up feeling perplexed. "Well, that was very weird. It was Maggie's boyfriend, Michael Brigham wanting to speak with me. He didn't tell me what it was about."

"What's weirder is that he called you at home. How did he get your home phone number? He's a lawyer, he should know better than to invade your privacy in that way. Perhaps we should look into Mr. Michael Brigham, Esquire. Are you sure you want to meet with him?"

"I'm sure. I had offered to talk with him if he wanted to. He probably just wants some support. It can't be easy burying your fiancée. Hey, it's ten-forty-five. Shall we get going? I need to pick up a sympathy card on the way, if you don't mind. I've also got to dry off this soggy doggy first."

Randy rarely returns to the house dry or clean. You'd think the obvious solution to the problem would be to get rid of the pond but it was built by my grandfather. It would be easier to get rid of the pain-in-the-ass dog but Martha won't hear of it. Talk about being in the sandwich population.

It took me about ten minutes before I had eventually dried the hundred-pound mutt off as best as I could and confined him to the kitchen until he completely dried off. It was a safe place for him to stay. There had been nearly two pounds of bacon fried up this morning and I only ate four slices meaning he had snacked on at least twenty rashes of bacon. I wasn't convinced that his stomach was finished doing its upchucking business. Something to look forward to after returning from the funeral.

Chapter 15

The funeral for Maggie was being held in St. Margaret's Anglican Church in downtown Cookfield. It's a beautiful piece of architecture built in an era when stone masons were admired for their skill meaning that it was at least two hundred years old. Architecture has gone down the toilet since that time as far as I'm concerned. I'm a bit of a renaissance girl that way – I love history, old buildings fascinate me and my favourite music is classical. I like nothing better (okay, there's one thing better!) than sitting down with a trashy novel about a medieval lord in his conquest for a beautiful maiden. He always managed to get his girl and they always lived happily ever after. They never needed the Internet or speed dating to get hooked up. I would have been very happy as a medieval princess, except of course for the lack of flushing toilets and toilet paper. My sister-in-law and I were talking about this very topic one day and my brother scoffed at the idea of me being a princess and said, "You? A princess? Only in *Shrek!*"

We drove to the church in Kevin's truck. I offered to drive but he gave me a, "Yeah! Right!" look and headed down the path to his truck parked out front of the house.

I had told Kevin that I wanted to sit close to the back and he was fine with that. I continued to feel very self-conscious about my appearance and preferred not face the general public for fear of frightening them.

The church was an immense building and even with a relatively large number of mourners present, the church was only a quarter filled. We sat somewhat inconspicuously half way down the church but everyone knew we were there when I had an uncontrollable fit of sneezing caused by the incense. I could see Michael Brigham sitting in the front pew physically consoling two women whom I recognized from Maggie's family photos as being her mother and sister, Sandra. Her sister appeared to be the most outwardly upset and cried continuously. Her mother just looked forward. It was difficult to see much more from our poor vantage point.

The service was very beautiful. Michael gave the eulogy and spoke at length in loving terms of Maggie as a strong, dedicated, hardworking woman, a much-loved daughter and sister and the true love of his life. He stopped several times during his five-minute speech when he became overwhelmed with tears. A friend of Maggie's read a poem and her sister read the passage from the Bible that is so often read at funerals, "The Lord is my Shepherd." I listened intently to Psalm 23 and it made me question why Maggie had chosen the path that she did? Why not call for help? Had she been lead down that path by another person? If so, by who? And why? Perhaps I couldn't accept Maggie's death because it would also mean accepting my failure. I was denying Maggie's suicide because I was having difficulty dealing with the pain of her loss and my inability to prevent that loss. The last five days had shaken my faith in my abilities to the lowest point ever and I needed to do something about it and get out of this pity pit – and do it now. That was it! I would meet with Michael, provide the support he needed as I had offered to do and then find some closure for the Denton case. Tomorrow, I was going back to work and start doing what I do well and that's be a Mental Health Nurse. Maggie would have wanted that.

Kevin nudged me. I guess I had been so deep in thought that I'd missed the cue to stand up and as a result was the only person remaining sitting. I quickly stood up in time to see the casket roll down the aisle with her family and closest loved ones following in its trail. Sadly, Maggie had planned to walk down this same aisle in a wedding dress with her new husband at her side. Talking about the potential groom, Michael smiled at me as he walked by and it was at this moment that Kevin grabbed my hand. I could have been wrong but it felt like he was holding my hand in a proprietary sort of way. It was probably wishful thinking on my behalf.

The immediate family was standing outside of the church doors shaking hands with everyone who had attended the service. It's one of those awkward moments when the people involved exchanged murmurs of support and the reassurance that the mourner would attend a reception. Kevin and I were the last ones out of the church and I figured that the receiving line would be over by the time we got outside but as luck would have it, Maggie's mother and sister were just as meticulous as she had been and had stayed to the end to extend their heartfelt gratitude to the stragglers.

There was no question that this was Maggie's family since she was the spitting image of her sister and her mother was just an older version of her daughters. I shook Mrs. Denton's hand and introduced Kevin and myself. I also apologized for my appearance and briefly explained that I'd been in a small accident over the weekend.

"Oh, you're Chailey. I'm so glad to finally meet you. I'm Susannah Denton and this is my daughter, Sandra." I turned and shook Sandra's hand. "Maggie had said such nice things about you and told me how helpful and supportive you were."

Yeah, helpful enough that she ended up killing herself, I thought. I felt a momentary shuffle behind me and an arm went around my shoulder. It was Michael.

"Susannah, Sandra. I'm glad that you finally met Chailey. She's been a gem." A diamond in the rough, maybe,

He turned to look at me. "Chailey, what happened to you? Are you okay?"

"Just a small accident," I replied. "Michael, let me introduce you to Kevin Harrison. He's a police officer and he also met Maggie."

"A pleasure to meet you, Officer Harrison. I'm always pleased to make acquaintance with the guys who keep our streets safe," Michael responded enthusiastically. "It never hurts to know the men in blue in case I'm pulled over by one of you."

"Yeah," replied Kevin. He sounded about as enthusiastic as a man waiting in the dentist's office for a root canal. In fact, he looked quite dark and unhappy.

"I must excuse myself," announced Michael. "Will we have the pleasure of your company at the reception?"

"Unfortunately we have other plans," replied Kevin. For some reason I felt like I was in the middle of a male pissing match and not on the steps of a church following a funeral.

Michael hurried off to greet another group of people. He reminded me of a politician. The group looked like lawyer types with everyone wearing tailored suits. I noticed that the ladies all wore nylons – the colours exactly matching their outfits. I bet they didn't own hundred-pound, nylon destroying dogs. I recognized one of the secretaries walking in the back of the crowd. Her name was Julia and I had spoken to her briefly when I visited the office.

Mrs. Denton had pulled an envelope out of her purse that looked like it was a card of some type and gave it to me.

"This is a small "thank you" card from us. I know Maggie would have wanted you to have this." She choked slightly on the last few words and I started to tear up.

"It's not necessary," I quietly insisted.

Mrs. Denton looked directly into my eyes and said, "Maggie would have wanted you to have this. Take it." She placed the envelope into my right hand and I accepted it from her.

In response, I learned forward and gave her a hug and told her, "Maggie loved you and her family very much. I can see why." I stood up straight again and told both Sandra and her mother, "If there is anything I can help you with, please don't hesitate to call me. You can always get hold of me through the police station."

"You already have helped," replied Mrs. Denton quietly.

Kevin put his arm around my waist and guided me down the steps past Michael and his lawyer groupies. Just as we were at the bottom of the steps, I heard a female voice call my name and saw Julia approaching us.

"Julia, how nice to see you. Let me introduce you to my friend and colleague, Kevin Harrison."

Kevin dutifully shook Julia's hand and smiled. Julia blushed furiously in response to his attention. "Julia was one of Maggie's friends and worked with her at the law firm. It was a lovely service, wasn't it?"

"Yes, it was. I know Maggie would have been proud to have so many of her friends there. Chailey, do you have a second? I want to talk to you about something."

"I'll be at the truck," Kevin dutifully replied giving us some privacy.

"Chailey, I just wanted to tell you how distressed I was to hear the accusations being made against Maggie. She never told me a word about taking money and she was such a nice person. She never said a bad thing about anyone. I can't believe she's guilty of theft." Julia started to tear up. "I'm sorry. I just wanted to tell you this so you won't think badly of Maggie. She didn't deserve any of this. I'm sorry, I need to excuse myself and get back to the office."

"I know Maggie was a good person. Take care, Julia, and stay in touch."

I walked over to the truck feeling overwhelmed with sadness. Kevin unlocked my door, opened it, helped me in and then went over to the driver's side. He was being a gentleman by giving me a few minutes to collect myself together emotionally. I tell you, the last five days had turned me into "Cry Baby Chailey".

Kevin got in and started up the truck. He was looking quite serious – the kind of look he had when I rear-ended him in his cruiser.

"What's with that Michael Brigham guy? If he touched you one more time I was going to deck him right then and there, funeral or not."

I thought this assessment was a little harsh. "He was definitely over the top today. Perhaps it was just the stress of the funeral."

"Maybe. I still don't like him. Would you like to go for a coffee? I'd love to take you out for dinner, but I'm working tonight."

My stomach did a little somersault. The kiss on Sunday night wasn't just a dream or a figment of my very active imagination. It really did happen. Someone other than the ninety-year-old dirty old man from the old people's home next door was interested in me.

"Sure," I replied as calmly as possible.

Kevin drove off to a quaint little coffee shop in the west end of town. I was thankful that he chose a place off the beaten track. The police department was a fertile ground for rumours to spread and I preferred to keep our "friendship" private – whatever "friendship" meant.

The day had warmed up considerably so I took off my jacket and enjoyed the heat of the sun through the truck window. We sat outside on the small patio enjoying the warm spring sunshine risking fate and the chance that we'd be seen together. I took the opportunity to ask Kevin about his son. He showed me a picture of Jake recently with Kevin. Like any proud papa, Kevin had twenty-two other photos in his wallet depicting little Jake's development from birth to the current ripe age of four. He was a cute little boy and I felt that familiar twinge of envy of every parent who has the joy of sharing their lives with a child. The only photo in my wallet was the one put in there by the company that made the product. The picture was of two beautiful blonde-haired, blue eyed children whom I'd named Hansel and Gretel. I think that they're nine and seven and such good children....

"Chailey, there's something I need to tell you. Tomorrow morning I'm flying out to British Columbia."

"That's great, " I replied. "You'll be able to see Jake."

"That's part of the plan. When Gillian and I separated and she moved out to BC, I thought about following her so I applied to various police departments out there and Vancouver Police Service called me about two weeks ago. They are paying for my trip and I have an interview with them tomorrow afternoon. Their goal is to recruit experienced officers to their department."

"Wow," was about all I could manage to squeak out. I wanted to add, "Before you move out there could you please sleep with me?" but that seemed a trifle inappropriate and a touch on the selfish side. Instead, I rose to the occasion and said, "I mean, that sounds pretty exciting. What a wonderful opportunity for you. They'll take you in a second. Heck, you're a great cop. Make sure that they give you a pay

increase. The best part is that you'll be closer to your son."
I babbled with a smile on my face. I should have received
an Oscar for that performance.

"Chailey, don't get ahead of yourself. It's just an
interview."

Yeah, I thought, and you're only the nicest guy I've
met in a long, long time. It's funny but when I was in the
hotel room with Gunman and contemplating my rapidly
upcoming early demise, one of the thoughts that upset me
the most was that I was going to die and the last person I
had sex with was my ex-husband. Now that was pathos. On
Sunday night, just before I went to sleep I started a list of all
the things that I want to do before I die. The list includes
having children either through birth of my own children
or adopting a child, bungee jumping, and so the list went
on. I was hoping that to cross off number one as soon as
possible, if you know what I mean, and I was hoping that
Kevin would help me with that little duty. Adam can *not*
be the last person I copulate with before I die.

"Hey, don't look so sad. I'm back on Thursday afternoon.
Can I have the pleasure of your company for dinner on
Thursday evening?"

"That would be wonderful." I replied. I felt tears
coming on so I changed the topic and quickly.

Once again, while enjoying some pleasant company over
coffee, the tranquility of the moment had to be broken by
my cell phone chirping.

"Hi Chailey. This is Sally Hannah." Sally was my
uncle's secretary. "How are you doing, honey? We've
all been worried about you." *All* meant that tightly knit
community with as much power and knowledge as anyone
at the police department, the secretaries.

"Not too bad, Sally. Thanks for asking."

"Your uncle asked me to call you. He knows you're on
light duties but he wondered if you would drop by his office
at three today. It's important or he wouldn't bother you."

"No problem," I replied.

"Come half an hour early and we'll have coffee."

Rumour has it that Sally is around the age of forty however she refuses to tell anyone her age. I adore her as does my uncle and he knows how lucky he is to have such a great secretary. I've begged Sally to come and work for me however she always laughs and tells me that Flo and I deserve each other, whatever that means.

It was already quarter to two and I told Kevin about my uncle's request to meet with me and my promise to meet Sally at half past two.

"I have to go home and get out of this monkey suit before I go on my shift at four. Do you want me to take you home or drop you off at the station? I guess that we should head out now."

"Home would be great. I need to change out of this ridiculous outfit into something that doesn't ride up my butt every time I move."

"Yeah, I noticed," said Kevin with smile.

Kevin pulled the truck up in front of my house.

"I'd invite you in but it's "Bridge Day"."

"Yeah, I meant to ask you, what's "Bridge Day"? And what the heck are the "Whiteheads" that you warned Abby about?" he asked.

"Martha invites her friends over for a Bridge game on Mondays. Annie McCann comes and she has arthritis and a bad hip and can't walk up the stairs so they hold the game here. They'll still be playing now. Martha makes them dinner and they shuffle off home to an evening of sitcom reruns awaiting the golden hour of nine o'clock when they can finally wash down a handful of sedatives and laxatives with a tumbler full of sherry and shuffle off to bed in anticipation of a predawn awakening ready to start the cycle again. My friend came up with the nick name, "Whiteheads", because all of them have one. Except Mabel from next door and her hair is definitely a shade of purple. We call her "Violet"!"

"Is your house ever empty?" he asked incredulously.

"Well, the house never seems empty. My apartment is occasionally uninhabited but that is not a predictable science. I don't mind since it makes life interesting. At least Martha helps with the garden and buys my groceries for me. Mind you, that only seems fair since she eats half of them. My sanctuary is at the top of the house in the attic – nobody goes up there unless invited."

"The attic sounds.. er, nice."

"Obviously, you've not heard about my attic. If you're really nice to me, I may show it to you some day." I felt like I was nine-years-old again and promising Jimmy Minion that I would show him my underwear if he showed me his pet lizard.

"Well, I'd better get going. Thanks for the ride." I went to reach for the door handle.

"Chailey, just a second."

I studied the road intently as though a five-car crash had just happened in front of me.

"The other night, when I kissed you, well, I'm not sorry I did that. But I shouldn't have knowing I was going to Vancouver for this job interview. I know this is a difficult time for you with Maggie and the hostage incident and so on. And as I'm saying all this all I want to do is kiss you again."

"I tell you what, you hang onto that thought 'til Thursday," I replied.

"No, you hang onto this thought!" He bent towards me, turned my face gently towards his and kissed me. It was a deep, sensual kiss. I felt his tongue sweep into my mouth and I suddenly felt warm all over. When he eventually pulled away I felt like my breath had been taken away.

"See you on Thursday, Chailey. Stay safe."

Chapter 16

I floated into the house. Kevin had kissed me and there was even some tongue involved!

The bridge game was in full swing in the dining room. There was no way I was disturbing those gambling grannies. Remnants of a lasagna lunch were strewn across the kitchen and there were a few bottles of wine on the table. Betty Butterfield was already snoozing in the wing chair. At least I hoped she was sleeping. I quickly checked her chest was rising. Last year, Ethel Dykman took a deep long "nap", or so Martha told me when I arrived home from work eight o'clock at night.

"What's Ethel still doing here?" I'd asked.

"Sleeping," replied Martha casually.

"And how long has she been snoozing for?"

"Since about two," she'd answered quietly. About as quietly as Ethel was breathing.

I was a little suspicious. The grey tinge on her face started to look more like skin tone and not just shadows as I had first thought. There was definitely a bad odour in the room and I was pretty sure it wasn't from the rotten feeling I had at the bottom of my stomach. My hunch was confirmed five minutes later by the paramedics who announced that Ethel was dead.

Having checked that Betty's chest was indeed rising and falling, I quickly slipped into my bedroom and quietly grabbed my daily uniform of jeans, T-shirt and sweatshirt to get changed in the bathroom. Bart was snoozing on the floor in his sleeping bag with Randy curled up beside him obviously avoiding contact with the mob in the dining room.

Ten minutes later I was out the house with clean clothes and a quick squirt of perfume ready for my next conquest of the day namely returning to work. I dropped by my office to see if there was anything important for me to look at before my appointments "upstairs".

Flo actually greeted me with, of all things, a hug. I was more than a little uncomfortable with this outpouring of affection however it confirmed my suspicion that the Ice Maiden really did have a heart. I was even more surprised to find two beautiful flower arrangements in my office. Usually Jody was the one with flowers as a "thank you" from some adoring fan. One arrangement was from my uncle and the other was from Flo and Jody. I should have figured as much because the flowers were arranged around an umbrella.

On my desk there was a massive brown cardboard box which had helium balloons attached. One balloon announced, "It's a Boy!" and the other said, "Happy Retirement!" The box was wrapped in "Do Not Cross Police Line" yellow tape. On the side, in black marker, was a simple message, "From your friends at the Cookfield Police Department." Now I was nervous. That could be anything from a cat and seven kittens to nuclear waste. I was, however, both surprised and thrilled to find the box filled with stuff. Chailey stuff! Chocolate bars, bags of chips, smutty romance novels, a pair of fuzzy, pink slippers, six bottles of wine and thirteen bottles of beer. The department smart asses had also contributed a box of tissues, a porno magazine (for men) and two packs of condoms. I wasn't sure if it was a care package or a box of locker garbage. Obviously the snack machine was now empty. There was a wonderful card signed by everyone including the dead-ground-hog guy. On the bottom it said, "Now stop reading this card and get back to work!" Yep! Things were starting to return normal again.

I climbed up the stairs slowly to the third floor to the executive area. Sally greeted me enthusiastically and gave me a hug. She was soft, warm and smelt like *Chanel No. 5*. We went to the Executive Lounge, unofficially referred to as the secretary's lunch room. The four other executive secretaries were already there and it was an enjoyable half-hour of chat. These women were always up to date on all the gossip so I listened intently to see if there was any news of my uncle doing the dirty deed with anyone but came up with zip. No one present proclaimed that they were shagging my uncle so I was no further ahead in my investigation for my aunt. There was no chance that anyone would disturb us since the bosses knew that their secretaries worked liked dogs for them and coffee break time was untouchable.

It was finally time to head into the meeting with my uncle. When I entered the room, a cold chill over me when I looked around and saw who was also present. It was like déjà vu from the interview about Slater. Not a good omen.

I sat down and my uncle started into the meeting straight away. "Chailey, I have invited you to join this meeting because we have become aware of important and yet also disturbing information..."

Yeah, so had I today. Kevin was going to a job interview in Vancouver.

My uncle continued, "Slater's accomplices were involved in another heist yesterday. Another person was shot. One of the culprits did not get way and was detained by police. Through interrogation, the man revealed that Slater had taken a large sum of money and jewels from the first robbery. The group was supposed to meet up to split the money. Slater was caught before that could happen."

I was listening closely. So far there wasn't anything that remotely interested me or that I even cared to hear. I figured the punch line was coming real soon which was a good thing because I needed the meeting to end soon. After all the coffee I'd drunk this afternoon, I had to pee so badly that my back teeth were floating.

"The suspect we caught revealed that Slater had informed his partners that you know where the money is located and assisted him to hide it."

I just about wet my pants when I heard that. "What! That's a lie! He's a freaking liar!"

"I know, Chailey. You need to calm down and sit down." I didn't realize that I was standing. "There's more," he added.

"More? Personally I'd say that's more than enough."

I sat down. That is, after I checked that I hadn't peed on the chair. My uncle continued on. "The man we have in custody informed us that the last suspect plans to come and make you reveal the location of the money."

"For the last time, I don't know where the fucking money is!" I was standing again.

"Chailey, we know you don't have it." It was Dave who had stepped up to the bat. Pretty brave on his behalf if you ask me.

"We are all well aware that you are innocent of any accusations made by these lying, stinking criminals. I don't think it takes a rocket scientist to figure out why Slater said this. He's obviously a psychopath trying to mess with people's minds."

"He's doing a good job, if you ask me." An appropriate moment for sarcasm, I thought.

My uncle picked up the ball. "What we are concerned about is your safety. We wanted you to be updated on the situation so that you know why you need to go into a protective setting."

"No, I won't hide. If you need to protect me then do. But I won't run away."

"You aren't thinking rationally."

That's just what I needed. A room of males telling me that I was irrational. "Yes, I am. If you hide me then that jerk won't be able to find me and will keep on hurting people in heists. He's on his own now and is more desperate than ever and will take more risks. Use me as your sacrificial lamb and he'll come out of hiding and you'll catch him. And you know that."

I could see a smile at the corner of twitch at the corner of Dave's mouth. The detectives knew I was right and had probably spent a whole bunch of time explaining why this should happen and the big wigs, including my uncle, had refused to listen.

"Chailey..." my uncle started to say.

"No, please don't "Chailey" me, uncle. You know I'm right so let's just go with it. I believe these guys will keep me safe. You know it, too. If we don't stop this guy now he will just continue hurting people and we can't let that happen."

He took a moment to consider the matter. "We need to discuss this further."

"Fine, discuss away. I need to excuse myself," I announced.

"We'll reconvene later at five o'clock. Thank you, for your input." He walked me to the door of his office.

I whispered, "Thank you for listening to me."

He whispered back, "When you started this job your mother chewed me out telling me that you wouldn't be safe and that you couldn't take care of yourself and so on. I told her she was wrong. There is *no* way that I'm going to let your mother be right." He smiled and I left the office.

The first thing I did *after* I went to the bathroom was to call Pete on his cell phone.

"Hey lady! How are you doing?"

"Great!" I lied.

"No you're not, I can tell," he replied. See, I am the world's worst fibber.

"Listen, I need to talk to you for a few minutes."

"Do you want to meet after my shift?" he offered.

"Actually, how about now? It's about Slater."

The "Slater" word tipped him off. "Now's good," he replied. "I'm down in Detention." The detention area in the police station is the holding area for prisoners.

I headed down the back stairs. I hate using the elevator and have had some pretty bad experiences in elevators. Last year in the spring, I dropped off some information to a man who lived on the seventeenth floor of an apartment building. The elevator arrived and I got on absentmindedly not paying attention to anything around me with my mind focused on where I was going to buy a coffee on my way back to the office and if I had a spare *Mars* bar in my car. By the time the doors closed and the elevator went sailing down to the ground floor, I finally noticed the really bad smell in the elevator and the dead man that it was coming from who was slumped in the corner. I screamed the remaining fifteen floors, scrambled off the death ride elevator and finally called to dispatch. Of course, I was too busy freaking out to remember to hold the elevator button, so I was horrified when it zoomed off to the eighth floor only to return with the dead guy. I finally remembered to hold the button and to prevent terrorizing the rest of the building. The dispatcher thought that I was joking when I radioed in the call and didn't send a cruiser until they received a 911 call from a very distraught tenant on the eighth floor.

Another time a female officer and I were taking a slightly intoxicated, suicidal man to hospital. On the way down from his sixteenth floor apartment, he whipped out his wiener and started pissing on the two of us. Neither of us wanted to grab him because each time we tried to, we were sprayed with his pee. Of course the guy had been drinking beer so he had a lot of urine on tap.

I almost hate elevators almost as much as I hate going to the Detention area. It's the place in the police station that someone is taken to after being arrested until the time that they are released or transferred to a detention centre. If you've ever been in one, you'll know that it's loud with people yelling and farting. It stinks with the smell of vomit, sweat, body odour and smelly feet. Kind of like the guys locker room three floors up.

I found Pete and several other officers in a "discussion" with some very drunken man who didn't want to be there and was causing quite a disturbance. The cops were putting up with a lot of crap and I've got to tell you, if someone barfed on my shoes as the drunk did to Pete, I'd be real upset. The drunk finally conceded to spending the night in the cell more because he passed out than volition. I chatted with the other cops who had the pleasure of "Detention" as they called it while giving Pete time to clean up his shoes before I dumped on him my problems of a different kind. The more I thought about the situation the more I felt like imitating the drunk and upchucking my cookies.

He walked me over to the interview room serenaded by the whistles and yells of the male prisoners who apparently appreciated my female presence. I figured those guys were probably drunk. Pete told them to shut up in a not so nice way that included the word "fuck"!

"Sorry to bother you but I needed to talk to someone, Pete."

"Honey, you know you can talk to me any time," he replied kindly.

I gave him a quick rundown on the situation.

"Chailey, are you positive this is what you want to do? I'm not so sure that this is a good idea."

"Pete, it's not a matter of wanting to do this, but needing to."

"You're pretty smart for being a chick and if anyone can manage this, it's you."

"Really?" I asked. I wasn't sure if I was more surprised that he thought I was smart or somewhat capable. I hoped he was right on both accounts.

"Yeah, really," he replied. "So, tell me what's happening with you and Kevin Harrison?"

I blushed at that one. "Nothing," I mumbled, knowing that he knew that I knew that it was a lie.

I went out into the hall to the cacophony of cat whistles. The way these Neanderthals went on you'd think it was Cameron Diaz modeling a bikini in front of them. There's something about putting a guy behind bars that makes him into an animal. If I walked past any of these guys on the street they wouldn't even blink an eye at me.

I thanked Pete for listening. I guess I just needed to babble to someone. I told him I'd call him later with the outcome of the meeting and headed back to the stairs and up to the detective's office.

Liam Fitzgerald was in thankfully and greeted me warmly telling me how relieved he was that I was safe.

"Yeah, safe but you are going to have to excuse my look."

"You look like Dicky the day after you head-butted him," Liam said smiling. "I'm glad you dropped by, I was going to call you. What's up?" he asked as we sat at his desk.

"Well, Kevin Harrison informed me that the case was concluded with the final cause of death deemed suicide."

"With the evidence from the law firm supporting Denton's involvement in corporate theft and the Coroner's Report, we have concluded that Maggie committed suicide. It's unfortunate that Ms. Denton was not up front with you when you met her since you could have supported her in making better choices. There was nothing to suggest otherwise, Chailey. As you know we arrested the man who we believe to be the prowler and he denies any involvement with Maggie Denton. He's a petty thief with a long criminal history for breaking into houses during the day while people were at work. When we suggested he had any involvement with a death he gave us all the information on the break-ins he'd done with no lawyer present."

"What about the gun, Liam? I wouldn't have the foggiest idea where to get a gun and I'm convinced that Maggie who was Miss Manners wouldn't know how to buy a bag of pot, let alone, buy a gun."

"I take it from your comments that you'd know where to get a bag of weed." I wanted to answer, "From my tenants" but thought that little piece of information was best kept to myself. I blushed instead.

"We haven't been able to trace the origin of the weapon. It is definitely an unregistered gun. As with many suicide victims when they are really determined to kill themselves, they will find a way to do it." Kind of like guys wanting to get laid on a date, I thought. Another comment I kept to myself.

"Just for your information, we interviewed several coworkers who supported the Security Supervisor's claims that Maggie was secretive for several weeks and increasingly anxious several days before her death. We also checked on the whereabouts of her boyfriend, Michael Brigham who was in Mexico on his business trip. There's no evidence pointing us in any other direction but to suicide. I'm sorry Chailey, I know this has been hard for you to accept." Great, now I was sounding more pathetic than Dicky the Dick!

"Thanks, Liam. I've got to go."

"Stay in touch, Chailey. Let me know if you have any other information."

It was five o'clock and time to head back to the Chief's Office. I pretty well knew what the final decision was based on the presence of Paul Tayler who was the head of the unit that fulfilled undercover surveillance. My uncle got straight to the point.

"Chailey, based on the increased frequency and intensity of the attacks by Slater's group, the decision is to allow Eastwood to make contact with you thereby increasing the chance of apprehending him before anyone else is harmed. It is the opinion of this expert group that Eastwood sees you as an accomplice and therefore will not harm you. There will be a twenty-four hour a day surveillance team coordinated by Paul Tayler. Your tenants will be moved out of your house. PC Hartford will stay at your house at night." I presumed that he *didn't* know that last night Abby got pig drunk and had to sleep over because she couldn't drive home.

"Eastwood may not even make contact with you," my uncle continued, "however I have accepted the argument that he probably will. We will inform Slater that we have reason to believe that you know the location of the money. He will be allowed to visit with his lawyer after which point we can assume his lawyer will be directed to pass this information onto Eastwood. Of course, the lawyer will do this so that the money can be retrieved and he will get paid. Any questions?"

I wanted to ask if Kevin could replace Abby on Thursday and sleep over but figured that would churn up the rumour mill a wee bit and secondly, result in my uncle having a coronary.

"Chailey, Detective Tayler will meet with you now. I will be updated daily and I will decide when this project is to be terminated. Thank you everyone and good night."

I met for the next hour with Paul who basically explained the rules of engagement. I knew Paul through Pete and he was a smart guy with a great sense of humour. He did not, however, look anything like a cop which made him perfect for surveillance. He was about five and a half feet tall, skinny with short brown hair and Harry Potter glasses. He looked like a bookkeeper. Paul outlined the plan. The surveillance team would follow me during my day and evening and I would probably not even know they were there. I was required to update Paul daily on my schedule. My phone would be monitored. He showed me a picture of Mr. Eastwood. It was a mug shot of a brown-eyed ugly white guy who had a shaved head. He looked a little like my last blind date. No one was to know about the surveillance and I was to go about my normal business as usual. Any contact with Eastwood was to be reported immediately to the surveillance team. If he spoke to me I was to go along with the story that I knew where the items were, namely in a safety deposit box, but had to arrange a time to access them. A safety deposit box had been rented in my name.

"There's a few last things. There's a new Kevlar vest in your office. It's one that you wear underneath your clothes. Please start wearing it all day long." Okay, so they did notice I didn't have a vest on Friday night. Oops! "Any questions?"

"No. I do have a seven o'clock appointment with a client down town tonight. I'll be going alone without a uniformed officer."

"Oh, that's something else. When you are working over the next few days you will be working with the same uniformed officer each day who will be aware of the situation. If you have any questions, call me at any time. Your tenants are already out of your house enjoying life at the Sheraton Hotel."

"And how did you get them there?" I asked out of curiosity.

"Your uncle told them you needed some quiet time after last week's incident," he replied.

"And...?"

"And he offered to pay them to stay at the hotel," he added.

Just like rats off a ship! When this was all over I was going to demand a weekend at the Sheraton myself.

"We have no concerns at this time. We have put surveillance on you many times before."

"You have," I asked incredulously.

"Yeah. Didn't you know? We use you for training."

Oh-my-God! All I could think of were the times I'd driven to the coffee shop in my pajamas and the millions of times I'd surreptitiously adjusted my underwear in public thinking no one was watching. And I couldn't even begin to think of the number of sessions of topless sunbathing I'd had in the backyard.

"Don't look so worried. It's not like we videotaped you!"

I wasn't going to ask about still photos.

I gave him the details about my appointment, promised that I'd put on the vest and got ready to leave since it was already past six-thirty.

"Oh, by the way, Chailey, I wouldn't sunbathe topless again this week if I were you."

I left the office feeling very embarrassed. And to think that people saw me without my top on and I still didn't have a date.

Chapter 17

I returned to my office and found my new vest on the back of the door. It was designed to go under my clothes and it made me look bulky. Or should I say bulkier like a line backer for the Miami Dolphins. Perhaps it was the bruises that helped create that image. My stitches were burning so I slapped on some more cream which to be honest, didn't seem to be helping much. I felt like I weighed ten pounds heavier than when I went into my office. Of course, my dinner of a *Mars* bar and a package of *Skittles* candy didn't help relieve that feeling. I was covering several of the major food groups with a *milk* chocolate bar and *fruit*-flavoured candy - balanced but by no means a healthy meal.

I opened up my reserve supply clothing drawer and pulled out my black blazer. I also gave myself a quick squirt of perfume and deodorant and felt a little more dressed up and ready to go.

I called Paul to let him know that I was heading out. I went down to the parking lot to locate my car. The new windshield had been installed following the regrettable riot. The car had been backed in with lots of room on each side.

Now that was a first. Usually they park my car so close to the car beside mine that I have to climb in through the passenger door. This is a particularly good maneuver if it snows overnight and the snow is banked up on the passenger side and the only way in is to dig with a shovel. In the winter, the snow removal guys leave just enough snow in front of my car that it usually takes me a good hour to dig out. They probably watched me from the gym and made bets as to how long it would take me to dig myself out of the snow bank. So a proper parking job was a very kind and unprecedented gesture on the mechanic's behalf.

I couldn't believe my eyes when I got in the car. It was clean. Someone had actually *sanitized* my car. The dozens of chocolate bar wrappers, coffee cups and chip bags were gone. The floor had been vacuumed and the windows were clean. There was a little note sitting on the passenger seat that said, "Welcome back Chailey. We're glad you're safe. Please keep the car safe too." You've gotta to love those guys. It made me tear up again.

I drove across the downtown core to the restaurant. I noticed a cruiser was following me. So much for "unobservable surveillance". It took me a moment before I could tell that it was Kevin, so he had remembered my appointment and was obviously feeling a wee bit territorial. Michael was just a guy needing some support and it was my job to do it.

Michael had arrived early and selected a seat in front of the window. It was a wonderful spot with a full view of the whole road. Michael epitomized my image of a gentleman by focussing his attention on me the whole evening, ensuring my every need was being seen to and treating me with utter charm and respect. On the whole, it got irritating after five minutes. I guess I'm just not use to this kind of attention hence it was freaking me out.

I directed the conversation to my purpose for being there and that was to discuss Maggie. When Michael started talking about how Maggie had been over the last few months my curiosity was peaked. He stated that she had become secretive at work locking drawers excessively and becoming less and less communicative with her coworkers and eventually stopped talking to Michael. Her fears quickly expanded to outside of the work place believing that people were following her. Michael stated that he asked Maggie repeatedly what was bothering her and she kept him at a distance. One night in early April he had gone to her house with the purpose of making her share her concerns. Maggie admitted to him that she believed someone was sending her threatening letters. Michael had strongly encouraged her to call the police, however, she had refused to do so. She didn't have any samples and reportedly had burned each of the letters she had received. The letters told her to mind her own business and to keep out of the business that wasn't hers.

"I asked Margaret what that meant and she told me that she had become involved in some difficulties with someone at work. That's why she wasn't talking with people at work because she believed that people were spying on her. I checked with several of her co-workers and no one knew what Margaret was talking about."

"Did she tell you specifically what she was concerned about?"

"No, she just kept telling me that someone wanted to frighten her out of investigating an issue. You can talk to anyone at the firm; they will confirm my story. And then when she told me that a person was following her home at night and calling her on her phone and hanging up, I became frightened for her. I had a private investigator look into the situation and he found nothing. I've brought his report with me. My biggest fear is that Margaret was mentally ill and that her beliefs were actually paranoia.

"Now we know that it may have been her own guilt about the money theft that made her act this way. I can't believe she stole money from the law firm. That was so out of character for her. I continue to wonder why she did this. The only theory I have is that someone was pressuring her for money. Perhaps that was the basis of the letters. I just wish Margaret had confided in me."

"Did you tell the police any of this?"

"Not really. I know that I should have but I wanted to save Margaret the shame of being labeled mentally ill. It has taken me a few days but I now believe she killed herself. The guilty pressure about the thefts was too much for her. I feel dreadful that I left her here alone. Perhaps if I had been here I could have stopped her from hurting herself."

"You can't blame yourself, Michael," I told him. That guilt job was mine. I knew exactly how he felt. "If Maggie wanted to kill herself, she would have found a way. Maybe she waited for you to be out of the country. I guess we'll never know."

Michael asked if it would be okay for him to call me when he needed to "for support". I had come prepared with information on grief counseling which he accepted. It was left that he would call me at the office if additional assistance was needed.

Throughout our interaction coffee was served by a waiter along with a variety of little finger sandwiches with the crusts cut off along and a delicious assortment of desserts. I hoped that I wasn't going to be paying for this because my boss wouldn't be too pleased with this bill. Just in case I did have to pay for it, I pigged out making sure I got my money's worth. I could see a cruiser parked across the road and realized it was Kevin. Just as I had entered the restaurant I had heard him tell the dispatcher that he was taking lunch at seven o'clock. He must have shared his concerns about this meeting with Zack and Neil because they pulled over a total of five cars during the first hour of our interaction just in front of the restaurant. Sixty minutes later, Kevin and the boys switched spots resulting in Kevin doing another four traffic stops for the second hour. Policing is definitely a brotherhood and technically I wasn't a brother or sister - more like a cousin but still worthy of their protectiveness.

"Busy night for traffic stops," noted Michael. "Those men in blue are earning their money tonight."

"Yeah, they are, aren't they," I replied with a smile.

Michael must have misinterpreted my mood as being more positive than it was meant to be because the conversation turned personal. He asked me questions about my interests and my family as well as if I was seeing someone. I felt like I was on Star Trek with Counselor Troy "probing" my mind. Perhaps he didn't realize he was being inappropriate and that he was just getting into his defense lawyer mode. As a nurse I had been taught to only share personal information which would be helpful to the client. These were certainly *not* the kinds of questions I expected from a grieving fiancé. Perhaps I had given him the wrong impression and he was misinterpreting my wild pheromone emissions for Kevin as being directed at him. I don't know why I was so irritable. The itchiness on my face was bothering me but that was no reason for Michael to be getting on my nerves as much as he was. Perhaps it was just my mood. The guy had been through a lot and he had no reason for me to be short and snappy with him. I decided I'd save that bitchy mood for my ex-husband in divorce court tomorrow. I needed to get some sleep and thought it was time to call it a night.

Michael paid for the meal with his Platinum *VISA* card and then walked me out to the sidewalk telling me how wonderful I was and how helpful I'd been. He caught me off guard when he asked, "What did Maggie's mother give you in the envelope outside of the church?"

I was surprised that he'd even noticed.

"A "thank you card"." I replied. "She wanted to thank me for everything I'd done for Maggie." To be honest, I hadn't even read it because I'd been so bloody busy since I'd left the funeral.

"Well, she was right," added Michael. He then embraced me in a hug and gave me a kiss on the cheek. I pulled away but it was too late.

"Michael, you shouldn't..."

"I'm sorry," he interrupted, "but I feel such a closeness to you. Thank you so much for everything you've done."

He walked me to my car and I tried to keep my distance from him to avoid another hug or kiss or any body contact. Surprisingly, he just he shook my hand before I got into the car. I wondered if the hug and kiss were a show for the "Boys in Blue" or if he realized that he had stepped over the personal line. Kevin would probably be having a shit fit right now!

I drove away feeling completely done in. I waved to Kevin, Zack and Neil on my way back to the station. So Maggie may have been more paranoid than I first thought. But why would she kill herself if she believed someone was after her? I know that there are people who have believed that there was no way out of a situation so they harm themselves because it is what they perceive to be their only option but this tended to be rare. I was having a sneaky suspicion that I may have screwed up royally.

My face was on fire from the burning stitches. I was tired and bitchy. My head was bursting from being so "nice" for the past two hours. I returned to my office, signed off for the night on the radio, called Paul to tell him the same thing and drove home. Abby was in the living room watching a movie with Nick and apparently didn't need my company.

I wondered if my uncle knew he was paying Abby to stay at my house *and* screw her boyfriend, the Crown Attorney.

"You okay, Chailey?" Abby asked. "Your eye looks swollen."

"Yeah, I'm okay. I'm just going to bed. See you tomorrow." I could feel the joint sigh of relief when they knew I wasn't going to join them on the couch. Little did they have to worry, I was going to have the couch cleaned before I sat on their love cooties.

Randy wasn't around so I figured that Martha had taken him with her and he was no doubt terrorizing the guests of the Sheraton Hotel at this very moment. As long as he wasn't terrorizing me I really didn't give a damn!

Chapter 18

I went to bed but I didn't go to sleep. I couldn't with the itching and burning on my face. It felt like I'd been dragged over a gravel driveway and then someone had peed on my face. At 4 a.m. I finally got up threw on some clothes and banged on the living room door and told Abby that we were going to the hospital. When she eventually emerged she took one look at me, grabbed her keys, called into her radio that we were going to the Emergency Room and set off for a six-hour wait to see the doctor. Apparently every other resident of Cookfield needed emergency care tonight and the Emergency department was wall-to-wall people. Abby told me that I looked like hell and it wasn't until I looked in a mirror that I realized what she meant. My left eye was just about swollen shut and my lip was about five times its normal size. Even the nurse at the Registration Desk looked a little ill when she looked at me. When we were *finally* seen by the doctor he told me the obvious, that I was allergic to the cream, gave me antihistamines and some new cream and told me not to use the old stuff. I guess it takes seven years of medical school to come up with that advice.

Abby stayed with me at the hospital, meaning she slept in the corner of the ER waiting room. At least she called work to let them know I wasn't coming in on account that my face looked like it had been boiled. She dutifully drove me home and I had less than half an hour to get changed into my blue suit, which had been lying in a heap on the ground and get to the courthouse for my divorce hearing. Damn, the jacket was missing. I must have left it in Kevin's car. I grabbed another outfit and made it out the door in a less than ten minutes and ran into the courthouse with only minutes to spare.

I hated the idea of going to court. It reminded me of doing a class presentation in grade school. My worst experience *ever* was in grade six when the class presented on the solar system. Of course I got stuck with the seventh planet, the rude one which rhymes with famous. I couldn't stop giggling each time I said Uranus. The teacher didn't share my sense of humour and sent me down to sit on my seventh planet outside of the principal's office.

Judges are the adult version of school principals. They ask you tough questions, caution you not to lie and give you the evil eye.

My lawyer met me just outside of the courtroom and stared at me. "What the hell happened to you?" she asked. "You look like the victim of a wife-beating. That will look good in front of the judge."

"Geez, thanks Olivia. I had a little incident last week and then I reacted to the antibiotic cream they gave me. I've been in the ER all night and I feel as bad as I look."

Adam and his lawyer walked up to us. His lawyer took one look at me and took Adam aside. Within five minutes his lawyer approached us and told us that he would acquiesce to our demands. To be perfectly honest I had no idea what "our demands" were, but figured it sounded good. We all went into the courtroom, the lawyers did their legal stuff and we were out within fifteen minutes. It had taken six years to get this far and it was all over with no fireworks or histrionics. A little disappointing as far as I was concerned. My lawyer told me that she'd get all of the papers taken care of and she'd meet me at the end of the week to finish everything up. She had a smile on her face. No doubt she'd be driving that new BMW by the end of the day.

"Go home and get some sleep," she advised.

I followed her orders exactly and woke up at the absurd hour of ten o'clock at night. I got up, brushed my teeth, ate a piece of cold pizza left in a box on the dining room table and went back to bed again.

Wednesday I woke up at eight feeling quite refreshed. It's amazing what eighteen hours of sleep will do for you. I looked less like Rocky with the swelling having gone down and I could see out of my left eye again as well as move my lips normally. The bruises had turned an icky green but were actually starting to fade slightly. It was time to get back to work.

I was at the station by ten in the morning ready to start my day. It felt good to be back in the horse's saddle, which reminded me that Kevin would be back tonight. I'd have to call him and cancel our dinner date since I wasn't dining under surveillance. The rumours would have been flying high with that tidbit of information. I called the dispatchers to let them know I was ready to start my day. Flo wasn't in and there was a big sign on her desk stating, "Gone for the morning!" So much for advanced warning. There was also a memo on my desk from Jody. Apparently she was taking a month of stress leave. I figured it was related to my incident last week. That meant that the office was mine to enjoy alone. There was also a message from Sally Hannah asking me to call my uncle at my earliest convenience. Yeah, I'd get to that task early in the afternoon. I put a call into Kevin's apartment and left a message telling him that I couldn't meet with him tonight and that he could call me and I'd explain. Also, could he please drop off my jacket if he found it in his truck? Julia had left a quick message stating that she had some information that may be helpful and could I please call her at the office. The last message on my voice mail was from Liam Fitzgerald. That got my attention. I was just about to dial his number when Neil walked in.

"I'm here!" announced Neil as he walked into my office, sat on Jody's chair and put his feet up on the desk.

"Yeah, and...?" I asked.

"I'm your chauffeur for the day. You know, I'm your escort. They assigned me to you or you to me. I'm not sure which but does it really matter? By the way, you look pretty crappy. You need a makeover, Kermit."

I was just about ready to respond by calling him some off-colour but accurate names when I was rudely interrupted by the radio.

"Charlie 13 – we need you to respond to 7 Rosemary Lane to see Mrs. Robertson."

"She's lost her purse, right?" I asked. I'd been to Mrs. Robertson's home about fifty times this year already. Rosemary and Robert Robertson live on Rosemary Lane, I kid you not. Both are in their early nineties. She has memory problems and calls the police every time she misplaces something thinking that it has been stolen. She loses everything – her glasses, her purse and even her cat. The trouble is that she hasn't lost her phone and therefore calls 911 repeatedly. I'm usually sent over to help her retrieve her items and have a cup of tea.

"Actually, no, Charlie 13. She says she's lost her husband." Last time she lost her husband she had accidentally locked him in the shed.

"Okay, we're on our way."

It only took a few minutes to get to Rosemary Lane and Rosemary was standing outside looking very worried.

Neil was a sweetheart with her by leading her into the house, sitting her down and asking her what happened. She explained that she got up this morning and made her way down stairs and made breakfast for Mr. Robertson, as she referred to him, and he didn't come and eat. She looked everywhere for him but she just couldn't find him. She did, however, find her reading glasses. Neil told her to sit tight and we'd look around.

Needless to say I found Mr. Robertson first. He was in bed – dead. This was my second death discovery in two weeks. Rosemary had made the bed over him. I called Neil up to the bedroom and he confirmed my suspicions. He made the appropriate calls on the radio and we went down to talk to the deceased's wife. She was relatively calm when we told her the news and finally said, "Well, at least we know where he is." We stayed with Rosemary while the ambulance arrived and finally the coroner. We returned to the station to write up our reports and get ready for our next call of the day.

As always, it never rains, it pours. The dispatcher had us off again to see another person with questionable mental health concerns. Jessica Delaney was a fifty three-year-old woman who was currently in a laundromat causing a disturbance. Uniformed police were responding and my presence was requested.

It took us a good fifteen minutes to get across the downtown area during the rush hour traffic. There were two cruisers outside of the laundromat and we parked behind them. I saw one of the uniformed officers check to see if I had hit his cruiser and the subsequent look of relief when he saw Neil get out of the driver's side.

There was no question that this was the right place based on the small crowd of fifteen or so irate women banging on the doors of the laudromat shouting and screaming. We were in one of the tougher neighbourhoods in town which meant that the women were rough. They also weren't terribly respectful of law enforcement officers since cops had probably arrested their fathers, husbands and sons scores of times.

"Get that bitch out of there!"

"Where the hell have you pigs been? Long line up at the donut counter?"

"Get that nutbar out of there!"

"If she touches my whites I'll kill her."

"Who the fuck are you?" That one was directed at me.

The group of us split up thereby dividing the mob into three groups. Jessica was well known to these women as a drug user and former prostitute but today they felt that she was acting crazy. I don't know about you but anyone hyped up on crack looks pretty damned crazy to me. These women live in the streets where crack is just another addiction and *they* would know the difference. Jessica had shown up today looking for her baby. According to these "ladies", she didn't have a baby. Jessica had "evacuated" the building by yelling "fire" and pushed the last people out before she locked the door. The women were just about ready to lynch her since it was *their* washing she was chucking on the ground. Washing day was a weekly tradition in this end of town and nothing interfered with that. Jessica had not only interrupted this sacrilegious event, she was actually *touching* their belongings. The floor was totally covered in clothing and sheets both wet and dry thrown out of the washers and dryers by Jessica in her frantic efforts to find her child. Washing powder and fabric softener were everywhere and Jessica had somehow flooded the place with several inches of water. The crowd outside was getting really ugly now and they weren't a pretty group to begin with.

Two additional police cruisers had shown up to hold back the mob and help deal with Jessica who was obviously delusional. The owner had shown up in response to a panicky call by one of the patrons. He had been told in no unclear terms to get down here or the "ladies" vowed to burn down his building! Lovely!

Jessica didn't notice our arrival initially. She kept rooting through the piles of laundry.

"My baby! Where's my baby?" She continually screamed and cried uncontrollably. She obviously believed that her baby was somewhere in the heap of wet, soggy washing or even worse, in one of the machines. It truly was every mother's nightmare!

"Jessica, how can we help you?" I asked.

"Get away! You may be hurting my baby!" she screamed back as she launched herself at me. The cops were more than ready to react but it took four of them to wrestle her to the ground and handcuff her. Unfortunately I was not to be excused from the joy of rolling around on the floor when I got knocked over. I'm sure the cops did it on purpose. Within minutes we were all covered from head to toe in wet disgusting slime! Poor Jessica was beside herself with fear and grief. She really believed that her child was there somewhere. The women outside booed and hissed at Jessica and us as we made our way out to the cruiser. It took three cops to hold the crowd back. These three guys happened to stay clean and dry and I don't know how but Neil had managed to miss out on the gooey wrestling match. So much for thanks from the crowd. It made me want to go back one more time and grind my shoes into their wet clothes.

We took Jessica to the hospital where we were seen quickly due to the loud noise she was making with her hollering and screaming. I'm also pretty sure they wanted the wet, slimy police personnel out of their nice clean emergency room. One day I may actually go home from work without wet knickers but it wasn't going to be today.

Chapter 19

After my shower and change of clothes at the station, I dropped by the Squad Room to grab a cup of coffee and returned to my office to find Flo sitting at her desk with a strange expression on her face that I'd never seen before. I think they call it a smile. There was also a rose in a vase on her desk. The closest thing I'd seen to a flower on her desk was the picture on the side of a box of tissues.

"Hey, Flo. How was your morning off?" I asked as I headed towards the door of my office.

"Fine," she replied with a smile. "Don't go in there. Richard is making a phone call. It was confidential so he asked to use your phone."

"Sure," I replied. I sat down in the chair across from Flo's desk. She had aroused my curiosity so I asked, "Who's Richard?"

Flo blushed slightly or so thought. It was hard to tell with her drinker's facial pallor. "He's a detective. Chailey, can you keep a secret? Of course you can because you have no ability to lie, do you? Well, Richard has asked me out for dinner tonight."

Great, even Flo was going to have sex before I do. That reminded me, I needed to call Kevin and see how his trip was.

"Wow, that's wonderful," I replied with genuine excitement for her. Flo's husband abandoned her with two children nearly twenty-five years ago. Her children were fully grown up and had moved away and Flo was left alone in the nest drinking herself into oblivion with Jack Daniels as her best friend.

We chatted for a few minutes about where they were going for dinner until the door to my office opened and out walked Dicky the Dick.

"What the hell are you doing in my office?" I roared. Then it hit me. "Richard" was Rick Simmons.

I turned to Flo. "I'm sorry but that Neanderthal stays out of my office." I then turned to the "Dickstick" and yelled, "Get out and stay out!" as I marched into my office and slammed the door shut. Within minutes I had the window open, every cloth surface Febreezed and any remaining surfaces wiped with a Clorox wipe. I could tell that he'd touched everything probably just to get a rise out of me. It had worked. What a jerk! I tried to visualize Dicky walking out of my office to remember if his zipper was down and he had a smile on his face. I finally settled down long enough to start the stupid report. That is, I sat at Jody's desk. Neil returned looking a little more refreshed. He had to change after the women threw coffee at him while he tried to hold the mob back just as we were leaving the laundromat.

"Yikes! This office smells like my mother has been cleaning."

"Yeah, well "Dicky the Dick" was here using my office. He must have touched everything while making a "confidential" phone call."

"Yuck!" He got out of my chair and moved to the one opposite me at Jody's desk. I switched spots to allow Neil access to the computer so that he could use his time wisely to improve his Solitaire scores.

I took the opportunity to call Sally.

"Thanks for returning my call, Chailey. Your uncle would like to talk to you. I'll put you through." Neil made sexy kissing actions when I was talking to Sally. I told you, she was hot and untouchable making her all the more desirable.

My uncle's booming voice came on the phone. "Chailey, I'm just checking in. How are you doing?"

"Great, thank you." My radar was on full alert. My uncle had *never* checked in on me.

"Paul Tayler tells me there's been no contact yet. We can expect it to occur in the next few days. Err, Chailey. There's one more thing,…" he started to say.

Damn! I almost missed the bullet. Perhaps not the most appropriate phrase to use this week.

"Your Aunt Janice. Does she seem okay to you?" he continued.

"I spoke to her last Thursday. You know how she is, Uncle John. She worries about you. She thinks you have too much on your plate."

"So you think she's alright. She's been so distant recently and I'm worried about her."

I was very uncomfortable with this conversation. I would have been happier talking to him about Pap smears.

"Can you talk to her, Chailey? See if there is anything bothering her." I wanted to scream at him, "She thinks you're bonking someone and you think she's leaving you!" but I restrained myself.

"Uncle John, I'm not sure that I'm the right person.." I started.

He interrupted me. "Please Chailey. If your mother was here I'd ask her but she's not. You know I'd appreciate it."

Great, now he was using the mega-guilt complex. Nothing is worse than your surrogate father begging you to do something.

"Okay, I'll talk to her." Wonderful! Now I was stuck in the middle of my uncle's impending marriage breakdown.

My next call was to Liam Fitzgerald. I wanted to update him on my conversation with Michael Brigham. He was unavailable so I left a message for him to call me back. My final call was to Julia. I looked forward to hearing what she had to say and to check out Michael's claims.

"I can't talk for long. Maggie made me promise not to tell anyone this, but since she is dead, I feel I can tell someone. I hope she'll forgive me."

"I'm sure she will." Julia was killing me by keeping me in suspense.

"Maggie told me the day before her death that she was thinking of ending the engagement."

"What?" I hadn't expected that one. "Did she say why?"

"I did ask but she refused to give me a reason. It seemed so out of character for her. I think it was related to a man named Stephen."

"Who's Stephen?"

"I met him the day that Michael left town. I suggested to Maggie that we go for lunch to make her feel better since she was upset that Michael had gone away. We went to a restaurant in the Market Square and were walking back to the office when this man walked in front of us. I jumped but Maggie just stopped and said, "Steve." She looked like she'd seen a ghost. They just stood looking at each other with people walking by. Maggie told me to go back to the office and she'd be there in a few minutes. Thirty minutes later she was back in the office. I asked if she was okay and she said she was fine and that Steve was an old friend whom she was surprised to see.

"The next day, Steve showed up again at the office. He went up to Maggie and announced, "We have to talk". She said, "Later." He said, "Now" and they went out of the office. Maggie came back ten minutes later and she looked upset. I asked her if there was a problem and she said "yes" but she'd figure out a solution."

"Did she say anything else?"

"It was the next day and she told me that she'd had a bad night and someone was banging on her door and harassing her. I asked her about Steve and she said that everything was settled and she was happy with her decision. It was that day she told me she was thinking of ending the relationship."

"Does Michael know this?"

"Absolutely not. Maggie said she was thinking about this but definitely had not come to a decision."

"What did you think about all this?"

"Honestly I was shocked. They seemed so happy together and Michael was very good to Maggie. I told her to think it through and that it was probably cold feet. Every bride-to-be gets them."

I didn't get cold feet but I should have because Adam was keeping his feet warm in someone else's bed every night.

"Did Maggie ever talk about someone harassing her at work?"

"She showed me a letter about a month ago telling her to mind her own business. It was unsigned and Maggie thought it was someone was joking with her. I told her it wasn't funny and that she should report it to Security."

"Did you believe her?"

"No. Listen, I've got to go. Take care. Bye."

And that was it. So Maggie wasn't as lily-white as she made herself out to be. And who the hell was Steve? And what about the threatening letter. But from whom? And why? With nothing else to do I settled down to finally write my report.

****

I was just about finished when I heard a knock. I yelled at the closed door, "If that's you, Neil, I'm going to smack your bottom. I told you to leave me alone for thirty minutes. You've got seven minutes left."

The door opened and Kevin stepped in. "Is that bottom smacking reserved for Neil or can anyone get a piece of the action?"

"Kevin! How are you? Come on in. You're welcome here. It's just that Neil has been driving me bonkers with his inane chatter. I had a report to finish up so I sent him away. Never mind him, how was your trip?"

I've got to tell you, I was thrilled to have Kevin back and felt a warm flush come over me when he smiled. Now I know why you shouldn't date someone you work with. Just what you need is in the middle of an interview is to look up at your boyfriend and have your cheeks flush and your nipples pucker up.

"The trip was great. Jake is doing well. They offered me a good deal but there have been no decisions yet. How are you? Your bruises are fading and you are starting to look human again."

"Geez, thanks!" Nice to know your potential date thinks you're beginning to resemble a human being.

"I brought the jacket that you left in the truck."

I got up from behind Jody's desk to close the door. I didn't need Flo, Chairman of the Rumour Mill, listening to our conversation. I didn't realize it but Kevin had followed me to the door. He kissed me gently on the back of my neck.

"I missed you," he murmured as he nibbled behind my ears. A warm flush was threatening to engulf me with a wave of hot desire.

I turned towards him and he kissed me on the lips. At first he was gentle and then the kiss deepened. Oh-my-

God, I thought, I'm going to have an orgasm in my office. And we'd have witnesses with Flo on the other side of the door and Neil due back in exactly four minutes. That put a damper on my sexual desire. I guess Kevin noticed.

"What's wrong?" he asked huskily.

"Neil's going to be back any minute now."

"Don't worry. I've got my knee against the door." I had noticed that *something* was wedged between my thighs against the door. It was his knee, was it? I knew I couldn't move even if I wanted to so I hoped the door wouldn't budge either.

"I'll shoot anyone who comes through that door," he added. At that moment I believed that he would. Hell, at that moment I would have grabbed his Glock and done it myself!

It took us just a few minutes to realize that nothing else was going to happen. With both of us wearing Kevlar vests and with his belt containing a gun, nightstick, police radio, pepper spray, handcuffs and so on, we were like two turtles trying to make out stomach to stomach. Unsuccessfully, might I add. No wonder turtles do it from behind. It didn't help our level of frustration when the dispatcher called Kevin over the radio.

"Dispatch to 611."

"Shit!" we said in unison.

"That's me," he said to me. "Yeah, Dispatch?" he responded tersely into the radio. Not exactly good police radio protocol but not bad considering the situation.

"I'm sending you to 21 Nightingale Street for a burglary report."

"Ten-four," he replied to the dispatcher. To me he said, "When can we get together? You said in your phone message that you needed to cancel dinner. What's up?"

I gave him the *Reader's Digest* version of the events since he left. He didn't look too pleased.

"I don't want to have dinner with you with a surveillance team watching," I explained.

"As long as you stay safe, I don't mind. I guess we'll have to wait for dinner. It's the surveillance part I'm not so happy about."

"Dispatch to Charlie 13."

"Shit," we said again in unison.

"Charlie 13 we need you to respond to the main library..."

"10-4"

Well, this gig was up. Kevin bent over and kissed me briefly but passionately and then stepped away from me and the door. God this guy kissed well. I was hoping that the rest of his skills were just as good. At the rate we were going, I wouldn't be sleeping with him for another three months.

Neil was knocking at the door calling to me, "Chailey, we've got to go on that call."

"See ya," said Harrison as he opened the door, "and stay safe."

"Yeah, you too," I added. And then he was gone.

Neil was waiting outside of my office with a big grin on his face. "Big homecoming, huh? No wonder you wanted me out of the office."

I gave him my bitchiest glare and told him, "No more words!" He took the hint and headed out to the car and we were off on another call.

We went straight to Morrisella Street to the main library. Some lady was running around half naked causing a disturbance. They didn't say if it was the top part or bottom part that was naked but they were asking for Neil to help with the chase and for me to do the assessment on her. Apparently I had dealings with her before but her name didn't ring a bell with me. I was fairly sure that she hadn't done this before because I'm pretty sure that I'd remember it. On a personal level, I was hoping that they didn't have wanted posters at the library because I had several books more than a few months overdue. I was saving up to pay for the fines.

Neil had us over there real fast. He likes to pretend that he is driving in the Indy 500. Hey, I love to watch car racing on a racetrack, it's just that I don't appreciate being in a car hurtling along the city streets at more than the speed of light. I wasn't terribly excited about the prospect of chasing a naked lady around the library and would have gladly taken the long indirect route at a snail's pace.

We would have been at the library faster but someone stupidly cut off Neil so badly that he felt obliged to pull the idiot over and give him a ticket. It's interesting to drive around with different cops and hear what each officer's pet peeve is. It's the one thing they always see people doing and it drives them crazy. Well, at least it's something other than me that bugs them. Usually they let the offenders go when they drive with me because the major purpose of our calls is to see the people with emotional problems. Of course, when I'm driving with Abby we are going to mental health calls *and* looking for the Cookfield hunks. For example, Hatcher hates people who have plastic covers over their license plates (it's illegal too), Spencer detests people who drive through red lights and Dan Robertson gets upset with people who illegally change lanes. Neil can't stand people cutting him off and big women who don't wear bras and Zack gets annoyed at people who have oral sex while driving. Unbelievably, he has fined two people for this act. As for me, I say arrest every person who picks his nose while driving. They, meaning mostly men, do it as though no one sees them. You know it's just a matter of time until the culprit rolls it into a little green ball and pops it into his mouth. Yuck! It's one of the greatest distractions known to drivers.

There were several cruisers outside of the library so we weren't the only ones on the search and rescue mission. Sergeant Oliver met us at the front door and explained that the lady had come into the library this morning sounding very upset and confused. Her library card named her Penelope Lopez. The librarians weren't able to help her and she wandered off into the "History" section. This was after all the downtown library and was used by many as a safe sanctuary from the severe heat and cold elements. There were clean toilets and sinks to bathe in and a bevy of media to entertain the spirit. In other words, it was a hang out for many of the homeless and their buddies.

It was reported to the library staff that a woman who was approximately five feet, eight inches tall and weighing close to 150 pounds with shoulder length black hair was causing a disturbance and running around in the maps section on the fourth floor. She had only panties and socks on and was wielding a small pocketknife. I guess that wearing only your undies in the map section was considered unacceptable library behaviour, just like talking loudly in the library and bending pages in books. Those were definitely no-nos! Police records revealed that I had apparently seen her a year ago and had taken her to hospital at that time. I couldn't remember her but then I also forgot what I had for breakfast this morning. There were four male officers looking for her at this time – there were no female officers available right now. At least I wouldn't have to pat her down if she was naked. Neil and I accepted our fate and headed into the plethora of books hoping to avoid meeting Ms. Lopez. Perhaps while we were in there I could hack into the library computer and delete my overdue fines.

We chose the second floor since the other officers had taken the top two floors, which included the "Maps" section, so we figured we were safe. The security guards had emptied out the library temporarily and I could see the librarians huddled together outside the library like a flock of sheep being harassed by a wolf. The second floor housed the fictional section and I wanted to see if my favourite author's new book was in while I was up there. Five minutes after wandering through the maze of shelves and shelves of library books we of course ran into the now infamous Ms. Lopez. She was actually a very beautiful woman with a body that would make Madonna jealous. The problem with her body was that she had covered it from head to toe in fire extinguisher foam and was now directing the stream of foam towards us. Man that stuff is slippery. Penelope was laughing hysterically and appeared to be talking to herself. She definitely appeared to be psychotic and she may have even been high on drugs based on the way she was acting. To add to the view she had stripped herself naked. Neil had quickly radioed the other officers obviously not wanting to deal with this situation alone. He'd prefer to watch naked women wrestle in mud on a stage, not this.

I introduced myself. "Hey, Penelope, I'm Chailey. This is Neil. What's going on today? Why aren't you wearing anything?"

"What kind of name is that? Didn't you get the invitation, there's a festival here today!" she shrieked. Penelope fell over with laughter and gleefully rolled around on the floor. When Neil stepped towards her she scrambled up and grabbed the extinguisher and yelled, "No way are you stopping my fun, Kailey and the Pig!" and sprayed Neil with the foam.

"Fuck!" said Neil. He obviously wasn't impressed.

"And it's Chailey," I murmured under my breath.

I tried to continue on at a healthy distance from her. If she was going to spray me with foam I wanted it directed towards the computers so that it might fry the system and delete my file complete with the fines attached. It was a trifle selfish I admit but understandable all the same. I'd always had a lifelong fear of the "Library Cops" showing up at my door and taking me away to the place that people who lose books go. Kind of like a literary hell.

"Who invited you, Penelope?"

"The people invited me to bring joy to them," she yelled out euphorically. "God told me that the people needed me to make them happy so I'm having a party," she tried to spray me but I was quicker than Neil and jumped out of the way. Second time I wasn't so lucky and landed on my ass. We were in the back of the section behind the many stacks of books so the other cops could hear us but couldn't quite see us. Penelope was moving around providing a moving target which didn't really help matters while she babbled away laughing and giggling like a kid in a candy shop. She was obviously not well and needed to go to hospital. To add to the gaiety she started throwing books at us and pulled the fire alarm on the way by. Now we couldn't hear ourselves think or hear the radio. The four officers and the sergeant made their way over to us and then the fun really began. Penelope had no intention of letting the party end and kept spraying the cops with foam. They tried to spray her with the pepper spray but it had next to no effect on her and just made the cops cough and splutter and add to their misery. Every attempt to catch her was a failure since she just slid out of their grasp. Neil later described the experience being the same as wrestling a bowling ball basted with butter with only your hands. For me, it was like watching the Keystone cops mud wrestle - only better! As the grease match continued, books went flying and shelves were knocked over. We later learned that Penelope had lathered herself in exotic oils so that she'd be ready for the sexual encounter she had been promised.

After a good ten minutes of this fiasco, Penelope finally threw herself onto the ground on her back with legs and arms spread-eagled with her eyes closed and went completely mute. She refused to move or talk so the ambulance guys were called to take her to hospital on a stretcher. The cops were absolutely exhausted. As we left the library building someone had finally turned off the fire bells. Needless to say, Penelope was admitted to hospital. Poor Neil had to stand for two hours covered in oil and fire extinguisher foam. Every time he tried to sit on a chair he would slide off.

We made it back to the station at three o'clock and Neil took off for a shower and change of uniform while I wrote up my notes. There was a message on my voice mail from Liam Fitzgerald wanting to update me on several issues. He had spoken to the coroner who had adamantly stated that Maggie Denton had died as a result of suicide. Period and end of case. Secondly, Michael Brigham had called Liam about Maggie. He wanted to know what had happened about the investigation into the prowler. Liam had informed Michael that nothing had arisen from this case and that with Maggie's suicide, the case was closed. Apparently he wasn't happy about this and was formally complaining to the Chief of Police. Dicky would definitely be getting his hand slapped for this one. Heck, I'd put Dicky in jail and make him someone's wife if it was up to me. That's exactly why I'm not placed in positions of authority since I can't keep my temper under control.

I tried to return Liam's call with no success. I decided to call it a day to go home to shower and change myself.

Chapter 20

When I got home I checked my phone messages. One was from my mother telling me what a *fabulous* time she was having in England and hoping that I was doing well and staying out of trouble. Yeah, Mum, everything's great. I look like I was hit by a train, I haven't seen my dog in days, my ex-husband is mad at me, I can't get within ten feet of the first guy who had really wanted to date me in six years who is probably moving away 3,000 kilometers anyway, my tenants are enjoying a life of luxury at the Sheraton Hotel and a woman who I promised to keep safe is dead and I can't prove it was a suicide or not. Of course my only evidence so far is a left over casserole, an unlocked door and a cat with no food. Oh, did I mention, I'm also premenstrual. Everything is freaking great. Hope it's raining in England. I hit the "delete" button so hard that I broke a nail.

There was another message from my "bank manager" asking me to call him personally since there had been a slight discrepancy in my account. There was over half a million dollars in my account. Obviously someone was pulling my leg but I really didn't get the joke.

The final message was from Michael Brigham. Could I please contact him at my earliest convenience? I had decided earlier in the day that I needed to talk to Maggie's mother. I didn't know where she was staying so I tried calling Michael to inquire if he had that piece of information while killing two birds with one stone. He was "unavailable" according to his new Barbie-look-a-like secretary so I left a message with a request for Michael to leave me the name of Susannah's hotel. I waited half an hour for his reply and wasted the time away planning revenge on Zack and Neil.

Getting nowhere with both tasks, I realized that there are only a few hotels in Cookfield so I called around to find out where Susannah was a guest. I did a quick search through the "Hotel" section of the Yellow Pages and felt pretty strongly that I could skip the motels which rented by the hour and rounded off my list with three possibilities. My first call was lucky and I was talking to Susannah Denton in minutes, who not only agreed to meet me now but wanted to do it at Maggie's house. I called Paul to tell him I was doing a follow-up visit alone and gave him the address. He told me the guys doing the surveillance on me this afternoon just about pissed themselves laughing at Neil and me coming out of the library. Glad we could be entertaining. I also called Liam again and left a long and convoluted voice mail about Michael's information that a man had been investigated at Maggie's law firm.

I arrived at Maggie's house before her mother so I sat outside in the car and started thinking about my last visit to see Maggie. Not the visit when I found her dead but the one before that when I could still speak to her. It was last Saturday afternoon and I'd gone there to support her. I had driven over to her house from the station which only took me about ten minutes in the light evening traffic. I had taken the scenic route along Dunbar Street where all the hookers were hanging out ready to make a quick buck so that could get their next hit of crack that much faster. Not a nice life by any means. Some of the things those women do for twenty bucks I wouldn't do for twenty million bucks wearing a body condom.

Maggie had greeted me warmly and led me into the kitchen to make us a cup of tea. I normally don't accept drinks or anything from clients however Maggie's place looked cleaner than my own so I thought that it was safe. My worries were quickly put to rest when I realized that Maggie would have made Martha Stewart proud with her English tea set that matched her placemats and napkins. In my house you get a mismatched mug and a piece of paper towel. If it's a good day, the mug will be clean.

I had asked Maggie how she was doing and she told me that she was feeling much better. She'd had a relatively good night's sleep once she finally settled down for the night at two in the morning. She admitted that she was frightened by the events from the previous night.

"Why do you think that this is happening to you, Maggie?" I asked.

It was at that moment that I started sneezing. I knew straight away that she had a cat because my allergy was kicking in. I grabbed one of my allergy pills and popped it into my mouth. I'd be fine in a few minutes. I washed the pill down with one of the homemade shortbread cookies Maggie had just produced and placed on the table. They were my favourite kind with a little brushing of sugar on top. My inability to cook has been just one more failure to add to the list of my parent's disappointments in me. Divorced, childless, unable to cook... How do I manage to go on every day? My mother was trained as a chef so she was doubly disappointed in my lack of culinary skills. Mind you, I figure that my mother would suck as a Mental Health Worker so on that level we were even. Knowing her, she'd tell a depressed person to suck it up and if they were going to jump off the bridge then just get on with it and quit whining. My mother, the pragmatist! Of course, I didn't inherit anything useful like my mother's cooking skills. No, instead I have to inherit the Smith big butt and bad temper.

Maggie sat down and poured the tea seemingly trying to put off her answer as long as possible. I'd have to try this tactic the next time my mother asks me about my dating life.

"I've thought a lot about last night and wonder if it was my imagination kicking in. But I don't think so. Chailey, as you know I work as a legal secretary at a law firm here in town. My job involves confidential work which I am not at liberty to share with you. I hope that as a nurse you are able to keep our conversation confidential."

"Yes, I can promise you that I can," I replied.

"Good," she replied looking mildly relieved. "I wish I could discuss with you in detail the issues however I can't. But what I can tell you is that at work I have become aware of some irregularities in the office. I am trying to figure out if there really is a problem or not."

"Maggie, do you think that the problem with the prowler has anything to do with your work."

"No, that's crazy. It's just a coincidence that this is happening at the same time." Great! Now I was starting to sound crazy.

"I've been trying to get hold of Michael to get his advice as to what to do. The irregularities I think I've discovered aren't really that serious. I don't believe I'm in danger but I do worry that a person at the law firm may be in trouble. I just think that the prowler is just a coincidence but it has frightened me. I really don't think that these two things are linked. Michael is back on Saturday and I will talk to him about the situation at work. I know he'll give me good advice. He's such a dear."

Maggie certainly seemed calmer now and had a plan to deal with her work issues. What a contrast to the inconsolable, frightened woman we had met the previous evening. We chatted a little more and she told me about the trip to Egypt she and Michael had planned for the fall. Both had interests in history and were very excited about seeing the Egyptian burial sites. If I had been going on a trip with a boyfriend I'd go on a cruise ship and the only burial we'd be seeing would be in our bed. Maggie also told me about her boyfriend, Michael, an up-and-coming defense lawyer. The couple had announced their engagement the previous fall. Heck, when I got engaged all I got from Adam while having sex one night was, "Wanna get married?"

She showed me around her house, which was small but more than adequate for one person and would easily accommodate a couple. It was incredibly clean and tidy with not even a piece of paper out of place. The walls of the living room were painted a pretty primrose yellow with a cream-coloured area rug and a flower-patterned couch. Obviously she didn't own a black Labrador like Randy. There was piano sitting against one wall upon which she had numerous pictures. She was definitely a family person and shared with me who each person was in the numerous photos she had framed around her living room. There were family group photos including one of her sister's marriage four years ago. At least Maggie and I had one thing in common and that was our single status, or otherwise known in the family as the unmarried sister. Something else we shared was that we had both recently lost a father and Maggie talked about how hard it was to lose her father and how difficult it had been for her mother to readjust to life on her own.

Finally Maggie had told me about her family and her life growing up in Winnipeg. She loved the cold and snow so she must have been in seventh heaven living in that cold storage locker.

By the time I left two hours later I felt I had a good picture of Maggie as a wholesome, down to earth woman who wouldn't hurt a fly. She was my opposite. Everything she was, I wasn't!

Maggie had thanked me profusely for visiting and stated that she felt a little better for my visit. I thanked her for my substitute dinner which consisted of the half dozen shortbread cookies which made me feel better. There's nothing like eating a half-pound of butter for supper.

I drove back to the station feeling like I'd done something right that night. My conversation with Maggie had made me think about my own father and how much I missed him. He had died five years previously and there wasn't a day that didn't go by when I didn't think of him. What I wouldn't do to hear him yell "Shit!" as he threw the rope-less anchor into the river or watch him drive up behind my mum's car at a stop light, unbeknownst to her, and tap her car with his own. He was a typical Smith; workaholic, loyal, principled, quick-tempered but fun to be with. My mother basically survived his death however it took her several years to recover. I think that living with a Smith gives a person a certain amount of fortitude. Last year she met Ted and he has become her companion. They spend a lot of time together and started traveling this year. I don't think that their relationship is sexual but then I always denied that my parents had sex and had convinced myself that my brother and I had been the first invitro babies thereby not requiring the dirty deed to be done.

Susannah interrupted my thoughts when she pulled into the driveway. We met up at the front door.

"Thanks for meeting me, Susannah."

"I'm glad you called," she replied. "I've been wanting to talk to you but didn't want to bother you."

"You're no bother," I replied as we stepped into the house. I instinctively looked over to where the couch had been with Maggie dead and dripping on the cream rug. It was gone along with Maggie.

"It feels strange, doesn't it?" whispered Susannah. Strange, was an understatement. Personally I was having a panic attack.

"Yeah!" I said. What else could I say?

Susannah walked me over to the kitchen and I sat at the table while she bustled around in the kitchen making us tea. Like mother, like daughter. We chatted and she told me that she was gradually sorting through Maggie's belongings and that she hoped to be done within a week. The house was going up for sale the next day.

When Susannah finally sat down, I told her why I was there. "I wanted to talk to you about Maggie and how she seemed to you, Susannah? I met Maggie several times before she died and I didn't pick up any symptoms of depression. She seemed more frightened than anything else."

Susannah shook her head in agreement. "You're right, Chailey. She never said anything to me either. Maggie was excited about getting married and her trip with Michael. The only thing bothering her was work, and of course, the person harassing her. She told me that Michael was trying to help her figure out who was harassing her through letters. He'd hired a private investigator however he came up with nothing except that a man named Chesley had left the company under questionable conditions. This man has a history of assault but Margaret had very little to do with him. Michael was going to follow-up on that but I never heard back from Maggie as to what happened. Maggie was upset and it made her sound crazy. I have to wonder myself after everything that has gone on that may be she was mentally unwell after all."

"Michael told me that Maggie was being followed. He denied that anything came of the private investigation."

"All I'm telling you is what Maggie told me. I'm beginning to believe that Maggie was paranoid. You seem to be the only one who believes that it may not be a suicide. That Detective Fitzgerald is adamant that Maggie killed herself and he told me to avoid you because you were having troubles accepting this."

"He's right. I just can't accept this. Susannah, I am so sorry. I failed Maggie. I promised to keep her safe either from others or herself and now she's dead. Please forgive me."

It's moments like this that you start thinking of everything you've done wrong in your life; like losing your four-year-old niece at the fireworks display, smashing up your father's brand new, six-week-old Honda Civic or burning down your neighbour's garage. I had help with that one. Of course, I'd have to add marrying Adam to that list of losing hits.

"Chailey, honey, the fact that you are looking beyond the obvious proves that you are helping Maggie. We could both be wrong."

"Tell me about Stephen Williams."

Susannah visibly paled. "Why would you ask about Stephen?"

"According to her friend, Stephen was in town and Maggie was seeing him."

"Her friend must be mistaken. Maggie hasn't seen Stephen in years."

"Susannah, you're the one who making the mistake. Maggie has not only seen him, she was seeing him."

"But why?" It took her a minute to gather her thoughts. "Stephen and Maggie were high school sweethearts. They met in grade ten and were inseparable."

"What happened?"

"Maggie went to secretarial college and Stephen went to university but they were able to maintain a relationship.

Stephen dropped out after the first year, tried getting jobs and kept losing them. Eventually he became depressed and was hospitalized after an overdose. Maggie stood by him the whole time and they continued to plan the wedding. And then one day Maggie left home and moved to Cookfield. We woke up and found a note on the kitchen table telling us where to send her furniture and belongings. We were stunned by her decision."

"That sounds out of character for her."

"Absolutely. It wasn't until a year later that we learned what happened when she sent her father and me a letter. Maggie got pregnant. Steve pressured her to have an abortion. She felt terribly guilty and moved to Cookfield to leave her shame behind."

"Did you ever talk about this?"

"I tried to but she refused to talk. "One day", she'd say and now it's too late."

"Was Steve a violent person?"

"Not as far as I knew. I heard he moved away from Winnipeg but had no idea he made it here."

"How do you think Maggie would have responded to him showing up?"

"It's hard to tell. Maggie loved Steve very much. They had a special relationship. When Maggie left Steve I was stunned. The loss of that baby devastated her and it was the only thing that would have split them apart. That was six years ago. Maybe Maggie thought enough water had passed under the bridge and she could deal with him."

And maybe Maggie's guilt returned and she hurt herself. As if Susannah was reading my thoughts, she added her own. "When Maggie left Winnipeg suddenly, her father and I called the police. We thought she may have hurt herself. Steve being here changes everything. Perhaps she became despondent again."

She squeezed my hand. "By the way, what was on that CD that Maggie gave you?"

"CD? What CD?"

"Maggie left a computer disc with your name on it. She told me over the phone on Sunday night if anything happened to her to give it to you and you'd know what to do with it. I left it in the "thank you" card."

Hell, I can't take responsibility for a four-year-old without losing her. This sounded well out of my range of capabilities!

"Susannah, I left it in Kevin's truck for several days and he's been out of town. I only got the card today and I didn't get a chance to open it."

I heard a footstep behind me and Susannah looked up and jumped as did I.

"Open what?" I heard a male voice from behind me ask.

"Susannah, Chailey, it's only me. Don't look so scared. I didn't mean to frighten you."

Sure, I thought, creep up on us in a locked house where someone *died* less than a week ago and then pretend not to be scaring us. Michael was acting like a typical guy by being a jerk!

The jerk bent over to kiss each of us on the cheek. My radio suddenly came to life making me jump out of my skin. "Charlie 13, are you 10– 4?"

I replied that I was fine and was thankful that someone was keeping an eye on us.

"Michael, please join us. We were just talking about some of Maggie's interests in history. What was the name of the place you were going to on your Egyptian trip?"

I wondered why Susannah had suddenly changed the topic in conversation.

"That was Cairo. You know, the capital of the country. I'm sorry Susannah. I didn't mean to be sharp with you.

I'm finding it difficult to be back in Maggie's house." His voice caught with emotion. "I didn't mean to interrupt the discussion you lovely ladies were having. You were telling Susannah that you hadn't had time to open something. Pray do go on."

Shit! If I lied this guy was going to know it since he was a lawyer.

"Chailey was talking about a vacation fund. She hadn't had the opportunity to open an account to pay for vacations."

Wow! Susannah didn't miss a beat. That lie just slid out of her like a warm knife through butter. She should be a lawyer!

"Really? Well Chailey, you really need to learn to take care of yourself. Something like that will give you the protection you may need one day."

"Well, thanks for the advice. I've got to go. Lots of things to do." See, I babble when I try to lie.

"Please don't leave on my account."

"That's okay, Michael. I just wanted to touch base with Susannah to see how she was doing. Just out of curiosity, how did you know we were here?"

"You had called and left a message that you were looking for Susannah. Your secretary provided me with the information that you were with her so I put two and two together." Flo was dead meat for giving out my location.

"Well, I have to go as well. Thank you for meeting with me, Chailey. I go home in five days so I will be working here each day trying to get the house ready for sale."

Michael got up from his seat at the table and walked us out the front door. He put his arm around my shoulder as he walked me to my car. I could be imagining it but it was almost as if he knew that I was being watched. Susannah had followed us and gave me a handshake and then a hug and a kiss on the cheek.

"Call me," she whispered quietly enough that Michael couldn't hear.

Michael took his opportunity to hug me and give me a kiss also. Both kiss and hug were held a little longer than was required. I wondered if Michael had a little crush on me.

I drove away with smiles and waves to both of them. I also left with a little something else. Maggie Denton's house key! Susannah had pressed it into my hand when she shook it. Susannah wanted me to look in Maggie's house and she didn't want Michael to know. If Maggie was more paranoid than I thought then maybe the apple doesn't fall far from the tree and Susannah may share some of that paranoia. In the psychiatric world, it is referred to a "folie a deux". It seemed like Susannah was acting real strange as well. And why the sudden change in conversation when Michael showed up? He seems like the only normal one out of the lot. With the key in my hand I was coming back and this time without Mr. Michael Brigham or Susannah Denton breathing down my neck.

Chapter 21

For some unknown reason I was up at the unearthly hour of 6:30 on Thursday morning. If I had any premonition of how the day was going to unfold I would have rolled over and gone back to sleep. No, I had to challenge fate. I got up trying not to disturb Abby who was dozing on the couch. For being a "guard" she slept real well and snored like a gorilla. I putzed around the apartment getting my breakfast ready. I was one day closer to the weekend and I hoped that the surveillance schtick would soon be up so that I could *finally* have "dinner" with Kevin as well as spend a night out with my friends.

Usually I nip outside to collect my newspaper wearing whatever I happen to have on hoping that the neighbours aren't watching. Our newspaper man throws the paper onto the path and the ten-yard dash to get it at the end of the path is usually as much exercise as I can manage in any one day. The man who delivers the paper is eighty-six years old and has been doing this paper route since he was nine! He uses one of those rolling walkers and puts the papers on the seat. He only does about ten homes but he loves his job and when he comes collecting his money, he comes in for a cup of coffee and a chat. When you're under surveillance, one has to be appropriately attired to leave the premises which sadly meant getting showered and dressed first.

I sat at the dining room table with my jug of coffee and today's breakfast special; frozen waffles drizzled in Canadian maple syrup prepared by Chef Chailey. I was about to turn to the obligatory review of the horoscopes when a picture on the front page caught my eye. It was Kevin Harrison! And Pete McNeil! And, oh-my-God!

"Abby!" I screamed. "Abby, get out here."

She may have been sleeping but she was out in the dining room like a shot and ready to take a shot with her hand on her gun.

"What is it, Chailey? Are you okay?"

I just held the front page of the newspaper to her.

"Shit!" was all she could say.

The front headlines read:

POLICE NURSE UNDER SUSPICION

Chailey Smith, RN who works as a Mental Health Worker in the Cookfield Police Department is currently under suspicion for conspiring with Reece Slater. Slater is in custody and stands accused of murder following an armed robbery which resulted in the death of a security guard at the Burton Bank. Unnamed sources state Smith, niece of Chief of Police John Smith, split the money from the robbery which occurred one week ago. One accomplice was arrested this week and another remains at large. Smith was apparently taken "hostage" by Slater on Friday May 2nd. The police are continuing their investigation.

This story was printed under a photo taken by a reporter outside of the hospital obviously on Saturday morning when we went to visit Tim. Pete and Kevin stood on each side of me like guards looking grim and serious. I looked even grimmer as Frankenstein's bride with bruises and stitches.

I would have preferred my driver's license photo over this one.

"Who the hell leaked this out?" Abby yelled at no one in particular.

"Abby,.." I started to cry. Everyone was going to think that *I* was a criminal. I'm telling you, shit sticks, and this was some serious, sticky shit.

The phone rang. Abby grabbed it.

"Hartford." Someone spoke to her and she replied, "Too late, she's read it." Another pause. "Yeah, just a second."

"Chailey, it's your Uncle John. He wants to talk to you."

I shook my head, no. I was too upset. And to have his name smeared as well. My aunt would be having a bird right now. Mind you, if my mother was here, she'd cut the article out and put it on the fridge. It takes a lot to faze her. Abby told him that I couldn't talk right now.

"Okay, sir!" She put the phone up to my ear and said to me apologetically, "He told me to."

"Chailey, we will get to the bottom of this. We will demand a retraction and an apology from this newspaper and I will *personally* be issuing a statement at the station at nine this morning. We *will* find out who leaked this to the press. Don't worry, Chailey. This will be sorted out."

I managed to eek out a "Thanks". At this moment it all sounded to me like "Blah, blah, blah!" Abby spoke to him a little longer and then hung up the phone.

It rang again. Abby answered it again. This time it was Paul. And so the phone rang and rang until I unplugged the damned thing and put it in to the microwave. Out of sight, out of mind! If only my phone rang this often for dates. All I could think of was that my reputation was ruined and I'd never be able to return to the one love of my life and that was working as a Mental Health Worker.

The doorbell rang. Abby, who was acting as my newly appointed personal assistant, answered it. I could hear that it was a reporter. So the snitch gave the press my address as well. I could faintly hear someone ask, "Did Miss Smith have a comment?" Abby replied, "No! But I do, go to hell!" and I believe that the reporter probably had her nose broken when the door slammed on her. Too bad, so sad, go to hell!

Abby went into the kitchen and came back with orange juice for both of us.

"Drink up," she coaxed me.

I just about choked. It was a vodka screwdriver!

"Abby, we can't drink vodka this early."

"Sure we can. You're going to need it. I do. Bottoms up!" By the way, I don't want you to go out back."

"Why, Abby?"

"Because someone did something bad."

Of course, my first reaction was to go outside and the second I got out there, I regretted my decision. Someone had destroyed my garden. Every plant had been ripped out of the ground or stomped on, the magnolia tree had been cut to a stump. A message had been burnt into the grass with bleach or weed killer. It took me a moment to read the five-foot letters and figure out what it said, but the message was clear, "BITCH". It also took me a while to figure out what the strange smell was coming from the pond. It was bleach! Someone had poured bleach into the pond and my fish were floating tits up and dead. The garden was completely devastated and so was I.

And that was how one of the worst days of my life began. Let's face it, I'd been having a lot of these lately so you'd think I'd be use to it by now.

Paul showed up about ten minutes later and Abby hurried off to shower and clean up. We sat at the dining room table under which lay the newspaper ripped to shreds. He started asking me questions.

"Did you tell anyone about the surveillance, Chailey?"

I told Paul the only person I told was Kevin Harrison and that was it. In a fit of honesty, I explained that we were suppose to be going out for dinner and that we couldn't at this time because of the surveillance. I earned a raised eyebrow from Paul about the dinner and his only comment was "Kevin's a good guy." I felt badly about getting Kevin involved but I had to. I hadn't even told Zack.

Abby was dressed and ready to go in record time. Apparently our presence was requested at the press conference so I needed to dress "professionally". Since my jacket had been returned I was back to the blue suit with the short skirt.

We were wisely advised to sneak into the station through the back door to avoid the horde of reporters. Nobody gets this excited when we take a depressed man to hospital and save his life. No, but crucify someone who is doing their job and we have a mob of people to record that event. I would have preferred to sweep through the front reception with my head held high but even I didn't have the balls to do that.

We met my uncle outside of the press conference. I could tell he was really angry - the Smith temper was taking over.

It was pretty painless in the end. Mind you, the vodka and OJ helped build up my courage. Hopefully no one could smell alcohol on my breath at nine in the morning. I had eaten a *Mars* bar on the way over to cover the smell. I walked into the conference with my uncle and the police department's Public Relations Officer. My uncle read out a statement while I stood beside him trying not to throw up. The reporters asked questions which were answered with as little substance as possible and the whole ordeal was wrapped up in fifteen minutes. Despite the intense television lights blinding us, I could see at least twenty uniformed officers in the audience including Pete, Tim, Abby and Kevin. They all had their hard cop faces on. I could tell no one was happy. I had a momentary panic attack thinking that maybe they looked angry because they *believed* the lies that I was working with a criminal. That is until Kevin winked at me and Zack pretended to adjust his privates. Those guys had all worked overnight and then stayed for the press conference. I loved those jerks so much.

There was a meeting right after the "Meet the Press" session and it was held in the Chief's office. The meeting included Paul, Dave, John and several other detectives I'd never met before. Essentially the meeting involved my uncle ranting and raving and the crowd agreeing that an investigation was required. The surveillance was finished. At least Kevin and I could finally have a date. I wondered how long it would be before I could return to society without being viewed as a criminal co-conspirator. Perhaps someone would put a big fat scarlet letter "C" for "Criminal" on my chest. I left the meeting after fifteen minutes feeling unable to cope anymore. I was already craving another *Mars* bar and a cup of coffee to wash it down with. Abby had told me that she'd meet me in the Squad Room when I was done.

The gang was all there along with half the day squad. Apparently the citizens of Cookfield were going to have to wait a little longer for police services. Everyone was thoroughly pissed off. The conclusion of the group was that the problem was an internal one and they were all furious that someone had ratted out one of their own. I told everyone all that I knew which wasn't much and gradually everyone filed out to go home to sleep or were sent by the dispatchers to different calls. Ironically, one of the cops was sent out to see "Bridget" who was out on *Mary Marry Me* Bridge and was asking for me. I would have given my eyeteeth at that moment to be able to go out and help her.

Officially I was on duty with full pay - unofficially I was going home for the day and could return when the situation was resolved. Who knew when that would be?

There was nothing else to do at the station so Abby told me she'd drive me home so that she could catch up on her sleep at my place. The others were all going home too because they were all due back in at seven tonight for another night shift. Kevin stopped me on the way out and passed me a note and I quickly pocketed it. The way my day was going he was probably telling me he didn't want to go for dinner after all. I'd save the pleasure of reading that note for later.

It was ten thirty by the time Abby and I got to my place. It seemed so empty with none of my tenants invading my privacy or my dog digging up the back garden. Abby went straight to my room to sleep. I thought about going out to the garden to start cleaning up but couldn't face the "BITCH" etching in my lawn. I couldn't go to work and had no interest in cleaning since that's Martha's domain and it would have to wait until she returned to the Golden Manor.

By two o'clock I had played at least forty games of solitaire on the computer and won none, cleaned out the freezer and painted my toenails. I used sparkly nail varnish figuring I needed something to make me a little more glamorous. Something else that might brighten my day would be to open and read the card from Susannah so I pulled it out of my jacket pocket as I settled down at my computer desk. It really was a "Thank You" card signed by Susannah and her daughter. The computer disk was inside an envelope and a small note was written as follows: *Give to Chailey Smith, Cookfield Police Service if anything happens to me.* It sounded a little dramatic but showed me that she was probably paranoid and definitely upset about something. Wow, this should go to Liam Fitzgerald. Mind you, he told me not to bother him about this case unless I had clear evidence. So… that meant I needed to look at this disc to see if it was evidence just like Liam told me to.

The disc was made up of six documents with a listing of numbers. There were absolutely no words and I had no idea what it meant.

Okay, Chailey, I thought, this is a code. All you have to do is to figure it out. Time for a beer.

Five minutes later, beer in hand and no new ideas. There were two sets of lists. The first two pages had a column on the left with a jumble of numbers that were both minus and plus numbers. For example, there was "9-1–6–6". The column on the right consisted of large numbers. Most of those were in the hundreds of thousands. Time for another beer.

Forty-five minutes later and the only thing the beer was helping me to do was to make me pee and the riddle was giving me a headache. I had tried matching numbers to letters in the alphabet but it didn't go high enough. I gave up but decided to hide the CD in my bedroom drawers where no one would ever look – in my package of sanitary pads! What was strange was that everything in my bureau drawers looked askew and slightly out of place. I may be a slob in some areas of my life but my bedroom closets and drawers are maintained according to a strict code of order. Maybe Abby had been looking for something she needed. Not to worry.

My cell phone rang and I absentmindedly answered it, forgetting my current hate of the outside world. It was Michael Brigham. The man was like a bad smell at times and just wouldn't go away.

"Chailey, how are you? I've been so worried about you today when I read the paper. Is there anything I can do to help?" Okay, so he was being thoughtful and considerate making me feel guilty. Damn that conscience of mine.

"Actually I'm fine thanks, Michael. What can I do for you?"

"It's what I would like to do for you. You have been so good to me supporting me over the loss of Margaret. I thought I could at least lighten your day by taking you out for supper. Tell me which restaurant is your favourite and I will treat you to dinner."

After the day had gone so far, a dinner at my favourite restaurant sounded really appealing and I was all for it. I could put up with his drivel in order to get a free diner and I wanted to ask him about Susannah's claim that the private investigator had found a man named Chesley.

"That sounds great, Michael. I appreciate the offer. Are you sure you don't mind hanging out with a potential criminal based on today's newspaper report?"

"Chailey, you forget what I do. I'm usually paid to hang out with criminals. I would like to talk to you about your ideas regarding Margaret's death. I talked to Liam Fitzgerald and I was shocked when he told me that you have some concerns that maybe she was murdered. I'd like to hear what you have to say. If someone hurt my Margaret then I want that person prosecuted to the fullest extent of the law. Perhaps my experience as a defense lawyer can help us figure this out further."

Okay, so he had caught me hook, line and sinker. It's not like I had any alternate dinner plans – Kevin was working, Abby was out and with Martha gone, the only thing in the fridge for dinner was a left-over rice dish from Blimpey's on Sunday night and a container of apple sauce for dessert. Michael could be a pain in the ass at times, however, he did know how to treat a woman well and with that Platinum *VISA*, I could have a good dinner while fishing for information.

"Thanks, Michael. I really have nothing much to go on but I'd appreciate the opportunity to review the case as

I see it. I hope this isn't too painful to drudge this all up for you."

"Not at all, Chailey. I want to help put this case, and Margaret, to rest."

"I adore *Monet's*."

"Then *Monet's* it is. How about seven tonight?"

"Terrific. I'll see you there."

I felt a twinge of guilt knowing that I was having dinner out tonight when I should really be dining with Kevin. I decided that I was going to have to occupy my mind with something or I'd been cleaning the oven; the true sign of boredom. With nothing else to do I finally gave in and had a nap on the couch. The beer had caught up to me. Two hours later I woke up and decided that I was starting to act a lot like Bart and Harold. It was definitely time to get out of the house, but where to go?

Chapter 22

Having exhausted my repertoire of home-based activities proving that I really wasn't Martha Stewart's twin, I decided to escape from my house arrest. Wherever I went I needed to avoid nosy reporters and anyone else who might remotely recognize me. That meant church or the local beauty salon, neither of which I visit often. Susannah's "thank you" card caught my eye and reminded me that I still had Maggie's cryptic message CD. I crept back into my bedroom where Abby was sleeping and slid it out of my hiding spot without waking Sleeping Beauty who was snoring like a bear. I took her car keys not wanting to drive my own car with everything that was going on today. Okay, so that was my excuse. I just like to look cool driving in her Toyota Rav 4. With no surveillance team cramping my style, I didn't have to tell anyone where I was going; however, I did leave Abby a note telling her I was off to my lawyer's office, then to Maggie's and finally to dinner with Michael Brigham at seven. I also left my week-old cell phone number. I have been reduced to using disposable cell phones having lost three permanent cell phones and driven over an additional two in the past ten months.

My lawyer had left a message on my machine yesterday for me to drop by the office to sign some papers. It was my first stop of the day. Olivia greeted me enthusiastically as she always did.

"I need you to sign this paper." I presumed that it was for money to be deposited in her account so I was more than a little surprised to see the amount of $50,000.

"Wow! Fifty thousand!"

"Err, look again," advised Olivia.

"Holy Crap! Five *hundred* thousand dollars!" I sat down.

"Yes! And it's all yours. Adam cut a check for my fees separately. This paper acknowledges that Adam has transferred that amount to your account. Congratulations Chailey, you're half a millionaire."

So that message from my bank wasn't a hoax. Bells and sirens must have gone off when my bank balance went over zero let alone up to half a million dollars.

I put my head between my knees and hoped that the room would stop swimming around me. The last time I saw money in my savings account was when I met Adam and I had $7,637 there. I hadn't been paying attention to the divorce proceedings and had only asked Olivia to get back the money I'd paid for Adam's medical school at a grand total of forty five thousand dollars. Adam must be mightily pissed off right now.

I thanked Olivia profusely. My anxiety skyrocketed when she offered me the name of a good criminal lawyer in light of today's events. I left the office feeling dumbfounded. At least I could finally pay my hydro bill on time.

I drove over to Maggie's house carefully. Maggie's house looked as prim and proper as ever. There was a realtor's "For Sale" sign outside. It was a lovely home and it would sell fast in today's market. That's of course if people don't know that someone *may* have been murdered there. Nothing drops the price of a house more than a fresh murder. On the flip side, "open houses" of major crime scenes are pretty popular since people want to view the scene of the crime close up. They are usually pretty disappointed to find that the industrial cleaning people have been in to clean up the carnage.

I let myself in through the front door with the key that Susannah had given me. I found Kevin's note in my pocket at the same time.

His note read: *"No matter how down and out you feel right now, remember that you are loved by the people around you who know you the best. Believe in yourself because we all do. So NOW can we have dinner???? Fondly, Kevin"*

What a sweetheart!

I sat down to Maggie's computer feeling completely freaked out. Either Maggie or someone else had sat in this very spot to write a suicide note. As I slid the disc in, my fantasy was that some amazing, high-tech decoding program would kick in and decode the list. My dreams were quickly shattered yet again and the same jumbled numbers appeared on the document.

There seemed to be two patterns. Two pages had plus and minus numbers. The remaining four pages included numbers which, when I wrote them individually, ranged from 1 to 26. These were obviously the pages to tackle first since the letters had to match the twenty-six letters of the alphabet. I tried the obvious by matching the letters to numbers with "A" being 1, "B" being 2 and so on. This seemed too obvious and didn't work, especially since I'd tried this approach earlier today and it wasn't successful then either. I moved the 1 over to the "B" which made "C" number 2, "D" 3, etc. That didn't work either. I tried the reverse approach by assigning "Z" number 1, "Y" number 2, etc. but still no success.

This was important and Maggie had trusted me with this job. So far I had screwed up. Why the hell would she trust me in the first place? I can't be trusted to look after my dog let alone figure this out. Maggie and I were so different. There was an example of the blatant discrepancy in our interests right in front of me. Maggie had typed and posted a list titled; *Maggie's Choice of Desirable and Exotic People to Meet.* This was her list:

> *Queen Elizabeth*
> *Jack Kennedy*
> *Alexander the Great*
> *My Great Grandmother*
> *Pavlov's wife*

Me? I'd like to meet Moses, Elvis and Marilyn Monroe!

The more I looked at Maggie's list the stranger it appeared to me that it was posted on the wall. Maggie had nothing else on the wall, just this list. And to be perfectly honest, the people weren't all that exotic either.

I took the list down from the wall. It really was a weird list of people; who wants to meet Pavlov let alone Pavlov's wife? Maybe his dog, but not his wife. As I read through the list I had a hunch. I'm a renowned Scrabble player, although my friend Mary's skills far exceed my own, but as any good Scrabble player knows you need the big scoring tiles of "X", "Q" and "Z" to win the game. Maggie's list included all of these letters. I carefully reviewed the list and found that it included every letter of the alphabet. I was finally getting somewhere. So, maybe the list was the code. And then I did see the obvious. The first letters of the title spelt CODE!

I assigned the first letter "Q" a 1, the "U" a 2, the "E" a 3 and so on. Using the newly coded letters I attempted to translate the list. It worked! The list of numbers magically turned into a list of what appeared to be companies with hundreds of thousands of dollars listed beside each company name.

So, Maggie had a list of forty-five names with large amounts of money ranging from $50,00 to $250,00 attached to each name. So what? Well, Maggie worked for *Bell and Peters*. Maybe the companies had something to do with the legal firm. I looked around the cupboards for a phone book and was momentarily distracted by the level of organization Maggie had achieved and finally found a city directory. Within a minute I was on the phone to the first company, Burlington Foundries.

"Please connect me to your legal department," I requested the switchboard operator.

I was connected to some snippety administrative secretary who told me that their legal affairs were handled by *Bell and Peters*. Very interesting! I called a dozen more companies on the list and achieved the same outcome.

I dialed the phone number for *Bell and Peters* and asked for Julia. Thankfully she was at her desk.

"Julia. It's Chailey. I need to ask you a huge favour."

"Sure."

"I have some company names for you to check out. I need you to tell me who the lawyers were who dealt with the following companies."

"Chailey, I'm not sure I can do that."

"It's important Julia or I wouldn't ask."

The phone was silent for a minute while Julia did some mental gymnastics. "Okay, give me the names."

I randomly picked the names of ten companies from the list and gave them to Julia along with my cell phone number. "Call me as soon as you get the information. If you get fired for this, I promise you I'll get you a new job. I'm at Maggie's house by the way. Thanks Julia."

It was time for Sherlock to analyze the "plus and minus" number list. The money side of this list was obviously a sum of different amounts with the final total of $3,625,000. I took the list I had decoded and tried to match up amounts on both lists. For example, the DASS agency was listed at $65,000. There was an amount for $65,000 on the uncoded list with the same number of letters in the name. By laying all the letters of the alphabet in a line and matching the numbers to the letters, I broke the code. Maggie had assigned letter "M" (presumably for Maggie) as a 0. "L" to "A" were listed in ascending numbers with "L" being 1, "K" as 2 and so my list looked like this:

$$J 3 / K 2 / L 1 / M 0 / N -1 / O -2 / P - 3.$$

Descending numbers were used for the last half of the alphabet, hence, "N" was -1, "O" was -2 and so on. I was trying to decipher the title of the page when my cell phone rang. It was Julia. She quickly told me that Michael Brigham was responsible for all the legal transactions with the companies that I had listed. Just as she told me this I finally finished deciphering the title of the page. Michael Brigham's Bank Account!

"Holy shit!" I said.

"So, Maggie did leave you a list."

I jumped at the voice from behind me and dropped the cell phone. It was Michael and he crushed the phone with his shoe. Damn! Another cell phone shot to Hell!

"No, I .. err.." Crap, I was going to have to learn to lie a little better than this.

"The little bitch figured it out, did she?" he sneered. "I thought she had. That's why she had to die."

"You killed her?" I stammered. So much for my training to "look concerned, act surprised and deny, deny, deny!"

"No, she "killed" herself, remember Chailey? You found her with a self-inflicted shot to her head and the gun in her hand. The Coroner said so."

"Wait a minute, now I remember! You were so concerned about the gun. I should have picked that up. And I kept sneezing when I first met you. You must have had cat fur on you. Damn!" It was a case of too little, too late.

He had grabbed my hands and put them behind my back. I heard the unmistakable whirring click of handcuffs. Usually that sound turns me on but not tonight.

"Yeah, Chailey, you were a little foolish on a few things! Good job with decoding this list. I would never have figured this out alone." He grabbed the list and ripped it to shreds then directed his efforts to deleting the files on the disc. He opened a new file on the computer and started typing with gloved hands.

"A short and sweet suicide note for you, Chailey, don't you think?" That was his first mistake. No one would ever believe that I wrote a *short* note. I'm incapable of being brief and concise.

"I should have kept Maggie's note on file and used it for you tonight. By the way, you really do have a stupid name." This guy was nuts. And I should know since I am a Mental Health Worker.

"Don't look so frightened. I won't make you suffer. Maggie didn't."

He kept typing the note which read:

I cannot take the guilt of Margaret's death any more.

Today was too much. I am sorry. To all my family, I love you. Chailey

"No special hugs or kisses for that dumb cop Kevin Harrison who thinks he owns you," he added triumphantly.

I had to admit, Slater had been frightening but Michael was terrifying. How could this happen twice in a week? I have *never* been involved in any major type of violent incident in my work and now this was happening! My bruises weren't even gone from last week. The day I become a half-millionaire is the day I die. I don't think so buddy! I earned that money and I was bloody well going to spend it and I didn't mean on my funeral.

"Fuck you, Michael!" I tried to get up and run but he grabbed me by my hair and pulled me back on to the chair.

"Now listen you little bitch. I'm in charge here now. You remind me of Maggie. She tried to fight back and I didn't get a bruise on her, did I? Now for you. You've decided to jump off a very high spot. But I don't trust you. You are going to take something to give you the courage needed to do this deed."

Next thing I knew, he had grabbed my hair and yanked hard. Immediately my mouth opened and he started pouring a liquid down my throat. Vodka, I think. Something that was pure alcohol. He was patient letting me cough and splutter and then doing it again. Next he poured something in my mouth that felt like *Skittles* candy.

"Valium, my friend. To help you relax before you take the big plunge over the quarry."

Fuck, I hate heights. I responded in my traditional manner by vomiting.

"Jesus Christ, you're fucking disgusting!" I had spewed all over the computer, the floor and of course, myself.

"No problem, I've got more," Michael announced. He repeated the process spilling the vodka over me and the floor. "Well, off to our date."

Michael half-dragged me out to his BMW parked in the driveway. I managed to puke over him halfway down the path which really ticked him off. So sad, too bad, I thought. He had one of those handy-dandy gadgets that pops open the trunk from a distance. He pushed me in rather roughly and closed the trunk and then popped down the back seat that folded down. He had turned me so that he could see my face from the driver's seat.

Apparently Michael planned to lecture me while he drove around town. I had a minuscule of hope. Michael was taking my lack of fighting back as an indicator that I was succumbing to the influence of the drugs and alcohol. I knew not to wrestle with him because it would only make the drugs course faster through my body. Thank God for nursing school training finally coming in handy in the last forty-five minutes of my life! Secondly, he couldn't see my hands which I was expertly removing from the handcuffs. One lesson I had learned in the three weeks I *did* complete at police college was there are things you do when you handcuff someone to ensure that you keep them in handcuffs. Apparently Michael never learned these lessons at his hoity-toity lawyer school. When my hands were free I knew to pull the wires out of the lights to get attention from the police with burned out lights. This third lesson I learned from Oprah.

Michael was talking to me the whole time. Obviously he felt safe and secure.

"Margaret was getting too nosey. She figured out that I'd been removing money from the companies I was providing legal services to. More than six million dollars have been squirreled away in offshore accounts. I'll be leaving the country soon since I'm the "poor grieving fiancé" unable to cope with the death of my poor darling Margaret. I couldn't have done this without help. Everyone thought I was in Mexico but I gave away my tickets and paid someone to call Margaret from Mexico. I was here the whole time scaring the shit out of her every night."

"You were the prowler!" I blurted out. Duh!

"Yeah. And I also killed her. She was getting too close for comfort. Just like you. You just wouldn't leave it alone. Nosey little cow. Even Simmons tried to throw you off the trail. How did you get the CD?"

"Tooth fairy," I answered. It was getting harder and harder to focus. The drugs and booze were starting to take effect and I was finding it difficult to talk, let alone move.

"A smart ass to the end, huh? It was probably Susannah and that card she gave you. Simmons checked your office for it thanks to your unwilling secretary. No matter now. I've got the evidence and anyone who knows about it is dead. Or will be." And then he laughed hysterically.

Things were getting very blurry. I vomited again all over the trunk and the back of the seat.

"What's with you and this puking thing? Another few minutes and we'll be at the restaurant. I called ahead and made reservations. I'll wait half an hour, have a couple of cocktails, call you several times on your phone and make a big deal about you not showing up. And then I'll drive you to the quarry. Oh, did I mention, I plan to screw you before I throw you over the edge of the quarry. I would love to see your boyfriend's face when he learns from the autopsy that the last person who had sex with you wasn't him."

This was not what I had in mind when I didn't want Adam to be the last person I had sex with before I died. Be careful of what you wish for because you just might get it.

It seemed forever before Michael stopped the car, parked it and got out to close up the back seat. I heard him in the distant fog say, "Bye, bye, Chailey!"

And then he was gone. And so was the light. And that was my very last thought as I faded into unconsciousness.

Chapter 23

It was a very bright light. I closed my eyes. I didn't want to die. If I didn't go to the white light maybe I wouldn't die. I tried again. Nope! That was definitely a bright light. And voices! I could hear voices. They were speaking English. I always wondered what language they spoke in the after life.

"Am I in heaven?" I asked the bright light.

"No, honey. You're in the Cookfield General Hospital."

I opened my eyes fully. The light was a big, bright fluorescent one above my bed.

"How are you feeling, sweetie?" asked the nurse.

"Felt better," was all I could squeak out.

"You rest now. The doctor will be in to see you soon."

My body took her advice because I drifted off to sleep again. When I woke up it was dark outside but that Goddamn fluorescent light was still glaring on me like a spotlight.

I looked around the room. I could see Abby and Kevin sitting in the uncomfortable vinyl hospital chairs. Kevin must have seen me stir. Abby was fast asleep and snoring which is probably what woke me up in the first place.

"Chailey, how are you?" He came over and kissed me on the forehead. It was the sweetest, kindest gesture and it made me cry.

"Honey, I'm sorry," he said worriedly.

I smiled, "It's okay. Happy tears. Water. Want some water."

I sipped the water from one of those cool bendy straws. The effort of that small task sucked the life out of me and I drifted off to sleep again.

I awoke with a start. It was four o'clock according to the clock on the wall - a.m. since it was still dark outside. Kevin was right beside me as soon as I stirred. Abby's snoring was probably getting to him. The woman snores like a three-hundred pound wrestler and apparently she can sleep anywhere.

"Chailey, how do you feel?"

"I've felt better." Cool, I was actually making sentences.

"We've been worried about you. Brigham really doped you up with Valium and alcohol."

"Good thing I weigh a lot so my fat could absorb it."

"You must be feeling better, Miss Smart Mouth. I should let the nurses know you're awake."

"No, just sit with me. Tell me what happened? How did you find me?"

Over the next few hours Kevin and Abby told me how the events unfolded. The story was broken up with my little catnaps and interruptions by nurses doing silly things like changing the IV bag and checking my vital signs.

Like Abby, Kevin had slept throughout the day of the press conference. At six o'clock on his way to work he had dropped by the house to see how I was doing. He saw my car in the driveway so he assumed I was home and that Abby had gone to work since her Rav 4 wasn't there. There was no answer to his knocks at the door so he figured I was napping. In reality, Abby had been in the shower also getting ready for work and didn't hear him knocking. She never did see the note I'd left for her.

Upon arriving at the police station, Kevin ran into Sergeant Court at the front desk who commented on the Chailey situation and did Kevin know if they were questioning Michael Brigham. Why would they question Michael Brigham, he'd asked. Well, he was Slater's lawyer, wasn't he? He was also the same lawyer who'd been involved with Dicky the Dick's case last year when the guy went free. When he heard this, Kevin knew that something wasn't right and raced up to the Detective's Office to find that neither Fitzgerald nor Simmons were there. Kevin went down to the Squad Room at which point Abby showed up pissed off that I'd taken her car and not come home. Kevin got a call from Julia who was hysterical. She had heard Michael's voice before I dropped the phone. She remembered Kevin's name and phoned the station looking for him. Julia told him that I was at Maggie's. They raced over to Maggie's place, found my upchucked calling card on the front step and knew something was up. There was no response to calls to my cell phone and the secondary puke fest along with the suicide note did not resolve anyone's concerns. An alert was issued across the city for both Abby and Michael Brigham's vehicles.

The police found Michael quietly drinking cocktails at *Monet's*. It was seven twenty-five and he had planned to stay for five more minutes. He was arrested at gunpoint.

They quickly found me in the trunk of Michael's car unconscious and barely breathing. That was thirty-two hours ago. Unfortunately I had been diagnosed with aspiration pneumonia from breathing in some chunks of vomit into my lungs. The thought of that made me want to upchuck again. I still had a few more days to serve in this institution before I reached my hospital release date. I was expected to make a fully recovery. Hey, may be while I was here I could have the Botox team drop in to make some improvements!

Michael Brigham had barely said a word since being arrested. At the restaurant he reportedly said, "Only five more minutes and the bitch would have been dead. Damn!" That little bit of information gave me the chills. I hoped that those words earned him a smack in the head.

His accomplice, Rick Simmons, had been more forthcoming and sang like a canary. Michael and Dicky became associated through the Jones murder, the one when I had complained about Dicky's treatment of Mrs. Jones one year earlier. Michael had represented the accused and had become aware of Dicky's penchance for gambling and his desire to do anything for the right amount of money to pay off accumulated gambling debts. Dicky had obstructed the investigation into the Maggie Denton prowler case knowing that it was Michael. He had also gone through my office looking for the evidence under the guise of making a confidential phone call. Too bad Zack and Neil didn't leave the snakes in my drawer that day! Apparently Dicky had broken into my apartment as well. So I hadn't imagined someone had touched everything. The thought of Dicky going through my underwear drawer made me want to heave. The leak to the press was also compliments of Rick Simmons.

He proclaimed that all of these events were orchestrated by Michael Brigham who threatened to turn Dick into the authorities if he didn't follow Brigham's directions. He denied any intentions of hurting anyone and was very, very apologetic for everything he had done. Yeah, well he can kiss my ass. Neil and Zack later told me that Simmons has become a little clumsy. Every time he comes into the police station for an interview he accidentally bumps into people banging his nose making it bleed. It happened three times the previous day. He'd get no sympathy from me and as far as I was concerned, he could bleed to death. I didn't care how apologetic he was, the man helped someone to attempt to kill me. There were numerous charges against Dicky under the Police Services Act. Criminal charges were pending at this time. Nick was the Crown Attorney prosecuting the case against Dicky.

We finally got to the topic of Michael Brigham. Our esteemed lawyer was currently being held in custody facing charges of abduction and attempted murder of me. The police were further investigating the CD Maggie had left. The detectives would be talking to me as soon as possible.

"Michael told me that he murdered Maggie," I told Kevin. That was all it took to make the water dam break and the tears started rolling down my cheeks. "Poor Maggie. She must have been so frightened and scared. Everyone told her that she was crazy," I sobbed.

"Not everyone," replied Kevin. "You didn't. That's why she called you."

"But I let her down. She died."

"No, Chailey. She planned to meet you at her home. I believe that she wanted you to go with her to the police to give her story credibility. Michael must have figured this out in some way and got to her first. I hate to think what would have happened if you had shown up earlier. He may have killed you, too. Chailey, you solved Maggie's murder and Michael will never hurt anyone again."

That didn't help. It just made me cry more. Kevin has great shoulders to cry on and I am ashamed to admit it but I sobbed for a long time. I eventually cried myself to sleep and napped for most of the morning, which was a good thing since I had a long line of visitors to entertain for the remainder of the day.

When I woke up my Uncle John and Aunt Janice had arrived hand-in-hand. Apparently they had kissed and made up and romance had re-emerged in the Smith household. My uncle was obviously quite upset about the events that had occurred and told me that we could talk more in depth "later". He wasn't particularly adept at handling emotions. He had finally asked my aunt what was going on and she had asked my uncle the same question. They both confessed to preparing surprises for each other for their upcoming fortieth wedding anniversary. Each had become so involved in keeping the surprise a secret that they had become *secretive*. Uncle John had planned, with Sally's assistance, a cruise and Aunt Janice had planned a surprise party. Neither of them trusted me to keep their secret with my inability to lie and had concluded that it was better not to tell me in the first place. The party was next Saturday and the cruise ship sets sail the next day. As my uncle left he reminded me that the investigators would be in shortly.

"Oh, and Chailey, let's not tell your mother about this or she'll have my hide and then make you quit."

"It's a deal!"

An hour later Detectives Applegate, Fitzgerald and Tayler came in along with Nick Coomber, the Crown Attorney. Thankfully Kevin had returned from a break just before their arrival and they let him stay. They wanted a brief statement now and when I was feeling better a fuller recant of the story would be required. I did my best to give a step-by-step account but it was pretty rough emotionally to relive the events. I told them what events had unfolded in Maggie's house and how he had doped me up.

"He threatened to rape me before he threw me over the quarry. He wanted Kevin to know that he had raped me." I stumbled a little on the words but didn't cry.

It was the first time I said this out loud but it felt good to tell someone so that it wasn't just between Michael and me. The room went silent and Kevin went as still as stone.

Nick Coomber spoke up first. "Abby just walked by. Why don't you go and get her, Kevin."

"I'm okay," I told him as he walked out the door.

Abby came in a minute later. "Kevin will be back in a few minutes. He went to clear his head." You've got to love her honesty. More like he was pounding the crap out of a wall. The interview continued on while I gave them details of Michael's murder confession.

The computer crime cops had retrieved the data from the CD despite Michael having deleted the files. The information was being investigated as we spoke. They were impressed with my ingenuity. I knew my *Scrabble* skills would come in handy one day. The detectives were very understanding, especially considering they were guys, and didn't push too hard which was a good thing. I was on the edge emotionally *plus* I was premenstrual - a pretty ugly combination.

The detectives updated me on an interesting turn of events. Slater had given up his vow of silence and joined Dicky on the perch singing like a canary. Slater and Brigham had quite a history dating back ten years when Michael had represented Slater in a criminal matter. As psychopaths, both Slater and Michael were smart enough to know that they could profit from the other. Slater needed Michael's expertise and Michael benefited from learning about the finer aspects of being on the wrong side of the law. A perfect symbiotic relationship. As Slater's lawyer, Michael and had been contacted by Slater immediately following his arrest. Michael was also representing the other accomplice, Eastwood. The surveillance of me had been a complete and utter waste of time and energy since Slater had used Michael to help hide the loot. Slater trusted Michael to keep the money safe or Michael would be turned into the authorities by Slater. Michael had Slater by the short and curlies since he had hidden the money and wouldn't give it back unless Slater played by his rules. So the story from the police that Chailey Smith, Mental Health Worker, was involved in a criminal cover up was a big joke to this devious pair.

After yet another nap, the fun really started with the arrival of the Smith clan. David and Christine had brought the girls and Chloe brought a piece of horsetail which was quickly, and might I add tightly, tied around my finger for good luck. Great, just what I needed was something attached to my hand that was covering a horse's butt a day earlier.

Zack and Neil were next. It was so good to see my buddies that I started to cry. The guys were so uncomfortable with my emotions that they worked hard to make me laugh with tales of jokes and pranks that had gone wrong. The funniest had to be the day Neil had made up a fake bomb threat and anonymously sent it by e-mail to Zack. Unfortunately, he accidentally sent the e-mail to everyone in the police station which resulted in the building being immediately evacuated for hours. Of course Zack tried to outdo this and told us his own story about how he'd accidentally sat on his police radio leaving the mike open for everyone to hear while having a ten-minute raunchy and very colourful conversation about who had the biggest boobs and the cutest ass in the police department. The dispatchers couldn't cut in so the next thing people heard on the radio was a knock and Zack saying, "Hey, Sarge!" and the Sergeant replying, "Get your ass off that radio. NOW!"

Martha followed shortly after with her bridge group in tow. I think the nurses wanted the "Whiteheads" off the unit quickly fearful that one of them might croak considering their age. They were happy to leave only when the promise was made that they would visit the Gift Shop on their way out.

Bart and Harold followed in the wake of Golden Girls. They were pretty peeved that they had to vacate their first class digs at the *Sheraton Hotel* and return to their basement dwelling. Loralei had returned to sunny California leaving a depressed and lovesick Harold and Bart had been welcomed back to the nest. My boys brought me a Blimpey's burger and I gave them my meal tray which they lapped up the same way Scooby Doo eats Scooby snacks!

Even Adam dropped by. He was the culprit responsible for the disaster in my garden. He turned himself into the police and admitted that he had been so angry about the divorce settlement that he had taken it out on me through the one thing I loved. He was feeling overwhelmingly guilty as he should about his temper tantrum. Too bad he didn't feel guilty about all of those affairs he had. I guess for half-a-million dollars he was entitled to a temper tantrum. It's just that it was really, really bad timing!

Every cop in Cookfield felt the need to drop by and say hello. It was very sweet and I was embarrassed by the attention. About half way through the afternoon, I finally thought about my appearance and hoped that someone had washed the puke out of my hair which they had.

Even Jody made an appearance. She sat and wept for twenty minutes beside my bed and was finally left escorted home by one of the officers and no doubt was having sex with the man this very moment.

By nine o'clock I'd had enough and even sent Kevin home for some sleep. I had one more task to do before I called it a night. I picked up the phone and called the operator to help direct my call. It took a minute but a voice finally answered.

"Hi Susannah. It's Chailey..."

Chapter 24

It had taken me two days to get out of the hospital and another two to get the energy up to get out of bed. But now I was feeling much better and on the mend. Thank God for antibiotics.

The house was back to normal and I woke up daily to doggy kisses. Martha and the boys couldn't do enough for me by cooking and cleaning. I was learning to enjoy being spoilt. I was also enjoying time in my garden, which had been repaired, or as much as it could be, compliments of Adam. The lawn had been resodded, a new magnolia tree had been planted and I had plans to plant a green Japanese maple at the edge of the patio in memory of Maggie. I continued to experience guilt around Maggie's death and planned to meet with a counselor to help work through this and several other issues.

I was taking at least three weeks off work to fully recover. I was happy to be alive and thankful for the opportunity to be able to work again. Life just became a little more precious this week.

I had used much of my time off thinking about what I do as a Mental Health Nurse. I'm suppose to help the cops make decisions and help make the lives of mentally ill people better in some way or another. Sometimes I'm good at it and other times I'm not. There had been many times when I'd been caught up in people's delusional belief systems, having been there a few times before. Several years ago, while I was working on an inpatient psychiatric unit, I had been drawn into one lady's delusions. She told me that she had received a message from her father requesting that she call him. It was a long distance number so I dialed it for her on the office phone. She chatted for a few minutes with someone and left the ward's phone number for her father to call her back since he was obviously not available at that time. Two minutes after she hung up, the phone rang again. It was the RCMP calling from the Prime Minister's personal private phone line wondering who the lady was who had just called, why was she asking for Jean her "father" and how did she get this private number. Needless to say her "Daddy" never did call her from Ottawa and the patient never did tell me how she got the number.

Another time I was working with the rehabilitation department in the hospital. This position involved supporting people with psychiatric disorders in the community. One lady I worked with was incredibly fearful of going to work; specifically she was scared to travel to and from work. My job was to meet her at her apartment each morning and accompany her by bus to her place of employment where she functioned quite well. I'd do the same process in reverse in the evening. The only quirk this lady had was that she'd stand in the foyer of the apartment to wait for the bus to slow down as it approached the bus stop at which point she would shoot out the door like a bullet and into the bus. Thankfully the bus stop was just outside of the apartment building. The first time she did this I just about fell on my face trying to catch up with her. Interestingly she did exactly the same thing upon returning home. She'd time herself to exit the bus when the busy major road was clear and shoot across like Ben Johnson in the 100-meter dash. I learned to wear my running shoes and became as obsessed she was with my timing. Elizabeth refused to tell me why she did this and there were no notes in the chart explaining this behavior. Elizabeth had schizophrenia and was functioning relatively well on one of the new medications. One day I came back to the office on the bus and noticed that it was Maggie's regular morning bus driver who was driving the bus.

He recognized me and asked, "How's it going with Zap?"

"Zap! Why do you call her Zap?" I asked. "My name's Chailey by the way."

"I'm Ed." He added this in case I couldn't read his two-letter name on his shirt. "Yeah, Zap runs like the bats out of hell into the bus to avoid being zapped by the stun guns that she says are on all the balconies on the apartment across the road. She thinks they want to kill her to stop her important work." That was an interesting point since she packaged candy in a factory. "She's been doing this for more than twenty years. It was a lot easier for her to sprint when she was thirty."

I guess that every good psychiatric team needs a knowledgeable bus driver.

"Thanks." I said with a smile.

Since this had been going on for more than two decades, the team was pretty sure Elizabeth wouldn't change this behaviour even if her medications were changed. The enterprising occupational therapist bought Elizabeth a silver umbrella and told her that it was designed to specifically repel stun rays. Elizabeth was able to stand with her umbrella up at the bus stop and wait for the bus safe from stun guns and free from stress.

Other times we've believed someone has delusions or hallucinations and they are real. One elderly man called the police saying there were aliens in his attic. I was dispatched as well to find *illegal* aliens hiding from the immigration authorities. Of course, Maggie was deemed mentally ill when scary things were really happening to her.

I wasn't fearful of returning to work. It's just that the danger card had been flashed in my face twice in a span of a week and experiences like that make you think real hard about life and what it means. The fact that within seven days two men had attempted murder charges against them for trying to kill me shakes a person's sense of self. I kept trying to forget the phrase, "Third time lucky!" I tend to have vivid dreams and they were pretty relentless. Several times this week I'd woken up in a sweat completely freaked out of my mind with terror. The worst dream involved Slater trying to drown me in a bathtub in which Maggie was floating dead. Of course, I'd had a couple of Kevin Harrison dreams which had a much happier outcome. Friday night could not come quickly enough.

I was pretty sure that the idea of someone putting me in a trunk and locking me in would never, ever seem like a funny prank. I would be happy with being able to think about it without going into a full-fledged panic attack. I had never really thought of my job as dangerous. Sure, I go to every call with a man or a woman with a gun and that in it self makes every call a *gun* call. But most people I see have mental health problems that put them in crisis and that's why they call 911. When Rosemary loses her wallet because she has Alzheimer's disease she thinks her purse is stolen and calls 911, at least I can help. It must be terrifying for a mother to have her twenty-one-year-old daughter tell her she wants to kill herself and for the mother to have to call the police on her own daughter. Having me there does soften the blow a little. Yes, I could see and value my role but I still had some deep-seated worries about my abilities.

My thinking over the last few days has not been all deep and dark. I've spent more time relaxing on this patio in the last few days than I have ever in my life. I've also made some easy decisions over the past few days. Simple things like what colour I'm going to have my hair done next week and that when I get so old that may face looks like it needs to be ironed, I'm going to get a really simple job like being the *Wal-Mart* greeter. I hadn't told anyone about the money from my divorce agreement other than the Toyota dealer who had helped me pick out my brand new vehicle. He'd talked me into buying a Highlander, a red one, but I also refused to have one with one of those hand dandy gadgets that opens the trunks from a remote control. I didn't receive enough money to retire on but certainly sufficient funds to make my life a little more comfortable.

Of course the easiest decision has been if I was going on the date with Kevin. It was finally Friday, or "Date Day" as I like to refer to it! Kevin was picking me up at seven for dinner. Who knows how the evening will end? Kevin had been around every day and I was realizing more and more what a good guy he was. He had told me earlier in the week that he was planning to stay in Cookfield and had turned down a generous offer in BC. I told my uncle about Kevin's offer and how much money he had turned down financially and hoped that he may want to make amends. Kevin explained that he loved his son very much but his ex-wife had started a new life in BC and he had to respect that. Kevin felt that he belonged here. Talk about pressure to be a good date. I planned to be well worth everything he had given up in BC. I had no worries about that - I planned to be so good that the man wouldn't want to get out of bed again, let alone move to BC.

****

Sunday afternoon and I was at the airport with David, Christine and the twins. My mother's plane had landed forty-five minutes ago and she was due out any minute now. The twins had been counseled to stay quiet about the last few weeks' events and gifts given to them confirmed the girls' silence for at least a few days.

My mother finally appeared with Ted in tow, who was carrying two suitcases hopefully filled to the brim with gifts for us all. Kisses and hugs were shared with everyone.

"So what's new?" my mother asked.

I looked at the family and replied with a smile, "Not much. Now tell us about your trip?"

About the Author

Sarah was born in the village of Cuckfield, Sussex, England, immigrated to Canada at the ripe age of 11 and has lived in the Hamilton/Burlington area of Ontario ever since. Sarah attended Mohawk College and graduated with a diploma in Occupational Therapy in 1984. Within a year she was practicing in psychiatry and has been there ever since. In 1988 she graduated from McMaster University with her Bachelor of Health Sciences degree in Occupational Therapy and ten years later she earned her Masters of Education degree from Brock University.

Psychiatry has been the focus of her clinical practice including seven years on the Forensic Program at Hamilton Psychiatric Hospital, a provincial psychiatric hospital. In 2001, Sarah "escaped" from the hospital to work as a Mental Health Worker on the Crisis Outreach and Support Team or COAST, where nurses and other clinicians work directly with police responding to calls to people with mental health issues. It is a position she enjoys immensely and continues to holdss today.

Over the past two decades, education has been a core interest for Sarah and she taught in both the McMaster Occupational Therapy and Medical Programs and continues to work for the Mohawk College Occupational Therapy Assistant Program. Her newest venture is developing and coordinating a mental health training program for police.

Sarah's greatest passion is for her two daughters, Allison and Natasha, who keep her busy with their activities including basketball games and nights out at the barn horseback riding. As a family they enjoy traveling and visiting the cottage. Sarah's other two other passions are working in the garden and writing and she can often be found in the garden surrounded by the fruits of her labour writing about Chailey Smith's adventures.

Printed in the United States
136997LV00001B/2/A